Please return on or before the latest date above.
You can renew online at *www.kent.gov.uk/libs*
or by telephone 08458 247 200

CUSTOMER SERVICE EXCELLENCE

Libraries & Archives

00884\DTP\RN\07.07   LIB 7

D0270694

A MYSTERY WITH RECIPES

A CATERED HALLOWEEN

ISIS CRAWFORD

THORNDIKE
CHIVERS

This Large Print edition is published by Thorndike Press, Waterville, Maine, USA and by BBC Audiobooks Ltd, Bath, England.
Thorndike Press, a part of Gale, Cengage Learning.
Copyright © 2008 by Isis Crawford.
The moral right of the author has been asserted.

LIBRARY OF CONGRESS CATALOGING-IN-PUBLICATION DATA

Crawford, Isis.
   A catered Halloween : a mystery with recipes / by Isis Crawford.
      p. cm. — (Thorndike Press large print mystery)
     ISBN-13: 978-1-4104-1069-6 (alk. paper)
     ISBN-10: 1-4104-1069-2 (alk. paper)
     1. Simmons, Bernie (Fictitious character : Crawford)—Fiction.
2. Simmons, Libby (Fictitious character)—Fiction. 3. Caterers and catering—Fiction. 4. Women in the food industry—Fiction. 5. Cookery—Fiction. 6. Halloween—Fiction. 7. Murder—Investigation—Fiction. 8. Large type books. I. Title.
PS3603.R396C368 2008
813'.6—dc22   2008031004

BRITISH LIBRARY CATALOGUING-IN-PUBLICATION DATA AVAILABLE

Published in 2008 in the U.S. by arrangement with Kensington Books, an imprint of Kensington Publishing Corp.
Published in 2009 in the U.K. by arrangement with The Kensington Publishing Corp.

U.K. Hardcover: 978 1 408 42139 0 (Chivers Large Print)
U.K. Softcover: 978 1 408 42140 6 (Camden Large Print)

Printed in the United States of America
1 2 3 4 5 6 7 12 11 10 09 08

To Mike Ruffo.
Thanks for listening.

ACKNOWLEDGMENTS

I'd like to thank my family and friends for being there for me when I needed you, and DJM for his suggestions.

PROLOGUE

Amethyst Applegate turned the letter over in her hand. Then she put it down on the desk and looked at the envelope it had come in. It told her nothing. The envelope was one of those plain white, self-sealing ones that you could buy at any pharmacy or office-supply store. Her address had been printed out on a computer. There was no return address. As for the postmark, it revealed that the letter had been mailed from Longely two days ago.

She put the envelope down and read the letter again.

Dear Amethyst,

I've decided that it's time to renew old acquaintances. If you don't want everyone to find out what you did at the Peabody School when you were there, meet me in the Pit and the Pendulum Room at six-thirty sharp. I will be waiting for you. We have lots to discuss. Remember there's no statute of limitations on murder.

Signed, Bessie Osgood

"Bessie Osgood. Now there's a laugh."

She remembered Bessie all right. Bessie, with her braces and her pimples and those stupid glasses she used to wear. Bessie, who always used to roll her skirt up around her waist because she thought it showed off her legs.

Her calves were the only thin part of her, that was for sure. Bessie, who'd told the proctor that she'd seen her smoking in the bathroom and that she kept a flask under her bed. She'd almost gotten her thrown out of school for that, *almost* being the operative word. Fortunately, she'd been able to convince the proctor that she was being led astray by Bessie. Now that had been good. Poor Bessie. She should have taken the hint and gone home. Instead, she'd come up to her and told her she had proof. That she had witnesses that were going to testify against her. She shouldn't have done that. Amethyst tapped her fingers on the letter. But she'd shown her. Yes. She certainly had.

"Discuss," Amethyst muttered. She'd

discuss all right. That was ridiculous. You didn't discuss things with a ghost. Ghosts didn't talk. Bessie was dead and gone, and she should know, because she'd been responsible for Bessie's "accident." Poor thing, but those windows were low to the ground, and it was easy to lose your footing if you leaned out too far.

So the question was, who had written the letter? Who knew about what had happened at the Peabody School, and why was it coming to light now?

Amethyst folded the letter up, put it in the envelope, and slipped it inside her handbag. When it came down to it, she was pretty sure she knew who had written this, almost positive in fact. One other thing she did know: they were going to be very, very sorry. Evidently, they'd forgotten with whom they were dealing.

"Amethyst," her new husband called from downstairs. "We're going to be late if we don't get a move on pretty soon."

"One second, dear. I'll be right there," she trilled.

For a moment, she toyed with taking her knife along but discarded the idea. If she did, she'd have to change handbags, and that would ruin her outfit. No. She'd get who she thought it was in a not quite so

11

public setting later. Let them think she would go along with them. That would make the surprise that much sweeter.

She turned around and studied herself in the mirror. Not bad. Not bad at all, even if she did have to say so herself. The body was still good, and after she had a little work done around her neck area, she'd be perfect. As she went down the stairs, she smiled. It had been a while since she had had this kind of fun. She was looking forward to it. She really was.

CHAPTER 1

Libby looked at the darkening sky. In her dream the sky had been black with crows. They'd covered the tree limbs, and then they had popped out of her mother's pumpkin pie, and she'd woken up in a cold sweat. It had been a long time since she'd had dreams like that. God, she hoped they weren't coming back after all these years. She was wondering what the dream meant — dreams like that always meant something — when she realized that her sister was talking to her.

"It's dark out," Bernie observed as she muscled the van around a turn.

Libby grunted. The wind had picked up. Leaves skittered across the road. "A storm's coming in."

"So you're saying it's a dark and stormy night?"

Libby looked at her sister and shook her head. "That was bad."

Bernie grinned. "But irresistible."

Libby smiled despite herself. Her sister could always make her smile. That was one of the things she loved about her. After a moment, Libby went back to looking out. The road they were on twisted its way through the woods as it went up the hill. Every once in a while, she caught sight of their destination floating above the trees. The view was not reassuring.

"You should have taken the main road," Libby said. Their van wasn't really equipped for driving on dirt and gravel.

Bernie shrugged. "It'll be fine. Nervous?" she asked.

"About the job?" The truth was Libby always got a little nervous before a catering job. It was just the way she was constituted.

"No. About working at the Peabody School."

"Why should I be?" Libby asked. It was not that she didn't know the answer to Bernie's question; she did. She just didn't want to admit it.

"After all, the place is haunted."

Libby snorted.

"People have seen them," said Bernie.

"Them?"

"The ghosts, Libby. The Peabody School even has a blurb in the book *Haunted*

14

Houses in New York."

Since Libby didn't believe that everything that was in print was true, she felt no need to comment. She wished Bernie would slow down. The van wasn't that stable to begin with, and when it was fully loaded, well. She closed her eyes and tried not to think about the consequences of going off the road. They'd packed the van well, but there was only so much one could do.

Bernie took her eyes off the road for a second and looked at her sister. "Well, I think that having a Halloween Haunted House in a real haunted house is a neat idea."

"I never said it wasn't," Libby replied as she did a quick mental recap of the menu they'd be serving.

She and Bernie had decided to design the menu around the theme of waffles. Somehow they'd seemed right. Then she'd seen a recipe for them in the food pages of the *New York Times,* and she knew that she and Bernie were on track.

Given everything that was happening in the world these days, people wanted comfort food, and waffles certainly fit the bill. In addition, you could dress them up or down. They appealed to everyone. And because they would be served in the evening, instead

15

of during the morning, you had that whole fish out of water thing going on. Not only that, but from a business point of view, waffles were cheap to make. The ingredients cost next to nothing, and it took about five minutes to mix up the batter.

Libby was particularly proud of the chocolate brownie batter waffles she'd dreamed up. The finely ground black pepper gave them a particularly nice kick by balancing the sweet and the hot. Of course, the other waffles weren't bad, either. They would serve four kinds: regular, Belgian, the aforementioned chocolate brownie, and pumpkin. The waffles would be garnished with appropriate homemade ice creams and sauces: whipped cream and strawberries for the Belgian waffles, vanilla ice cream and hot fudge sauce for the chocolate brownie waffles, maple sauce and vanilla ice cream for the regular waffles, and a poached apple compote with cinnamon ice cream for the pumpkin ones. Naturally, they were providing maple syrup, apple butter, and homemade apricot and strawberry jam as well. Just thinking about the waffles quieted the butterflies in Libby's stomach.

As they rounded another turn in the road, flocks of crows in the treetops swirled up in the air; they came down again as the van

16

passed by. The birds' disapproving cawing followed the vehicle around the next bend.

"There seem to be more and more of them every year," Libby said.

"There are. Someplace in upstate New York has a crow hunt to get rid of them."

"We should try that."

Bernie laughed, "In Longley? The PC capital of the world? I don't think so."

Libby didn't answer.

Bernie looked at her. Something was bothering her sister. Had been for the past couple of weeks. "Are you all right?"

"I'm fine," said Libby.

"Positive?"

"Positive," Libby repeated.

"You and Marvin are okay, aren't you?"

"I said everything is okay," snapped Libby.

Bernie resisted the impulse to make a smarty-pants comment. Her sister was clearly lying, and things weren't all right, but now obviously wasn't the time to push. Libby would tell her when she was ready. She always did. Instead, Bernie changed the subject.

"There it is," Bernie said as the roof of the Peabody School came back into view. "Our home away from home for the next week. Well, just the evenings really."

"Personally," Libby said, "I've always

17

thought that whoever designed this place had a severe case of indigestion." She sighed. Boy, did she wish they weren't doing this. Halloween was one of A Little Taste of Heaven's busier times, and being out of the shop during the evening meant that they'd be staying up till two and three in the morning prepping the next day's food.

"Lots of work," Bernie said, echoing her sister's thoughts.

"But," Libby continued, "the money —"

Bernie finished the sentence for her. "The money is too good to pass up."

"It certainly is." Libby took another gander at her younger sister's outfit. "I don't see how you can work in that. Isn't it a little . . . snug?"

Bernie looked down at the skintight black dress she was wearing, took one of her hands off the wheel, and waggled her long bloodred fingernails in front of Libby. "Don't worry. I'll manage. I always do."

"I know."

And even though Libby wouldn't say it to anyone, for reasons she couldn't understand, that fact annoyed the hell out of her. By the end of the evening, she would be sweaty, and her clothes would be covered in stuff, but Bernie would look as if she'd just stepped out of the shower. If she were wear-

18

ing the shoes Bernie was wearing, she'd trip and go right into the food. It wasn't fair. She looked down at her sneakers and sighed, then gazed at the school again.

"The place does look like a haunted house," she conceded.

"That's what I just said, Libby."

"No. You said it was a haunted house. There's a difference."

Libby frowned as the van slid on the wet leaves. They went around another turn. A sign that read WELCOME TO THE LONG-ELY VOLUNTEER FIREMEN'S HALLOW-EEN HAUNTED HOUSE sprang into view.

"I'll say one thing for Mark Kane," Libby said. "He did a good job remodeling the place.

"Bree told me he spent almost a million dollars."

"He could toss some our way." Libby began digging around in her bag. "Why is there never any chocolate when you need it?" she asked as she dumped the contents of her bag on her lap.

"Because you probably ate it already."

"I didn't."

"If that's what you want to believe, fine with me."

Libby continued rummaging through the contents of her bag. She had her wallet, her

19

tissues, her appointment book, business-card holder, Swiss Army knife, cell phone, and a bag of glazed cashew nuts, but no chocolate bar. She didn't remember eating it. Could she have left it on the counter of their shop, A Little Taste of Heaven? Libby began throwing everything back in her bag.

"I'll tell you one thing, though," Libby said to her sister. "I sure wouldn't have wanted to go to boarding school here."

"Me either," Bernie agreed. "Way too isolated. And Bessie Osgood going out the window . . ."

"The place may not be haunted," Libby mused, "but lots of bad things have happened here."

"Probably bad feng shui."

Libby rolled her eyes.

"Mock me if you want, but if I were Mark Kane, I would have had this building cleansed before I took it over," said Bernie.

"What is The James Foundation for Scientific Reasoning, anyway?"

"It's a scientific think tank. . . ."

"Whatever that is," replied Libby.

"I think it's a conservative think tank."

"Meaning?"

"I'm just telling you what Bree told me," said Bernie.

"She probably doesn't know, either,"

Libby grumbled. "No reason she should," she added as she picked a piece of lint off her denim jacket. "She just sold him the property and got a nice fat commission."

"We're definitely in the wrong business," Bernie observed.

"You really think that?" Libby asked.

"No. I love what we do," Bernie said as she swerved to avoid a rock lying in the middle of the road.

"Me too," Libby replied. If she thought about it, she couldn't imagine her life without the shop.

"So what do you think happened to the Reverend Peabody and his wife, Esme ralda?"

"I think he killed her and threw her body in the Hudson and died of a heart attack a year later," replied Libby.

"They both died on Halloween night, one year apart. Don't you find that a little strange?"

"Not really. Can we change the subject?" Libby asked.

Bernie shrugged. "If you want. Okay. What do you want to talk about?"

"I'm just wondering if we brought enough waffle machines with us?"

"Of course, we brought enough. We did the math, remember?"

"We could have miscalculated." Libby bit at her cuticle again.

"You always say that, and we never do. You worry too much," said Bernie.

Which Libby knew was true. After all, waffles weren't the only things they were serving. The van was packed with apple squares, lemon squares, pumpkin bars, brownies, chocolate chip cookies, sticky buns, pear crumb cake, banana bread, pumpkin pie, and apple walnut cake, among other things, as well as gallons of spiced cider and chai. In addition, they had containers for coffee and for hot water for tea in the van, as well as fifteen large jack-o'-lanterns, which they were planning on using for decoration. They should really be fine.

"We're here," Bernie said as she rounded the last turn.

She put the van in park. It shuddered. Not a good sign. The last time she'd taken it in for an oil change, Sully had told her the transmission was going.

Libby frowned. "I would never have picked this place to do business out of."

"Me either," Bernie agreed as she yanked up her panty hose. "But Bree said he fell in love with the place. Said it would suit his needs perfectly."

A moment later the door to the back

entrance swung open, and Mark Kane came bounding out.

"And here's the man of the hour," Libby said to Bernie out of the corner of her mouth as he came closer.

Bernie nodded. He looked exactly like he did when he'd first come into their shop: like the successful entrepreneur, the go-to guy.

"Glad to have you two on board," he said. "I can't wait to have a piece of your apple pie. I went in yesterday, and I had to settle for a slice of cranberry-apple. Not that that was bad. It was amazingly good. I've gained about ten pounds since I've been here, and I put it all down to your shop."

Libby laughed. The guy could be charming, she'd give him that, although she never quite trusted men who were like that.

Mark gestured toward the mansion. "You like what we've done decoration-wise?"

"Love it," Bernie said.

"You don't think the heads on the spikes and the severed limbs dangling from the window are too much?" asked Mark.

"Maybe a tad," Bernie allowed.

"In the ads I stated that no one under twelve would be admitted," said Mark. "There are plenty of other places for young kids to go, and I wanted to do something over the top without having to worry about the little ones' sensibilities."

"Good thinking," Libby said. She couldn't imagine the nightmares a kid would have after seeing something like this.

"And we're having everyone sign a liability waiver," Mark said.

Bernie giggled. "Like they did for some of the horror movies in the fifties."

Mark grinned. It made his face look slightly lopsided. He snapped his fingers. "I knew I forgot something. A doctor and an ambulance."

"And the nurse," said Bernie. "Don't forget the nurse."

Mark's grin grew wider. "I'll see what I can do."

"So it's going to be a good show?" Bernie asked.

Mark rubbed his hands together. "A good show? It's going to be a great show. The best this town has ever seen. Forget the guy in the sheet jumping out at you and yelling boo and the dime-store skeletons hanging from the door frames. We're going to do much better than that. Come on. Let me show you what we've done since you were here last."

"We'd love to," Libby told him, "but we have to get the batter in the fridge." She consulted her watch. "Plus, we need setup time. We're behind schedule as it is."

"Not to worry," said Mark. He removed his phone from the clip on his belt, called someone, and spoke for a few seconds. "I just told Carl to come out," he explained after he ended the call. "He'll unload the van for you."

"I think I'd rather do it myself," Libby said. She really didn't like the idea of someone else handling their stuff. Actually, *didn't like* was putting it mildly. *Hated* would be a more accurate term. Who knew what they would do to it.

"Come on," Bernie said to her. "It'll be fine."

Libby could feel herself start to flush. No. It wouldn't be all right. The rule was no one touched their stuff. And Bernie knew it, too.

Mark jumped in. "Carl's worked in restaurants all his life. Anyway, there's no reason why ladies as lovely as yourselves should have to carry heavy things." Before Libby could answer, Carl appeared. "Tell him what to do," Mark ordered.

Bernie did.

Libby took a deep breath and told herself not to say anything now. She would talk to Bernie later. She forced a smile. "Let's go," she told Mark.

He rubbed his hands together. "Good. I'm going to scare you to death."

"I can hardly wait," Libby muttered as they went inside.

CHAPTER 2

Libby looked around the hallway they'd just stepped into. It had been totally transformed since she'd been there two weeks ago. The walls were now painted a dull gray and festooned with cobwebs.

Meat hooks hanging from the ceiling rattled menacingly. The floor looked old and dusty, except for the splatters of what, Libby decided, was supposed to be blood. The overhead fluorescent lights flickered on and off, painting shadows on the walls and floor. Libby sniffed. The place even smelled musty. The only things that looked modern were the EXIT signs over two doors down the hall.

Mark jerked his head in their direction. "The fire marshall insisted on those. I tried to talk him out of it — I think it spoils the mood — but it was a no go."

"I would think so," Libby said as she took a couple of steps forward.

No doubt about it. Mark was definitely getting on her nerves. She stopped for a moment in front of a sign on one of the walls, which said, THIS WAY TO THE EXECUTION. A black arrow pointed to the door on Libby's right. Then she moved over to the square wooden table pushed against the wall. On it sat a cash box, a bunch of forms, and a black cup filled with pens.

"The releases I was telling you about," Mark said, pointing to the pile of paper.

Bernie nodded. A notice on the table stated that the price of admission was thirty dollars.

"A little high, isn't it?" Libby commented.

Mark shrugged. "Hi tech always is."

Libby was about to tell him that was why she liked low tech better, but before she could, Bernie was pointing down the hall.

"I'm a little confused. The kitchen is the last door on the left, isn't it?" asked Bernie.

Mark nodded. "Correct. The corridor we're using for the Haunted House loops around and ends up in the kitchen and the dining room. This is the back part of the mansion. The oldest part. The part where they say Esmeralda is buried."

"Who says?" Libby asked. She wished she could have found her chocolate. That way she wouldn't be so grumpy.

Mark waved his hands in the air. "People say."

"Well, then I guess that's okay. I mean, if dogs said it, then it wouldn't be so good," replied Libby.

Mark shot Libby a puzzled look. Obviously, he hadn't gotten what she was saying. He took a step away from her as he glanced around. Even better. He probably thought she was nutty.

"God, you wouldn't believe how many rooms this place has," Mark said. "And they all connect with one another in weird ways. Tracing the wiring was a nightmare, and I thought the guy that put in the fiber optics was going to quit on me. Let me tell you, we had a hell of a time getting this place up to code."

"That I believe," Bernie said.

Mark nodded toward the door that was marked ENTRANCE. Below it was written, ONCE YOU COME IN HERE, THERE'S NO TURNING BACK.

"Shall we?" he asked.

"You know," Libby said, thinking of everything they had to do, "we really *are* running out of time. Why don't you and Bernie go ahead, and I'll start in the kitchen."

"Nonsense," Mark replied. "This will only take a few minutes. No more than five, I promise. We'll just do a quick walk-through."

Libby was about to say they didn't have five minutes when she caught Bernie glaring at her. Even though her sister hadn't said anything, Libby knew what she wanted to say: something along the lines that Mark was new in town, that he was wealthy, and that he could throw lots of business their way. Which he wouldn't do if Libby pissed him off. So Libby just nodded her head and followed Mark through the door.

When she stepped through to the other side, Libby felt a puff of ice-cold air play up and down her spine. She jumped in spite of herself. Mark laughed.

"That's the oldest trick in the book," he said. "I connected a motion detector to a compressed-air tank."

Libby looked around. The room was totally dark for a second; then a strobe light began flashing. She could hear a faint moan rising and falling. Then she heard another sound. It sounded like a chain saw. It *was* a chain saw. The chain saw got louder. Out of the corner of her eye, she saw a woman over in the corner. Her arms were tied to a chain that was suspended from the ceiling. The woman started screaming. A man with a chain saw appeared from the far corner of the room. The woman's screams got louder as the man got closer.

Libby wanted to look away, but she couldn't as the man came nearer. She could feel her heart racing as the man lifted the saw. The flashes of light from the strobe bounced off the blade, making it dance in the light. *This is all a trick,* Libby told herself. *It's an optical illusion.* But somehow it didn't help.

There was a bloodcurdling shriek as the man raised the chain saw and brought it down on the woman's shoulder. Rivulets of something warm and wet ran down the left side of Libby's face. She couldn't help herself. She screamed.

"It's water," Mark said. "Warm water. It was my idea. Everything is computer con-trolled. We also have a state-of-the-art sound system with volume controls and directional speakers."

Libby jumped. She'd been so focused on the scene in the room that she'd forgotten that Mark was there.

"God, that looked real," Bernie said. She gave a nervous giggle.

"Holograms," Mark said. "We can adjust the images if we want. We can adjust the screams and the sound of the chain saw. I think the blood splatter is a nice touch, don't you? It gets everyone involved."

"Involved?" Libby could hear her voice rising. She took a deep breath and told herself to calm down, because what she wanted to do was throttle him. She took a second breath and a third before she regained control.

Bernie gestured around her. "This must have taken months to figure out."

"Not really," said Mark. "I hired a company, FX Productions, that specializes in this sort of thing. It took them a day and a half to set the show up." Mark shrugged. "I'm not good with technical stuff," he confessed.

"Just making money," Bernie observed.

Mark's grin flashed on and off. "Well, I've found that if you can do that, everything else falls into place. And this is only the beginning of the tour. Wait till you see what else FX has come up with."

"I'd rather not," Libby told him.

Mark reached over and took Libby's hands in his. "But you have to."

"She doesn't like gory stuff," her sister explained.

Mark patted Libby's hands and then let go. "The rest of it is just scary. Promise."

Libby was about to say that she didn't think that was much better when Bernie interrupted.

"Is the whole thing movie themed?" Bernie asked.

Mark shook his head. "Not at all. We have vampires; we have ghosts; we have a little bit of everything."

Libby realized she was still breathing hard. What ever happened to the days when going through a haunted house meant being blindfolded and having your hands forced into a bowl of oatmeal and spaghetti and being told that was someone's guts?

"After you," Libby said to Mark. She just wanted to get this over with.

He laughed. "My pleasure."

"Enjoying yourself?" Bernie asked him.

"I have to confess that I am. I feel like I'm watching my baby take his first steps," said Mark.

And with that, they opened a door and stepped out into a hallway. Smog rolled around their feet and drifted upwards. *A fog machine,* Libby thought. She jumped as a bony hand dropped down in front of her.

"That's Bob," Mark said.

Now that Libby looked closer, she could see the outlines of someone's arm.

"He's one of our actors," added Mark.

"Actors. That's a laugh," came a disembodied voice out of the ceiling.

"Bob Small?" Bernie asked.

"How'd you guess?" came the voice from the ceiling.

"Your voice," said Bernie.

"When did you —" Libby began to say, but Bernie kicked her.

Bob finished the sentence for her. "Get out of jail?"

Libby rubbed her shin. "Yes."

"About two weeks ago," replied Bob.

"Comfortable up there?" Mark asked.

Bob snorted. "Yeah. If you like being in a coffin."

Mark patted his hand. "Don't worry. We'll have someone come and relieve you in two hours."

"Two hours?" Bob squeaked. "What happens if I have to take a leak?"

"We already discussed that. You hold it," Mark told him as he guided Libby and Bernie toward the center of the room. When he got there, he stopped. "I like to give people a second chance," he practically whispered.

"Very noble," Libby observed.

Mark shot his cuffs. "No. It's just what I call enlightened self-interest. You give a guy like that a second chance and he's yours for life. See, we have Bob to set the mood, and then you come over here and see this." He pointed to a big black coffin that was seemingly rising out of the floor.

There was a creak as the coffin's door began to open. A squeal of laughter came from a skeleton as it sat up. He had an eye patch over his left socket and a long mane of white hair that came to his shoulders. He stared straight at them and shook a bony finger.

"Soon you'll look just like me," the skeleton cackled. "Just like me. Eat, drink, and be merry. We don't have six-packs in the graveyard." Then he lay back down as the coffin door started closing. A minute or two later, the coffin was gone.

"It comes up through the floor," Mark explained. "People crossing a point on the floor trip a sensor that raises the coffin."

"Sensor?" Libby asked.

"Yeah. It works on the same principle as a doorbell," Mark replied.

"Like the one we have in the store, which alerts us when customers come in," Bernie added.

"I know," Libby said.

"Well, I was just explaining it in case you didn't," Bernie mumbled.

"But I do," insisted Libby.

Mark cleared his throat. "This is really a throwaway. Something to get you calmed down after the chain-saw scene and before the next thing." He paused for effect. "Because the next thing, as my father used to say, is going to knock your socks off." Mark walked to the door marked EXIT, opened it, and said, "Ladies, welcome to the Pit and the Pendulum. I have to say, I think that Poe would have approved, were he alive today."

Libby took a look around. The walls were mirrored, and in the center of the room was a raised platform. Four steps led up to it. On that platform was a long table, draped in a red cloth. Up above the table, a sharp-looking, curved blade swung back and forth, going lower with each swipe.

"You have to get closer to get the full effect," Mark said as he gave Libby a little nudge. She took a few steps. There was a headless body lying on the table.

"See," Mark said. "You stand in the center and you see your head being chopped off."

"Lovely," Libby said. She gritted her teeth and took another step. Never let it be said that she wasn't a good sport. "What's that?" she asked, pointing to the woman's head sitting on the first step from the top. It stared up at her. It looked incredibly life-like. It also looked familiar. Very familiar.

"Shouldn't the head be sitting in a pool of

blood?" Bernie asked.

Mark didn't answer her. "Wait," he said instead, and he put out his hand.

Libby stopped.

"Give me a moment," Mark said.

Libby noticed he was frowning. "Is something wrong?" she asked.

Mark didn't reply. His attention was focused on the head.

"Well, is there?" Bernie asked while she watched Mark take another step forward. She had a bad feeling in her gut. "Is that a hologram?" she asked. "Because it looks pretty solid if it is."

Libby watched as Mark stretched out one of his feet and gave the head a tentative tap with the toe of his shoe. It began rolling down the steps . . . bump, bump, bump . . . and then it kept going until it stopped at Libby's feet.

This is not a hologram, Libby thought. *Holograms do not make noises like that.*

And then she had another thought.

The head was not made of wax. It wasn't made of plaster. It was flesh and blood.

Libby didn't know how she knew. She just did.

And then she knew how she knew.

Libby stared at the face staring up at her. She'd recognize those eyebrows anywhere.

"It's Amethyst Applegate," she cried.

Which was when Libby started screaming.

CHAPTER 3

Sean Simmons took a bite of his pumpkin bar. "Not bad," he remarked. "Not bad at all."

As he brushed a small piece of the pumpkin bar off his lap, he thought that in the normal course of things, his daughter Libby would have taken those words as fighting words. Tonight she hadn't even blinked. In fact, she hadn't said much since she and her sister had come running in, yelling about what had happened down at the Peabody School.

Not that he was surprised. Some places just had bad karma. Of course, he hadn't said that to Bernie and Libby when they'd told him about this job, because he didn't like to talk about certain things. Now he was thinking that maybe he should have. Then he pushed that thought away. Better to concentrate on the known and leave the rest to all the weirdos out there.

"You've added a touch more cinnamon, haven't you?" he said.

Libby's eyes widened fractionally. "How can you ask me something like that at a time like this?" she demanded.

"I thought you liked talking about food," Sean commented as he turned his wheelchair slightly so he could look out. The wind had picked up and was blowing the leaves on the street into the air. He could hear the creak of the store sign as it swayed back and forth. It looked as if a cold front was coming through.

"I do, but I don't want to talk about food now," Libby said.

Sean turned to face her. "Well, what do you want me to talk about?" he asked.

Not that he didn't know. Bernie would say he was being disingenuous, but he'd found in his years as chief of police of Longley that it was better to let the witnesses, especially if they were in a state of shock, introduce the story themselves.

"We want to hear what you have to say about what happened at the Peabody School, of course," Bernie said.

"But I wasn't there," Sean reminded her.

Libby leaned forward and pointed at her sister. "And we wouldn't have been, either, if it weren't for her."

Bernie snorted. "Like I knew what was going to happen?"

"If we had been setting up like we were supposed to, we wouldn't have been there. We would have been in the kitchen," Libby snapped.

"We were cultivating a potential customer, which, in my humble opinion, was worth the ten minutes we were going to spend having Mark show us around," Bernie countered. "Besides, it was interesting to see how the place was rigged up."

"Not to me," said Libby as she put her hand on her forehead. "I'm going to have nightmares for years."

"Oh, don't be so dramatic," Bernie snapped.

"It's true. I am," Libby wailed.

Bernie groaned. "Which you're going to blame on me, just like you do everything else."

"That is so unfair," Libby retorted.

"Girls," Sean said before Bernie could reply.

Both of them turned to him.

"Enough," said Sean.

"But," Libby began.

Sean held up his hand. "I mean it. This bickering —"

"We're not bickering," Bernie objected.

41

"Fine," Sean said. "Whatever you want to call what you're doing doesn't do no one —"

"Anyone . . . ," Bernie corrected.

Sean glared at Bernie. She'd been like this ever since she'd learned to talk. "Any good. So do you have to give the retainer back? Is the Haunted House closed down for the duration?"

Libby and Bernie both shook their heads.

"It's opening tomorrow afternoon," Bernie volunteered.

Sean snorted. "You're kidding."

"Nope. That's what Mark told us."

"This has to be the fastest processing of a crime scene in the history of the town. But then what do I know? I'm an old man," said Sean. He tapped his fingers on the side of his chair. At least in his day, they would have kept the crime scene closed off for a couple of days. He'd learned to his cost that if you rushed, you always missed something.

Bernie took another sip of her Scotch and put her glass down. "Well, it is a big fundraiser for the volunteer fire department."

"And money always wins," Sean said after he'd taken another bite of his pumpkin bar. "You better bake some more of these. You know what people are like. The more gruesome the crime, the more people want to

42

see where it took place and the hungrier they are after they've seen it."

"Yeah," Bernie said. "When business is slow, we should just kill someone."

Libby glared at her. "That's disgusting."

"But true," Bernie countered. "Every time we're involved in a case, the shop is packed."

"I wonder why?" said Libby.

"People are nosy," Sean said. "Look what happens when there's an accident. Everyone always slows down."

Bernie frowned as she thought. Finally, she said, "Or maybe it's because we miss that kind of stuff on some primordial level. You know, in the old days, they used to have public hangings and torture. Now there's nothing like that. Maybe that's why haunted houses and horror movies are so popular. People like to be scared and disgusted."

"Not me," Libby said firmly. "Not in any way, shape, or form. In fact, I don't think I want to go back there."

"You don't have to if you don't want to," Sean told her.

Bernie untwisted her legs and stood up. "Yes, we do. We have a contract."

Sean took a final bite of his pumpkin bar. "I think a beheading might count as a cancellation clause, don't you?" he asked after he swallowed. He'd love a cigarette now, but since the girls didn't know he'd gone back to smoking, he couldn't ask them to get him any.

Libby folded over the empty wrapper of the chocolate bar she'd been eating and creased the line with her thumb. Then she did the same thing again.

"I'm serious. Maybe I won't go," she announced.

"Why?" Bernie said. "What more can happen? Anyway, then we'd have to give back the money, which we can't exactly afford to do."

Sean watched his eldest daughter run her thumb across the edge of the wrapper again. She didn't say anything.

"For real," Bernie said to Libby. "What more can happen?"

"Someone could cut off our heads," Libby replied.

Bernie rolled her eyes. "Please. You can't be serious."

"Of course, I am. Why wouldn't I be?" said Libby.

Sean coughed. The girls turned back to him.

"You know," he said. "Amethyst has . . . had . . . a lot of enemies. I don't think this crime was committed by some nut looking to get his jollies off. I think it was committed by someone looking to kill Amethyst. So you two have nothing to worry about."

"My sentiments exactly," Bernie agreed.

Libby stood up. "But you don't know that for a fact."

"It's true, but that's what my gut tells me," said Sean.

Libby plucked at the top button of the shirt she was wearing, then absentmindedly rearranged the magazines on the table over by the wall. "She wasn't well liked, was she?"

Sean wiped his fingers on the napkin in front of him. "That's one way of putting it. Look at what she did to Bob Small."

Bernie put her hand to her mouth. "I can't believe I forgot to tell you. We saw him today. He was working at the Haunted House, as a skeleton."

Sean raised an eyebrow. "Now that's interesting."

Bernie sat back down and took a sip of her Scotch. "I bet the police are going to pick him up in a hurry. I'd be surprised if he's there when we go back."

Libby shook her head. "I don't know. I can't see him doing this. He's just not the kind of guy who would chop someone's head off."

"In my experience, you get someone angry

enough and you'd be amazed what they can do," Sean said. "Remember Bernard? He weighed what? One hundred pounds, if that? He was so shy he could hardly look you in the face when he talked, and yet he managed to kill his two-hundred-and-fifty-pound girlfriend, drag her out of the house, and put her in the trunk of his car before he was caught, and that was only because he couldn't get the lid all the way down, so he tied it shut. If he'd gone to Boy Scout camp and practiced his knots, he might never have been found out."

Libby frowned. "Bob Small went to jail because he stole stuff."

"No," Sean said. "Bob Small went to jail because he gave Amethyst a top-of-the-line BMW off the lot of the dealer he was working for so she could get to work and back while she had her car fixed. But instead of doing that, she took off to Florida with a guy she picked up at a bar and totaled the Beamer. Bob lost his wife and his job and spent a year in prison because of her little shenanigans. If that's not a motive, I don't know what is."

Libby was about to reply when the door buzzer rang downstairs.

"You think Bob is guilty?" Bernie asked her dad as Libby went to see who was at

46

the door.

Sean shrugged. "Don't know, but if I were the investigating officer, I'd like Bob for it. He had motive and opportunity. Of course, like I was saying, Amethyst had plenty of enemies in town. Considering all the things she pulled, it's a wonder someone didn't do something like this before."

"She liked to make trouble just because she could," Bernie observed as she studied one of her nails. She really needed to get them done. And talk about getting things done. She was developing frown lines. Maybe it was time for a little Botox. Character lines were nice, but no need to go too far.

"Some people get a real kick out of that," Sean said.

"In this case she got kicked back."

Sean grunted. His attention was focused on the footsteps running up the stairs.

"Who the hell is that?" he asked as two men burst through the door. Libby was right behind them.

She gave her father an apologetic look. "They insisted on coming up."

"It's okay." Sean could feel himself relaxing. He glanced up at the two men approaching him. "Well, well, Curtis and Konrad Kurtz," Sean said. "I haven't seen you

47

boys in a while. Still got the same bad haircuts, I see."

Both men stopped. They shuffled their feet. Konrad hugged the tape deck he was carrying closer to his chest.

"We don't drink anymore," Curtis volunteered. "That night was the last time."

Sean laughed. "Yeah. That was quite a night. How many guys did you send to the ER to get stitched up?"

"Six," Konrad said. "But like Curtis said, we don't do that no more."

Curtis raised his hand. "I swear. Except for Thursday night bowling, when we have one or two brews."

"Sometimes three," Konrad said. "But that's the max. Honest." He nodded toward his stomach with his chin. "We're hardworking family men now."

"That's a good thing," Sean said.

Both men nodded solemnly.

"We're working for Mr. Kane," said Curtis. "Maintenance. Before that, we worked for the housing complex off Ridge Road."

"That's very nice," Sean said. "So what brings you boys out this time of night?"

Curtis adjusted his suspenders. "It's about what happened at the Haunted House."

Sean waited. When nothing else was forthcoming, he told them to go on. There was more shuffling of feet; then Konrad spoke.

"See, we got this other hobby besides bowling and being volunteer firemen. Only it ain't really a hobby. It's more like an avocation. We go all over doing it. Some people think it's silly, but it's serious."

Curtis pointed to himself and puffed his chest out. "We're professional ghost hunters. We even went to school for it. We got certificates to prove it."

"You went to school?" Bernie asked. "What school?"

"The Vincent Ludovic School for Paranormal Phenomena. You can look it up on the Web if you want to. We are trained professionals," said Curtis.

"I'm relieved," Bernie said. "I thought you might be fakes."

Sean motioned for her to be quiet. "Go on," he said.

Konrad shot Bernie a reproachful glance. "Well, we are the real thing. Being twins and all gives us a certain knack for it."

"I didn't know that twinness gave you a leg up in that department," Bernie said.

"It's true," Konrad told her. "Boy Scout oath of honor. Me and Curtis been doin' this for a while now. We done the Perkins Place and the graveyard over at Three Trees.

We even done this house over in Parker, PA."

"And how do you ghost hunt?" Sean asked.

Konrad motioned to his tape deck with a nod of his head. "We get tape recordings. You can't hear anything if you're just standing there, but if you ask people questions, sometimes you can hear their answers when you play the tape back. It's called EVP. Electronic voice processing."

"You mean electronic voice phenomena," Bernie corrected.

"There was a program on TV about that," Libby said.

"That's where we got the idea from," Konrad said. "And like I just said, it turns out we got a real talent for it."

"I take it this has something to do with why you're here?" Sean asked.

As Sean watched Curtis and Konrad nod, he noticed that they didn't really look like twins at all. Curtis was blond and skinny, while Konrad was broad and dark. But they had the same mannerisms and dressed alike.

"Okay. I think it's time you told me what this is about," said Sean.

Konrad and Curtis looked at each other. After a few seconds, Konrad said, "Well, Mr. Kane hired us to be ghost hunters for

50

this haunted house thing, and we jumped at the chance because there are actual ghosts in there, and lots of people have seen them. There's Reverend Peabody; and his wife, Esmeralda; and Bessie Osgood, the kid that died, the one that was related to your wife."

Libby turned to her dad. "You never told me she was related to Mom."

"She was a distant cousin," Sean said.

"Why didn't you mention it?" Libby asked.

Sean shrugged. "There didn't seem to be any need to."

"Mom never mentioned it at all," Bernie said.

"Well, she wasn't one to mention painful subjects," replied Sean.

"Painful?" Libby repeated.

"People said Bessie committed suicide," said Sean.

"That's not what Bessie says," Konrad interrupted.

Sean raised an eyebrow. "And you know this how?" he asked.

" 'Cause, she told us. She told us other things, too. We got it right down on this tape recorder," said Konrad.

There sure was a lot of nuttiness out in the world, Sean decided as he looked at the two men standing before him. "Fine," he

51

said. "But how does that explain why you're here?"

"We're here," Curtis said, "because we know who killed Amethyst."

"So go to the police," said Sean.

"We tried, but they didn't want to listen to our tape," said Konrad.

"And why do you think we will?" Sean asked.

"Because," Curtis said, taking over, "you always listened. You listened to our side that night."

"That was different. It was my job to listen," said Sean. "There was a brawl between you and eight other guys, and I wanted to know what started it."

"And you let us go," Konrad said.

"The Myers brothers were punks."

"So you gonna listen, or what?" Curtis asked.

Sean shook his head. He was definitely getting soft in his old age. But what the hell. Why not? It wasn't like he was going out anywhere tonight.

"Sure," he said. "Play the tape. Let's hear what you got."

CHAPTER 4

Bernie watched Konrad put the machine down on the table in front of her dad's wheelchair. It was one of those old-fashioned reel-to-reel tape recorders.

"Where did you get that?" she asked.

"From my uncle's basement. It's real old. Almost an antique," replied Konrad.

"It looks it," Bernie said.

"But it works better than cassette players or those new voice recording things. It picks up more stuff," said Konrad.

"I used to have one of those in the eighties," Sean remarked. "My wife made me throw it out. Me, I like to keep things like that."

"That's because you're a pack rat," Libby observed.

"No. You just never know when something is going to come in handy," said Sean.

"Like Konrad said," Curtis replied, "this deck works real fine."

"I didn't say it didn't," Bernie said. "I just said it was old."

Konrad held up his hand. "Listen now." Everyone fell quiet and leaned forward. "Here we go," he said, and he clicked the switch.

Bernie heard someone that sounded like Konrad say, "Are we on?" Then Curtis answered, "We're rolling," and then she heard a lot of static and white noise.

After a minute Curtis stabbed the air with his finger. "Did you hear that?" he asked excitedly.

"I hear static," Bernie said.

"No. Listen harder. There's Bessie," said Curtis.

"I'm sorry?" replied Bernie.

"Focus," Curtis said.

"I'm trying," said Bernie. And she leaned forward, closed her eyes, and concentrated. She thought she heard someone say, "Get out. Get out," in a hoarse whisper. A chill went down her spine. She shook her head. *Bernie, get a grip,* she told herself. This evening was affecting her more than she'd thought. Now her hearing was playing tricks on her.

"You heard something, didn't you?" Konrad asked her.

"I'm not sure," Bernie said.

"That's Bessie," Konrad said. "Here." And he stopped the tape and played it again.

This time Bernie didn't hear anything except a hiss. There were no words.

"I didn't hear anyone talking this time," Bernie said.

"Sometimes that happens," Konrad said.

Bernie turned to her father. "Did you hear anything?"

Sean shook his head, but the way he shook it made Bernie wonder if he had.

"I know I didn't," Libby said, but Bernie noticed her sister had the look she had on her face whenever she had one of her dreams.

"But you have to have heard it," Konrad said. "I'll make it louder." And he turned up the volume. Now the room was filled with earsplitting static.

Sean winced. "It reminds me of someone drawing their nails across a blackboard."

As Curtis leaned over the tape deck, Bernie decided if he got any closer, he'd be in it.

"See," Curtis said, stabbing the air again. "There's Bessie."

Bernie shook her head. All she heard was a hiss. Maybe she heard a word. Home? House? No. There was nothing there. She was just hearing things because Curtis was suggesting that she do so. This was a subtle form of hypnosis.

Konrad began pounding his leg with his fist. "I can't believe you can't hear this. She's telling us she cut Amethyst's head off."

"I don't hear anything," Libby said.

Bernie straightened up. This was giving her a headache. "You know," she said to Konrad, "it's been a really bad day, and I want to finish my drink, take a shower, and go to bed."

Konrad turned to Sean. "You heard something, didn't you?" There was a pleading note in his voice.

Sean shook his head. "Sorry. I can't say that I did."

"Let me rewind it, and we can try again," said Konrad.

Sean held up his hand. "Let's not. Instead, why don't you turn it off and tell me what you think Bessie Osgood told you."

Konrad looked at Curtis, who shrugged and nodded.

"Okay," Konrad said.

Bernie breathed a sigh of relief as Konrad flicked the switch up. The room became blessedly quiet.

Konrad and Curtis exchanged another glance. Then Curtis turned to Sean and said, "She said she cut off Amethyst's head."

"That's it?" asked Sean.

"What do you mean, 'That's it?' " Curtis demanded.

"Well, did she say anything else?" asked Sean.

"She says why she did it," said Curtis. "Here" — his hand moved to the switch — "you can hear for yourself."

"That won't be necessary," Sean said quickly. "Why don't you tell me instead?"

Konrad shrugged. "It's simple. She did it because Amethyst threw her out the window, and she wanted to get even."

"I see," Sean said.

"So you don't believe us?" Curtis cried.

Sean grimaced. "I believe you think you heard that."

"No. We heard it," Konrad insisted.

Curtis nodded. "We did," he said. "Her voice was as clear as a bell jar."

"Bell. The expression is 'clear as a bell,' " Bernie corrected.

"That's what I said," Curtis told her.

"No. You said 'bell jar,' " Bernie repeated.

"They're the same thing," Curtis retorted.

"No, they're not," Bernie said, and she went over and took another sip of her Scotch. As she was putting her glass down, she looked over and saw Libby eating the

57

piece of pumpkin bar her dad hadn't gotten to yet. She glanced away before she caught her sister's eye. She was having a hard enough time keeping a straight face as it was.

"The problem is," Bernie said to Curtis, "that ghosts are incorporeal beings."

"They don't get diseases," Konrad cried.

"No. Incorporeal, meaning 'without substance.' They don't have hands to grip axes or chain saws or whatever was used to cut off people's heads."

"They have energy," Konrad protested. "They can do amazing things. We learned that in our class. Right, Curtis?"

"Right, Konrad," said Curtis.

"I'm sorry, but ghosts don't go around lopping off people's heads, no matter how good the reason they have," Bernie told Konrad.

Curtis put his hands on his hips. "That shows you how much you know. Ghosts can do anything they want. They can move chairs. . . ."

"That's a poltergeist," Bernie snapped.

"*Poltergeist* is just a fancy name for a different type of ghost," Curtis told her.

Bernie threw up her arms. "I give up."

"That's because I'm right," Curtis replied. Then he turned to Sean. "She's awful excitable, isn't she?"

"I am not!" Bernie yelled.

Sean held up his hand. "Let's talk about something else for a moment, if you don't mind."

"I don't mind," Curtis said.

"That was a rhetorical question," Bernie informed him.

"The question is," Sean said hurriedly, cutting Bernie off, "isn't Bob Small related to you?"

Curtis looked at his feet.

"That's what I thought," Sean said. His legs weren't doing too good anymore, but that didn't mean his memory wasn't as good as it ever was.

Konrad drew himself up. "Maybe he is our cousin, but so what?"

"The *so what* is obvious," Bernie retorted.

"Are you saying my brother and I are lying about this?" Curtis said. "That we have ulcerated motives?"

Bernie laughed. "You mean ulterior motives."

Curtis's face began to get red.

"She's not saying that," Sean said quickly. Curtis and Konrad had had bad tempers when they were younger, and Sean was pretty sure that despite what they said, they still had them.

"Then what is she saying?" Curtis asked.

"She's saying you are hearing what you want to hear," said Sean.

Konrad lifted up his tape deck. "Come on, Curtis," he said to his brother. "Let's get out of here. No point in wasting anyone else's time."

"What did you want us to do?" Sean asked Konrad.

"We wanted you to prove that Bessie Osgood killed Amethyst Applegate, of course," said Konrad.

"Of course," Sean repeated. He could just imagine what his pal Clyde would say when he heard about this one.

Curtis shuffled his feet for a moment, then said, "We'll pay you."

"Money is not the issue," Sean told him as he moved his wheelchair a little to the left so he could watch Mr. Wilson walk his Chihuahua, Merlin. It always amused him to see such a big man with such a little dog. At the moment Merlin was trying to subdue a jack-o'-lantern on someone's doorstep by peeing on it.

"Then what is?" Curtis asked.

"There is no way to prove that Bessie Osgood killed Amethyst Applegate. Even if you had a viable tape, it wouldn't matter," Sean said after Mr. Wilson had rounded the corner. "I've never heard of ghostly testimony being accepted by the DA. And let me go further. The original crime happened over twenty years ago, and if I remember correctly, opinion was divided as to its cause."

"The dead have just as much right to justice as the living," Curtis protested.

"You're going to have to take that up with the judicial system," Sean told him. "I'm sorry, but there it is." He sighed. Why did Curtis and Konrad make him feel guilty? They shouldn't, but they did. "So do you have anything else you want to tell me?" he asked in the ensuing silence.

Curtis and Konrad looked at each other. They both cleared their throats.

"We don't think it's fair," Konrad blurted out, "that Amethyst got Bob in trouble before, and she's done it again."

"Bob loaned her the car," Sean said. "She didn't put a gun to his head and force him to."

"That's true. But she sweet-talked him into it. If he hadn't met her, he'd be all right now," Curtis said. "He'd still have his family and his job."

There was no arguing with that, Sean decided. "Do the police have Bob in custody yet?" he asked.

"No," Konrad said. "But they're gonna."

"He's a convicted felon, and he was there," Curtis said. "Of course, they're going to pick him up."

"True," said Sean as he spied Mr. Wilson heading back around the corner. He was carrying Merlin in his jacket pocket.

"The guy needs a break," Konrad continued. "And it's especially frustrating for us because we got the proof, and no one will listen to us." He lowered his voice. "Even our wives think we're a little wacko with this stuff."

Sean pursed his lips while he thought. "I'll tell you what. How about if me and the girls look into this?"

"That's all we want," Curtis said.

"But if whatever we find leads in the direction of Bob Small, that's the way we're going to go," said Sean.

"I keep telling you that Bessie Osgood did it," Curtis said.

"Maybe she did, and maybe she didn't," Sean said. "Maybe someone else did. That's what we're going to try and find out."

Konrad and Curtis nodded. "We'll leave the tape for you," they both said at the same time.

"Appreciate it," Sean said. "Tell me, how about the Reverend Peabody or Esmeralda?

You heard anything from them?"

"Dad," Bernie cried.

"I was just asking," Sean replied.

"To answer your question," Curtis said, "we haven't yet. But we intend to try. Mr. Kane said he'd pay us a thousand bucks if we get their voices."

"Dad," Bernie repeated after the two men had left.

Sean looked up from the newspaper he'd picked up. It was two days old, but that was the way he liked his news. Past its prime. It gave some perspective to it.

"What?" he asked.

"I can't believe you agreed to do that," said Bernie.

"I don't see why not," Sean retorted.

"Because Curtis and Konrad are crazy," said Bernie.

"A little strange maybe, but not crazy. After all, everyone has their private obsessions," said Sean.

"But Dad," Bernie continued. "You just said that you thought Bob Small chopped off Amethyst Applegate's head."

"No," Sean corrected. "What I said was that if I were the police, I would like him for it. That doesn't mean that I think he did it."

"But Bob Small had motive, means, and opportunity," Bernie wailed. "Those are your words."

"I know. But I think he's too obvious," replied Sean. "Over the years I've found that things that come wrapped up in pretty, neat little packages with bows on top of them rarely are what they seem."

"So you're saying that you think that Bob Small was set up?" Libby asked.

"I'm saying it's a possibility," Sean replied. "Which is why we should come up with a list of Amethyst's enemies and everyone who had access to the Haunted House and cross-reference them."

Bernie sighed. "It's going to be a lengthy list."

Sean cast a longing glance at his paper. "I'm aware of that."

"And we're doing this why?" asked Bernie.

"Because the case interests me, and because I don't want to see our redoubtable chief of police put the wrong man in jail," said Sean.

"Lucy could do that," Libby agreed, referring to the chief of police by his nickname.

"Lucas Broadbent has done it," Sean said. "Several times." He turned to Bernie. "And while you're at it, see what you can find out about what happened to Bessie Osgood."

"You're kidding, right?" Bernie asked.

"Not in the least," said Sean. "My gut tells me she's at the root of this in some way or other."

"Is this the same gut that told you to go west to Mr. Leonida's house when you should have been going east?" said Bernie.

"Just humor an old man, will you?" said Sean.

"Fine," Bernie said. She finished the last of her drink. "Maybe Curtis and Konrad do have something. After all, Halloween is the time of year when ghosts are supposed to come visit us mortals, the time when the veil between the two worlds is at its thinnest. The Celts thought so two thousand years ago. Who am I to argue?"

Libby groaned. "You don't believe in ghosts, do you, Dad?" she asked.

"No. But I believe in bad luck places. And I think the Peabody School falls under that category," said Sean.

Libby frowned. Maybe the money they were getting wasn't worth it, after all.

"Oh, come on," Bernie said, looking at her sister's face. "I told you nothing else is going to happen. Trust me on this."

Libby got up. "You know," she said, "whenever anyone tells me that, I've found that the opposite is usually true."

Then, before Bernie could reply, Libby went downstairs to bake some more pumpkin bars. Baking always made her feel better. And, anyway, her dad was right. They were going to be swamped tomorrow.

CHAPTER 5

Bernie looked at the three pumpkins she'd just carved to put in front of the shop's doorway. The first looked like a witch, the second looked like a cat, and the third one she'd carved into the shape of a goblin, complete with a wart on her nose. *Thank heavens for how-to books,* Bernie thought. What did people ever do before them? She removed her apron and dusted off her shirt. Black parachute silk and powdered sugar definitely didn't mix. But at least for once she hadn't gotten any pumpkin glop on her clothes.

She looked over at her sister, who was working away in jeans, a flannel shirt, and a T-shirt. Libby's clothes made more sense, especially when one was dusting powdered sugar on apple bars, but Bernie could never bring herself to wear outfits like that. What was the point? They were boring. And she had a reputation to uphold. People expected her to dress impractically now. It was part of who she was.

Bernie brushed a speck of powdered sugar off her black Dolce & Gabbana pants and checked her shoes for smudges. They were black suede and three inches high. Definitely not made for the kitchen, but she wasn't planning on being here for much longer. She had stuff to do for her dad.

"I'm going now," she said.

"I can see that," Libby told her sister, but her eyes remained focused on the pie dough she was rolling out. She'd done six pumpkin pies already and she had six more to go for the Haunted House. Her pumpkin pies always went fast. Maybe that was because she started out with real pumpkin puree instead of the canned stuff. The color was prettier, and the flavor and texture more delicate.

"Do we need anything?" Bernie asked.

Libby stopped for a moment and thought. "A couple of gallons of cider and some red food dye. I want to make two more batches of devil cookies for the display case. Everyone seems to be enjoying them. And if you're stopping by Sam's Club, we could use some more chicken breasts for our red ginger chicken."

"But I got some yesterday," Bernie protested.

"We don't have any left."

"Have you looked in the cooler?"

Libby went back to rolling. "Check if you don't believe me," she told her sister.

Bernie repositioned her bobby pin to stop her bangs from falling in her eyes. That was the problem with letting your hair grow in. It just went every which way. But, on the other hand, it did hide her crow's-feet. "We sold that much?"

Libby shrugged. "It would seem so."

Maybe they had, Bernie thought. Or maybe someone was stealing the chicken. Except she couldn't believe that Googie or Amber would do something like that. Shrinkage was a definite problem in their business, but Googie and Amber had been with them for years.

"We should keep better track of our inventory," Bernie said.

"Yes, we should," Libby agreed.

Bernie realized that they had this discussion every six months or so, and nothing ever came of it.

"And I vote that you be the one to do it. And be back by three-thirty," Libby added. "Don't forget, we have to be serving by five-thirty at the Haunted House."

"I haven't forgotten," Bernie said. "I don't think this talk will take that long."

At least she hoped it wouldn't. She was going to talk to Felicity Huffer, who used to work as a proctor at the Peabody School. Bernie had spoken to Felicity's daughter earlier this morning and been told that Felicity lived in the Pine Bough Manor, a residential home for older adults. Now there was a euphemism if ever Bernie had heard one.

"I told her she could stay with me," Felicity's daughter had said. "But she doesn't want to. I'm sure she'll be happy you're coming. She loves talking to people, and I can't get up there until later in the evening. In fact, I'll call her now and make sure it's all right. Sometimes she gets a little grumpy."

"Don't we all," her dad had said when Bernie told him what Felicity's daughter had said. "Of course, if I remember correctly, she always was a bit irascible," he'd added.

"Maybe you should go," Bernie had told him. "After all, you're the one that suggested this."

Her dad had waved the suggestion away. "She always liked your mom better than me. In fact, she never liked me at all."

Bernie was wondering why Felicity Huffer hadn't liked her dad when her sister put down her rolling pin and wiped her hands off on her flannel shirt.

"So," Libby asked her sister, "are we really going to do this?"

"Investigate Amethyst's death?"

"I'm not talking about baking cookies."

"Yes, we are."

"Why?"

"I figure Dad's done enough for us. Maybe we should return the favor."

"I guess you're right," Libby said doubtfully as she tugged at her bra.

"I know I'm right, and your sisters are still lopsided," Bernie informed her.

Libby tugged on her left bra strap a little more. "Better?" she asked Bernie.

Bernie nodded. "You need new bras. In fact, you need new everything."

"After Halloween," Libby said. "When I have a little more free time."

"Why do you hate to shop?"

"Why do you like to shop?" Libby countered, and she turned back to her pumpkin pies.

On the way out, Bernie stopped and had Amber pack her up a box of pumpkin chocolate chip cookies for Felicity.

"You know," Amber said as she taped the

71

box shut, "you ought to make sure someone isn't doing a remake of Michael Myers's *Halloween* at the Haunted House. Maybe there's this homicidal maniac hiding in one of the rooms, with a chain saw, just waiting for you to arrive. You should keep your cell phone out just in case."

This, Bernie thought, *is what happens when someone watches too many horror movies.*

"If we get diced up, you'll be the first one I'll call," Bernie promised as Amber handed her the box full of cookies. "In fact, I'll leave my cell on so you can hear every bloodcurdling scream. Now go wait on Mrs. Stein." And with that, Bernie walked out the door.

She stood in the street for a moment and took a deep breath. It was one of those glorious late fall mornings. The air smelled spicy — like cinnamon and cloves. The sun was still warm, and the leaves remaining on the trees were crimson and gold. Most of the houses on the other side of the street had decorations in their windows: there were witches and goblins and black cats. There were tombstones in the yards. There were jack-o'-lanterns on people's porches. In a week the street would be full of parents and children in costume knocking on doors and yelling, "Trick or treat!"

Halloween had been her favorite holiday when she was little. She still remembered her best costume ever. Her mom had made it, and she thought it was the prettiest costume she'd ever seen. It was a blue taffeta dress with a sparkly sash and pale blue wings and a wand. And she'd had a crown on her head and ruby slippers on her feet. She'd gone as Glynda the Good Witch from *The Wizard of Oz,* and she'd gotten so much candy, the pillowcase she'd carried was half full by the time her dad made her come home.

Halloween was still her favorite holiday. Every year she and Libby opened A Little Taste of Heaven and stood in the doorway and gave out homemade candy and cookies. They labeled every bag they gave away so parents would know where the treats had come from, which the parents seemed to agree with. Otherwise, they'd have to serve the prepackaged stuff, which would be a shame.

Bernie sighed. It was a pity that they wouldn't be able to do that this year, but they wouldn't be at the shop; they'd be serving at the Haunted House. She'd definitely miss seeing the little kids come parading by, but what could she do. Mark was paying them well, and they needed the money, although she wasn't sure that any amount of money could compensate for what she and Libby had seen last night. Whenever she closed her eyes, she could see Amethyst's head rolling down the stairs. She could still hear the bump, bump, bump that it had made.

Bernie shuddered and tried to think of something else, but she couldn't. The image was fixed in her mind. She kept wondering how it had been done. The person couldn't have used a chain saw. That would have made too much noise. So maybe the weapon was an axe. Which meant someone might have found it on the premises. Or someone could have brought it in. It was really impossible to know.

Or someone could have used a fiber-optic laser beam. She'd just seen someone cut glass with one a few weeks ago. Of course, things would be clearer when the coroner did the postmortem. From what Clyde had told her dad, it was scheduled for tomorrow.

She hadn't looked closely enough to see if the cuts on Amethyst's neck were smooth or jagged. She'd been too shocked. Of course, if she didn't want to wait for the PM, she could always ask Marvin to find out. His dad would know since both parts of Amethyst's body were resting in his funeral home. Bernie took another deep breath and got in the car. Maybe Amber and Libby were right, Bernie thought as she started up her vehicle. Not that she would let either of them know that. Maybe she and Libby shouldn't go back. Maybe there was some crazy person there, waiting to claim another unsuspecting victim, although that was not what her father thought.

If he did, he would never have allowed them to go back there, no matter what the circumstances. And he was usually right about these kinds of things. Thirty years in law enforcement had given him pretty good instincts. It was a thought Bernie consoled herself with as she drove over to see Felicity Huffer.

The lobby of the Pine Bough Manor was practically deserted when Bernie walked in. There was a small cluster of people gathered around a bulletin board, and she could hear the tinkle of music and someone exhorting everyone to "breath in and out and focus on letting your energy go out into the world."

A vision of people walking their energy on leashes became lodged in Bernie's mind. She shook her head to clear it and looked around. There was a fountain over by the far wall, with some goldfish swimming in the pond by the base. The dining room stood off to the right.

Three large ficus trees stood in pots over by a large picture window. The floor was carpeted in a pale green tweed, while the furniture was covered in light tans. As Bernie approached the reception desk, she decided the place reminded her of the lobby of a moderately priced hotel.

The woman at the reception desk smiled when Bernie asked for Felicity, and pointed over to the sofa in the back of the room. "She's waiting for you," the woman said. "She's very excited. In fact, I believe she has something to give you."

Bernie wondered what it was as she made her way over to the sofa she'd been directed to. At first, she didn't notice anyone there, and then she saw a small, kid-sized figure dressed in beige. It wasn't until she got closer that she realized that the figure must be Felicity Huffer. If she were taller than four feet eight, Bernie would have been surprised.

Felicity turned as she heard Bernie approaching and smiled. "You're Rose's daughter, aren't you?" she asked in a voice that seemed way too loud for the body it was coming out of.

Bernie allowed as how she was.

Felicity patted the space next to her. "Sit," she said.

Bernie sat.

"Your mother was a dear woman. Very refined. And an excellent cook. I understand you and your sister have inherited her ability," said Felicity.

"I hope so," Bernie said.

Felicity pointed to the box of cookies Bernie was holding. "Are those for me?"

"Yes. Of course. They're pumpkin chocolate chip cookies from our shop, A —"

Felicity cut her off. "I know the name. Even though I'm ninety, I haven't lost my mind. Though there are those that would like to think so," she finished darkly. "I'm sure the staff will like them. I can't digest anymore," she explained. "I exist on a diet of rice, bananas, and bread."

"I'm sorry to hear that," Bernie told her.

Felicity waved her words of sympathy away. "It doesn't really matter. At my age, everything tastes the same to me, anyway. So my daughter tells me you want to hear about the Peabody School."

Bernie nodded. She didn't think she'd ever seen anyone this thin before. It was as if she was looking at an anatomy illustration. For the first time, she actually understood what the term *skeletal-looking* meant.

"Your mother was heartbroken about what happened to Bessie, you know," Felicity said.

"She never talked about it to me."

"I'm not surprised. She was a woman who liked to keep unpleasant things to herself. It was a big tragedy," Felicity said. "Bessie was a good girl. Studious too. She could have done something with herself. Not like some other people I could name." Felicity frowned.

"So what happened?" Bernie asked.

"She went out the window. I was the one that found her." Felicity's voice trembled slightly. "Terrible. Truly terrible. The windows were very low. Almost French windows. All you'd have to do is lean out of them to fall. One push and there you'd go. It wouldn't even take much. Of course, some people say she jumped. Others say she fell, that what happened was an accident. But I don't believe that for a moment. I didn't then, and I don't now. I think she was killed. I think she was killed out of spite and jealousy."

As Bernie leaned forward to better hear what Felicity was saying, she caught Felicity's musty scent: dry, brittle paper mixed with the aroma of lavender water.

"So you know who killed her?" she asked.

Felicity put her hand up and coughed into it. "I know, but I never told anyone."

"Why not?"

"Because," she said when she was done coughing, "I could have lost my job."

"How so?" Bernie asked.

"Well, I didn't have any proof, you see. And the girl's family was very rich, very powerful." Felicity paused for a moment. "I needed that job. If I had lost it, I don't think I could have gotten another one. Some people think that Zinnia was the one, but even if she was, it was Amethyst that put her up to it. She was a bad seed. I know it's not fashionable to use that expression anymore, but it's true. That's why she was there, you know. Because her parents were afraid of her. Her mother told me that in one of her visits. Sweet woman, too. Imagine being afraid of your own child. But things happened when Amethyst was around. Bad things."

"Well, this time something bad happened to Amethyst."

"So my daughter told me. Which, of course, is why you're here. You want to know if I can shed any light on the situation."

"Exactly," Bernie said.

Felicity laughed. It was more of a rattle, actually. "Of course, I can."

Bernie waited. Felicity didn't say anything for a moment.

Then she said, "Do you like games and puzzles?"

"As well as anyone else," Bernie lied. In reality she didn't like them at all.

"Are you good at them?"

"Moderately," Bernie replied. "I'm good at crossword puzzles."

Felicity made a dismissive noise. "I'm talking about a real puzzle."

And she reached behind her and presented Bernie with a brown paper bag. It was crinkled and splotched with grease here and there. This brown paper bag, Bernie thought, had seen better days. It didn't smell too great, either. It smelled as if it had been storing things that Bernie didn't want to think about.

"Well, look inside," Felicity snapped.

Bernie did, with a great deal of circumspection.

"Take everything in there out," Felicity ordered.

Bernie reached in gingerly and pulled out an old View-Master and a wooden puzzle box that was covered with smudge marks.

"Thank you," Bernie said, not knowing what else to do.

"Take them with you," Felicity instructed. "And on your way out, see Odella at the reception desk, and tell her it's time for my nap."

"What are they?" Bernie asked, nodding toward the items that had been in the bag.

Felicity looked at her with an unmistakable expression of annoyance on her face. "They're the solution to your problem, of course. I just told you what you wanted to know."

"I'm sorry, but I must not have been paying attention."

"The box and the View-Master," Felicity told her. "The answer is in those. Especially the box. The View-Master not so much."

"I don't understand," Bernie stammered.

"What's to understand? I just told you. The answer to the question you want me to answer is in the bag. Solve the puzzle and you'll find it."

"What puzzle?" Bernie asked. She was at a total loss.

"The one in the bag," Felicity snapped. "Honestly. These days people expect you to do all their work for them. When I was younger, we had to figure things out for ourselves. Now go. Go."

CHAPTER 6

Sean looked at the items Bernie held out to him. She put them on the table in front of him.

"Interesting," he said, picking up the View-Master. "I used to have one of these when I was a kid." He held it up to the light. "Have you looked at the pictures?" he asked.

Bernie nodded. "When I got in the car. They're all pictures of the Peabody School."

When Sean was done, he put the View-Master down and picked up the wooden box. He studied it for a moment. "I haven't seen a puzzle box like this in years." He played with it for a moment, then put that down as well.

"So what do you think?" Bernie asked her dad when he went back to sipping his coffee.

"Felicity could be playing a joke," he mused. "It would amuse her to think that I was spending my time over these things. That woman always was a pain in the ass, not to mention being a real nut job."

"So why did you send me there?"

Sean gave a slight shrug. "I thought she might have mellowed. Evidently, I was wrong."

"Do you think there's anything in what she gave me that will help?"

"I'll play around with the puzzle box for a while, but I don't think there's going to be anything in there." He sighed. "Boy, that woman can hold a grudge."

"What do you mean?"

"She never forgave me for marrying your mom."

"But why?" Bernie couldn't believe someone wouldn't like her dad.

"Felicity was your mom's babysitter at one time. She was quite attached to her — probably too attached — if you get my meaning. And she disapproved of me. She didn't think I was good enough for your mom. I don't know if anyone would have been. She thought your mom deserved better then being a policeman's wife. And maybe she did. I thought she would have forgotten about that by now, but evidently, she hasn't." Sean frowned. "Oh well. On to Plan B."

"And what is Plan B?"

Sean looked at his daughter. "Can't you guess?"

"Find out who had a motive for killing Amethyst?"

Sean beamed. "Exactly." He always felt good when he'd managed to teach something to his children.

It was going to be a long list, Bernie thought as she went into her room to change into her Halloween costume for the Haunted House. Today she was going to go as a witch. Of course, the bottom of witches' dresses traditionally didn't have ruffles lined in pink, but so be it. She wasn't going to be wearing the kind of homespun cloth witches in thirteenth-century Europe would wear. It would be way too scratchy.

Libby was waiting for her sister downstairs. She and Amber had already packed everything and were in the middle of loading the van.

"Now be careful," Amber warned when Bernie appeared. Libby closed the doors of the vehicle. "Here," Amber said, pressing two small medallions into Libby's and Bernie's hands. "This is for just in case."

Libby looked down at the silver hand with an eye drawn on the palm. "Just in case what?"

"It's to ward off the evil eye," Amber explained.

"There is no such thing as an evil eye," Libby said. "That's just a superstition."

Amber gave her a reproachful look. "Don't you know what happens in movies when the hero or heroine refuses to wear the protective amulet?"

"They get chopped up into hamburger," Bernie replied.

"Exactly," Amber said.

"Fine," said Libby, as she put the amulet around her neck. "See. Feel better now?"

Amber nodded.

Libby shook her head as she drove down the street. She liked Amber, but there were some things about her she just couldn't understand — like her fondness for horror movies. "What did dad say when you showed him the bag?" Libby asked as they turned onto Ash Place.

"He said Felicity was always a little crazy. He said that stuff could be her idea of a joke."

"Lovely," Libby said. "Are you planning on wearing that hat this evening?"

Bernie patted her hat. "Why? What's wrong with it?"

"It's just very large." Libby could see

herself knocking it into the pumpkin pies by accident.

"Witches always wear large hats."

"I wouldn't know. I've never made an actual study of it."

Bernie glanced appraisingly at her sister. "You should get in costume, too, Libby."

"I don't like costumes," Libby said. "You know that."

"You don't have to go as the Cowardly Lion."

"I'm not going as anything," Libby said firmly. "Besides, it'll be hard to serve people."

"Not if you're wearing the right thing. Come on," Bernie pleaded. "It'll be fun."

"No," Libby said as she turned onto the road that led to the Haunted House. "I always feel ridiculous."

"For Halloween night, you can go as . . ." Bernie paused for a moment while she thought. "I've got it. Fruit of the Loom tighty whities."

"That's it," Libby yelped.

"I'm kidding."

"No, you're not."

"You have to admit it would be funny."

"Not to me."

"We'll get you a nice costume," Bernie told her soothingly. "Something sexy."

"I don't want my boobs hanging out."

"But they're nice boobs."

"Yes, they are," Libby agreed. Marvin thought so, too. She just didn't think it was appropriate to show them off when she was serving food.

"We'll do funky." Bernie snapped her fingers. "Wait. I know. You can come as Esmeralda's ghost. That would be really freaky."

"I'll see." Libby demurred. She reached over and turned on the radio, signaling that she didn't want to discuss dressing up anymore.

Ten minutes later they were at the school. Libby parked as close as possible to the entrance that led to the kitchen.

"Loading and unloading are the parts of this job that I hate the most," Bernie grumbled.

"Tell me about it," Libby agreed as she lifted a carton filled with cider out of the back of the van.

It took them about twenty minutes to unload the van and about half an hour to set up. They decked the long tables with the orange and black checkered tablecloths that Libby had found at the dollar store. Then Bernie arranged the decorations: five carved jack-o'-lanterns, pots of mums, and three small candles featuring Casper the Friendly Ghost. She stepped back and looked at the results.

Maybe she should forget about Casper. After all, there weren't going to be any young children. But then some adults liked cartoony stuff. After another moment of debate, she left the candles on the table.

"You know," Bernie said as she began laying out the paper cups, napkins, and spoons and forks, "we should have had bobbing for apples."

"Too messy," Libby said firmly as she began setting out the waffle irons. "There'd be water all over the floor, and then we'd have to worry about someone slipping."

"But it would be fun," Bernie protested.

"Undoubtedly," Libby said as she began setting up the workstation for the waffles. "But that's not the issue."

She could just see it now: someone walking by and slipping on the floor because it was wet, grabbing the table for support, and having the whole thing come down. Then they'd get sued. No. Bobbing for apples was out of the question. She checked her waffle supplies. They had the homemade strawberry and apricot jam, the hot fudge sauce, the apple compote, whipped cream, maple syrup, and strawberries, but no butter. She went through the box again. No. It wasn't there. She explicitly remembered telling Amber not to forget to pack it.

"Damn," Libby muttered. She should have checked everything over herself. This was what happened when she got lazy.

"What's the matter?" Bernie asked.

"Amber forgot the butter."

"No biggie. I'll run back and get it," Bernie told her. She looked at her watch. She had a half hour before they opened. Shouldn't be a problem at all.

"And bring some of the glazed walnuts while you're at it," Libby said. They would go well with the maple syrup.

Bernie nodded, put on her jacket, and hurried out the door. Libby turned back to arranging the cookie bars on the platters she'd brought. She probably should have brought some of their larger serving plates, but these would have to do for the moment. She'd just put one platter down and was busy taking the pumpkin pecan bars out of their Tupperware container when she heard a door slam.

"Bernie?" she called out, even though it was way too early for her sister to have gotten to the shop and returned. Maybe she'd forgotten something.

No one answered.

Suddenly, Libby was aware of how quiet the room was. And how large. Another door slammed.

"Bernie?" Libby repeated.

Her sister's name echoed in the silence.

"Hello?" Libby cried.

No one answered.

"This is ridiculous," Libby said out loud.

Obviously, the sounds were being made by people walking back and forth in the hallway. She looked down. She didn't remember doing it, but somehow she'd taken the amulet Amber had given her off of her neck and was clutching it in her hand. This was what came from listening to Amber and those ghost-hunter freaks. Libby shook herself. She hated when she got like this. She was acting the way she had when she was five.

Libby shook herself again, took a deep breath, and went over her to do list, holding it in her mind the way she was holding the amulet in her hand. She had to focus on finishing setting up. She had to finish plating the cookies, pouring the waffle batter into jugs, putting out the pies, slicing up the pumpkin loaves, arranging the drinks, and setting up the urns for hot coffee, tea, mulled cider, and hot chocolate.

She started humming Bob Dylan's "It

Ain't Me Babe" to herself. That always helped. She didn't know why, but it did. It had since childhood. She was finishing up overlapping the pumpkin chocolate chip cookies when she felt something funny around her.

It was like static electricity on her arms, neck, and shoulders. Then she felt a blast of cold air on her cheeks. She felt the hairs on the back of her neck stand up. She didn't know how she knew they were doing that; she just did. *It isn't a figure of speech. They really do that,* she thought as she noticed the goose pimples on her arms. Suddenly, she was very, very cold. Colder than she'd ever been. The air around her seemed wavy, as if she was looking down the road on a hot summer's day, with the heat beating down on her.

A young female voice whispered in her ear, "See you later, alligator." Then she giggled.

Libby whirled around. For a second, she thought she saw the outline of a girl wearing a button-down oxford shirt and a long, pleated skirt, and then the image vanished. A moment later the prickly sensation on her skin and the coldness surrounding her were gone as well.

Libby told herself she was imagining

91

things. Or that she was going crazy. But she knew she wasn't. Her mother was right. She was weird.

Libby cleared her throat. "Are you Bessie Osgood?" she asked.

There was no answer. *Of course not,* Libby thought. What had she expected? Some sort of rapping? Two raps for yes, one rap for no?

Yeah, right. There had to be another explanation, had to be, even though she knew in her heart there wasn't. Maybe this was some kind of trick. If it was, she didn't think it was one bit funny.

She went out in the hallway and took a look around. Bob Small, who was wearing his skeleton costume, waved at her as he walked past. *Guess they haven't arrested him yet,* Libby thought. She wondered why. Her dad had been sure that Bob Small would be behind bars by now, and he usually wasn't wrong about things like that.

"Did you see anyone out here?" she asked Bob.

"The Ghost of Christmas Past. Whoops. Wrong holiday."

"Seriously."

"Nope." Bob shook his head and hurried along.

For a moment, Libby thought about going through the rooms of the Haunted House, but she quickly ruled that out. She didn't have the time, and even if she did, what was she looking for?

She didn't know. That was the problem.

CHAPTER 7

Marvin looked at Libby, who was perched on her bar stool, trying to make a bird out of a cocktail napkin and failing.

"You actually saw a ghost," he said.

Libby smoothed the napkin out and tried again. "I didn't say that. I said it seemed as if I saw a ghost."

"Seemed?" Marvin repeated.

"Seemed," Libby said firmly.

"Well, I'm still envious. I've never come close," said Marvin.

Brandon put the beer Marvin had ordered down in front of him and then got Libby and Bernie their Irish coffees. "Not once?" Brandon asked after he'd given Bernie a quick hello kiss. His shift was over, but his replacement hadn't come in yet.

"Never," Marvin said. Then he pointed to the napkins with R.J.'S BAR AND GRILL printed on them in green and blue. "These are new," he observed.

"The owner's son is starting a printing business, and his dad is trying to help him out," said Brandon.

Marvin nodded as Bernie turned toward him

"Has your dad ever seen a ghost?" she asked.

"Nope. He doesn't believe in them," replied Marvin. "He says that when you're dead, that's it."

Brandon surveyed the bar. Everyone seemed satisfied for the moment, so he asked his next question. "Do you believe in ghosts?"

"Not in the least," Marvin said, with a great deal of conviction.

"He's had plenty of opportunity to see them, too," Libby pointed out.

Bernie lifted up her glass, changed her mind, and put it back down. "Not really," she said. "Ghosts tend to haunt places."

"Like funeral homes," Brandon said.

"No. Like places where they died a violent death. Personally, I think they're some sort of leftover energy that's just stuck there," said Bernie.

Marvin frowned. "I agree with my father — for once — on this one. I think when you're dead, you're dead. You go in the ground, and that's the end of the story. You don't go to heaven. You don't get reborn as something else. You just disappear. In all the time I've worked with my dad, I've never seen or felt anything that was vaguely ghost-like."

"How long has your dad been a funeral director?" Brandon asked.

Marvin took a sip of his Brooklyn Brown and wiped his mouth on one of the napkins on the bar. "Maybe thirty years. Maybe thirty-five. I'm not exactly sure."

Libby toyed with her glass for a moment and then took a sip. She could feel herself begin to relax. Who was it that said that Irish coffee was the perfect mix of fat, sugar, and alcohol? "I think I was meant to see Bessie Osgood's ghost," she blurted out.

"Obviously," Bernie said.

"No. I mean, I think someone wanted me to see her," said Libby.

Bernie raised an eyebrow. "Someone?"

"The someone who did this," replied Libby.

Bernie snorted. "And who would that be?"

"I don't know," Libby told her.

"But why would someone do that?" Brandon asked Libby.

"Because," she replied, "Curtis and Konrad are ready to swear that Bessie Osgood killed Amethyst, and my seeing her backs up their story." Libby explained what the ghost hunters had told her dad.

"Those two guys are nuts," Brandon scoffed. "They also believe in UFO's. In fact, one of them offered to hook me up with a ride."

"And you didn't go?" Bernie asked.

Brandon laughed.

"I think," Libby continued, "that what I experienced in the kitchen might be an attempt to keep us from investigating any further. Whoever did it is betting that we'll buy into this fantasy they've created."

"From the way you describe it, you have to admit it's a pretty elaborate fantasy," Brandon said.

"Exactly," said Marvin as he picked a handful of peanuts out of the bowl and began to shell them. "The sensations, the cold, the vision. If what you experienced was created by someone, the question becomes, how was it accomplished? Who has the technical know-how to do this?"

"That's easy," Bernie said. "FX Productions, the outfit that set up the show."

"What do we know about them?" Marvin asked.

Brandon whipped out his iPhone. "I'll Google them and find out." A moment later he said, "Here they are. They seem pretty legit to me." He passed the phone to Bernie.

"Expensive," she said after she'd read the company's Web page. "Lots of references." She handed the phone back to Brandon.

"I bet they can't be too pleased that they're involved in something like this," Brandon said. "There's a contact number. Maybe I should give them a call and see what I can find out."

"Sounds like a plan," said Bernie. She tapped her fingernails on the base of the glass holding her Irish coffee. "And in the meantime, maybe we should talk about who disliked Amethyst."

"Now that," said Brandon, "will be easy." He excused himself for a moment to wait on the people down at the end of the bar.

Marvin swept the peanut shells onto the floor and looked around the place. R.J.'s never seemed to change. There was the dartboard over on the right, the pool table by the window, the tables for two shoved up against the wall, the historical pictures of Longely hanging slightly crookedly on the wall, the spindly ficus tree fighting for life in the window, and the peanut shells on the floor.

"There aren't many people here," he observed.

"Monday nights are always slow," Libby replied. "You know," she continued, "I just realized that they never put up any holiday decorations around here."

"A good idea if you ask me," Bernie noted. She sucked her thumb. It was still sore from using the edge of a spoon to dig out the seeds from all the pumpkins she'd carved in the last two days.

"Our regulars come here to drink, not to be reminded of Halloween," Brandon noted as he planted himself in front of Bernie. "The only decoration they need is a glass."

"I don't understand. How can you not want to be reminded of Halloween?" Bernie asked.

"Because they don't," said Brandon. "They want to forget everything when they come in here. That's what serious drinkers do."

Libby interrupted. "Can we get back to Amethyst?" she asked, annoyed. She felt as if no one was taking this seriously enough.

"Sure," Brandon said. He unscrewed the top of a bottle of water and took a drink. "I'll tell you who's on the top of my list. Inez Colley."

Bernie took another sip of her Irish coffee. "I thought she went off to Arizona."

"She did, but she came back," said Brandon.

"When?" Marvin asked.

Brandon looked at the ceiling while he calculated his answer. "About three months ago, give or take a couple of weeks."

"Where's her husband?" Marvin asked.

"Still in the monastery in Kyoto. I don't think he's coming back from Japan," Brandon replied. "A guy who works for his former boss told me Kevin was taking the precepts, or doing whatever it is you do to become a Buddhist priest."

"Usually, it's the criminal, not the victim, that finds religion," Bernie noted.

Marvin took another drink of his beer. "Obviously, not in this case. Do we know what happened specifically?" he asked.

"No," Bernie replied.

"Yes," Brandon said at the same time.

"How do you know?" Bernie demanded.

"Because he told me," said Brandon.

"He did?" asked Bernie.

"Yeah. He was drunk off his ass," said Brandon.

"And you never told me?" said Bernie.

"A man never reveals what another man tells him when he's under the influence of alcohol," Brandon said.

Bernie rolled her eyes.

"Hey," Brandon said, "I have my code of ethics. But I'll tell you now because it's important."

Bernie patted her chest. "Be still, my heart."

"Do you want to hear this or not?" said Brandon.

"We want to hear it," Marvin said.

"All right, then," replied Brandon as he took another sip of water. "You know that Amethyst was working for Inez's husband, right?"

Libby nodded. "As an office manager."

Brandon leaned forward. "Well, according to him, one night, when they were working late, Amethyst slipped something in his drink, had sex with him, and videotaped it."

Bernie snorted. "Yeah, right. Poor Mr. Innocent."

Brandon shrugged. "It's possible."

Bernie rolled her eyes. "But not likely."

"Okay. Not likely," Brandon agreed. "But I definitely believe what Kevin said happened next, which was that Amethyst threatened to show the tape to his wife unless he paid her off. Which he did by refinancing his house and taking a loan out on his business."

"Stupid," Marvin said.

"It must have been quite a tape," Bernie

101

observed.

"I'd say," replied Brandon as he scanned the room again. "So here was Kevin, thinking the problem was taken care of, when Amethyst came back, asking for more money. Kevin freaked. He wimped out and took off for Japan to become a Buddhist monk, leaving Inez without a pot to pee in."

"Nice guy," Marvin commented.

"But, Brandon, Inez doesn't know about Amethyst, so she can't want to kill her," Bernie protested.

"She does know. Kevin told me he left Inez a note," said Brandon. "Explained everything in it. Asked her forgiveness. Blah. Blah. Blah."

Libby blinked. "Wow. Poor woman."

Brandon took another drink of water and screwed the top back on the bottle. "I saw her at Sam's Club last week. She doesn't look so great."

"I can imagine," Bernie said. "What's she doing now?"

"She's on a cleaning crew," replied Brandon.

"You're kidding," Bernie cried.

"Nope," said Brandon, shaking his head.

Libby clicked her tongue against the roof of her mouth. This was a woman who used to come into their store and order four hundred dollars' worth of food at a go without batting an eye.

"Jobs are tight these days, and with her problem, this was the only job she could get, and that's only because Ian felt bad for her," Brandon explained. "My friend Ian White runs AAAPlus Clean."

"Didn't she work in a lab doing something with remote sensing?" Libby asked.

Bernie finished her Irish coffee. "She did before she got married and became Mr. Rich Man's wife and started drinking and got two DWIs. Now, I'm sure she couldn't get a security clearance to work at Wal-Mart." Bernie stretched. "I'd say she had a motive to kill Amethyst."

"I'd go for the husband," Libby said.

"Yeah," Bernie said. "But Kevin is in Japan."

"Good point," Libby said. "And Inez has never been too stable."

"Just because she threw a tantrum in our shop when she found out we were out of broccoli cole slaw and we had to call the police to get her out?" Bernie asked.

"Something like that," Libby said.

"You want me to find out if she's working tonight?" Brandon asked.

"So late?" Libby asked.

"That's when Ian's crews work," said

Brandon. And he punched his friend's phone number in and walked to the end of the bar. A few minutes later, he was back. "Funny thing," he said. "But she's cleaning at the Foundation as we speak."

"Huh," Bernie said. "Curiouser and curiouser. I think we should go have a chat with her."

"Now?" Libby said.

"When better?" Bernie asked.

"Tomorrow is better. I want to go home and go to bed," replied Libby.

"Then Brandon and I will go," said Bernie.

"We will?" Brandon asked. "I thought we had other plans."

"First things first," Bernie said firmly.

"And then we can go to my place," said Brandon.

Bernie grinned. "That depends on your performance."

Brandon leered. "My performance is always stellar."

Bernie laughed and ate a peanut.

CHAPTER 8

Bernie watched the Peabody School rise in the moonlight as Brandon rounded the bend in the road. She hugged herself as she turned toward Brandon.

"This would make a great set for a horror movie," she said.

"Yeah," Brandon said. "The only thing it lacks is bats and a belfry."

"It has a colony of bats."

"I was being metaphorical." Brandon pointed to the top of the building. "It also has a widow's walk."

For a moment Bernie thought she saw a faint shape, a large, light spot in the dark, but when she looked again, it was gone. *Probably an optical illusion,* she told herself.

Brandon headed toward the main entrance. "Senior year, Ben Altman bet me I couldn't get all the way up there on Halloween night."

"And did you?"

Brandon shook his head. "I chickened out before I got to the second floor. I thought I heard voices."

"Maybe you did. Maybe someone else was in there."

"There were no cars in the lot."

"Maybe it was a couple of squatters," said Bernie.

"Maybe. But I wasn't about to stay and find out."

Bernie rubbed her arms. For some reason, she was cold. "You think Libby saw something earlier this evening?"

"Definitely. Don't you?"

"Yeah. I do. She was really freaked out."

"Do you think she really saw Bessie Osgood?" asked Brandon.

"Don't tell anyone, but yeah. I think she did."

"Freaky."

"Halloween is a freaky time of year."

Brandon turned into the parking lot. "There's the cleaning van," he said, changing the subject.

Brandon parked right beside it, and he and Bernie got out.

"And no cops," Bernie observed. According to Clyde, they'd packed up and left the crime scene a couple of hours ago. "Did your friend Ian say anything about Inez?"

106

Bernie asked Brandon as they walked to the front door.

Brandon zipped up his jacket before replying. "He said she was a mess. He thought she was drinking again."

"No surprise there," replied Bernie.

"I guess not. He told her she had to have a doctor's note if she called in sick one more night," said Brandon.

"Another DWI and she's going to be going to jail for a long time," said Bernie.

"She's going to be going to jail for an even longer time if she killed Amethyst," replied Brandon.

"True," Bernie agreed. "And she could have. After all, she knows how lasers work."

"If that's what was used."

"I'm guessing fiber-optic laser wire," Bernie informed him.

Brandon stared at her. "Where do you get this stuff from?"

"Well, I was reading an article on a new piece of work Jacobs is doing."

"Jacobs?"

"The sculptor, uncultured one."

"I'm cultured. I like yogurt."

Bernie faked a groan. "Anyway, it got me thinking that that would fit the bill. It's light. It's quiet. It's easy to manipulate."

"Why not a samurai sword or a machete?"

"Not enough blood."

"Maybe she was killed somewhere else and moved."

"Maybe," Bernie agreed. "But I don't think so."

"Your feminine intuition tells you this?"

Bernie chucked Brandon under the chin. "Exactly. I could be wrong. Who knows," she mused. "Maybe the person who killed her used a piece of flexible, glass-coated glazier's wire."

Brandon shook his head. "Sometimes you scare me."

"Then don't piss me off." And Bernie pulled her turtleneck up till it covered her chin. She definitely should have brought a scarf. "Did Ian say how many nights a week they cleaned here?" she asked, changing the subject.

"Five."

"That's a lot for an office, isn't it?"

"Evidently, Kane's a clean freak."

"So they were here last night?"

Brandon nodded. "But they don't clean the Haunted House area."

"How come?"

"Kane doesn't want them to. He said there was too much delicate equipment in there. Touch the wrong thing and kablamo. There goes one of the exhibits."

"Who does the cleaning then?" asked Bernie.

Brandon shrugged. "I assume the volunteers do, but you'll have to ask Kane."

"And Inez was here cleaning the Foundation part?"

"That's what Ian says."

By now Bernie and Brandon were at the door. Brandon put his hand on the handle. "So, what are you going to say to Inez?" he asked.

"I'm going to ask her if she killed Amethyst."

"Seriously?"

"Yes, seriously. Just like that."

Brandon threw back his head and laughed. "And you expect her to say, 'Yes, I did'?"

"No. I just want to see how she reacts."

Brandon pulled the door open. "A waste of time if you ask me."

"Do you have any other suggestions?"

"Yeah. Let's go back to my place and talk about this first."

"After," Bernie said and walked inside.

Brandon sighed and followed.

The Foundation was not what Bernie had expected. She'd psyched herself up for a scary mansion, and she'd gotten a generic office instead. For a reason she couldn't explain, she felt oddly disappointed.

The lights were on in the hallway, and Bernie could see that Kane had done some serious remodeling. Now the walls were white, instead of wallpapered in paisley, and wainscoted, and the floor was a sea of gray carpeting.

There were metal-framed pictures on the walls, mostly featuring trees and flowers and grass. About twenty feet in was a reception desk, and just after that was a modern black leather sofa and a coffee table with fanned-out magazines. In the background, Bernie could hear Aretha Franklin competing with the hum of a vacuum cleaner.

"Boy, this has sure changed," Brandon observed. "I remember all this weird wall-paper and dark wood and crystal lamps hanging from the ceiling."

"So it would appear," Bernie said as she cautiously opened the nearest door on the right. A small plaque on the door read MS. LONG. "I guess Kane was telling the truth when he said the site they're using for the Haunted House is the last place they have to remodel."

Bernie peeked inside. The room was small and generic. It contained a desk; a monitor, keyboard, and mouse on the desk; a standard-issue office chair; a wall full of bookshelves, which appeared to contain reports; and stacks of reading material on the table by the door. The room was devoid of any personality. Looking at it, Bernie decided she could be in any office anywhere in the world. For all intents and purposes, the old Peabody School was gone except for where the Haunted House was. And soon that would be gone, too. It made her sad. She carefully closed the door behind her and started down the corridor.

"Let's go find Inez," she said.

Brandon hurried after her. "The sooner the better as far as I'm concerned," he told her.

"So you've said," Bernie retorted.

They walked down the corridor. When they got to the end, they followed the music and turned left. Aretha was louder now. So was the vacuum cleaner.

"How many people are on this cleaning crew?" Bernie asked.

"Ian said three," Brandon replied.

They made another left. Bernie began to feel disorientated. The place was like a rabbit warren, all sharp, angled turns. One hallway led to another, and the white walls and gray carpet and overhead lights made everything look the same. Half of the rooms looked as if they were unused. By now the words to "I Heard It Through The Grapevine" were pulsing through Bernie's head. She paused in front of the door where the music was coming from.

"Let's do it," Brandon said and pushed open the door.

They stepped into a paneled conference room. A vacuum cleaner was parked by the far wall. A large, gleaming wooden table sat in the center of the room. The air smelled of furniture polish. A man in coveralls was bent over the table, spraying its surface with Pledge and wiping it down.

Bernie went over and tapped him on the shoulder. He jumped and spun around. It took him a minute to focus his eyes. Whatever he was on, it had taken him someplace else.

"Sorry," Bernie shouted. "We're looking for Inez."

The man blinked. He made an effort to look at Bernie. She smiled encouragingly.

"Is she around? We need to talk to her," Bernie explained.

She'd expected that he'd ask why, but he didn't. If anything, he seemed annoyed at being interrupted. He shrugged and pointed to the door on the far wall.

"Through there," he told her. "She's cleaning the bathrooms. At least that's what she's supposed to be doing. Whether she is or not, I can't say." He nodded toward Brandon. "Hey, pal. How's it going?"

"It's going, Josh," Brandon said. "It's going."

"You can say that again," Josh said and went back to waxing the table.

"How do you know him?" Bernie asked when they got outside.

"His brother was in our class."

"He was?"

"Matt Keller."

"That's Matt Keller's little brother?"

Brandon nodded. "Yup."

Bernie shook her head. She remembered him as this blond little pain that was always following Matt around. Now he looked about fifty and was missing half of his teeth.

Brandon must have read her mind, because he said, "That's what happens when you live on the streets. You want me to talk to him while you go have a chat with Inez and see if he can tell us what she was doing last night?"

Bernie nodded and went off to find Inez. She located her a little while later in the ladies' room. The door was propped open, held in place by a large garbage can. When Bernie walked in, she could see Inez leaning against one of the sinks, smoking a

113

cigarette. Bernie did a double take. Inez must have gained at least fifty pounds since she'd last seen her. Inez's face had that round, puffy look drinkers' faces got. Her waist had vanished, replaced by a layer of fat that ballooned over her belt. Even her hands looked pudgy.

"What do you want?" she asked Bernie.

Suddenly, Bernie decided that Brandon was right. This wasn't such a great idea.

"To talk to you, Inez."

Inez took another drag of her cigarette and blew the smoke out of her nostrils. *Just like in some B movie,* Bernie thought.

"You want to know why I haven't been in your store?"

"Not exactly," replied Bernie.

"I don't have time to talk to you. I've got work to do."

"So I see," said Bernie, nodding at the cigarette.

"Well, I'm going to answer your question for you, Miss Girl Detective," said Inez.

"Can you make that Ms. Girl Detective?"

"You think you're smart, don't you?" hissed Inez.

"Yes, I do. Now what's the question you're going to answer for me?"

"The one you were going to ask me about Amethyst. I didn't kill her. The police already questioned me. And let me go. Go talk to Bob Small. He was there."

"So were you."

"No. I was here cleaning."

"That's what I said."

"Shows you how much you know," Inez sneered. "You can't get from here to the Haunted House section of the mansion. They sealed it off when they remodeled. You have to go outside and around."

"And what's to prevent you from having done that?" asked Bernie.

"I was with Josh all the time I was here. We were cleaning the offices."

"It takes two people to do that?"

"That's the way Ian says to do it, so that's what we do," said Inez. She took another drag of her cigarette and flicked it in the toilet.

Bernie folded her arms over her chest and leaned up against one of the sinks. "Maybe you set up some sort of remote device."

"And how would I have gotten Amethyst there?"

Bernie shrugged. "I don't know. Wrote a note. Called her and set up a meeting. You're smart."

"I'm not smart enough," Inez said.

"Why do you say that?"

Inez pointed to one of the toilets. "That's

what I let my life turn into."

Bernie didn't say anything, because what Inez said was true.

"I'm glad Amethyst is dead," Inez continued. "She deserved everything she got. I only wish she had suffered more. She ruined my life. If it weren't for her, I'd still have my husband and my house. Look at me." Inez pointed at herself. "Look at the way I look now. Look what I'm doing. I shop at Wal-Mart, for God's sake. But I didn't kill the bitch. I wish I had, but I didn't. If I had, I wouldn't have been so merciful. Talk to Bob Small. Talk to Zachery Timberland."

"Zachery Timberland?"

Inez laughed through her nose. It was not a nice laugh, Bernie thought.

"Yeah. Zachery Timberland. Ask him about his daughter Zoe. Ask him what she's doing now."

Bernie was about to ask Inez what Zoe was doing now when Brandon appeared at the bathroom door.

"She and Josh were together last night," he said as he stepped inside the ladies' room. He looked around. "I've always wanted to see what one of these looked like on the inside."

"Well, now you know," Bernie replied. She

turned to Inez. "You could have both done it."

Inez snickered. "If I were going to do something like that, I certainly wouldn't choose a chucklehead like Josh for my partner."

Brandon tugged at Bernie's arm. "Come on. Let's go."

"Listen to your boyfriend," Inez said.

"I'll go when I'm ready," Bernie said, even though she knew Brandon was right. She'd gotten as much as she was going to get from Inez this go-around. Staying longer wasn't going to help anything.

She was turning to go when Inez called out to her.

"I have a question for you," she said.

"Yeah?" said Bernie.

"How the hell do you walk in those?" She pointed to Bernie's stilettos.

"Very carefully," Bernie said. "Very carefully, indeed. And I have a question for you."

"What?" Inez snarled.

"Have you met Bessie Osgood?"

Bernie watched Inez's mouth wobble. It was as if someone had taken a giant vacuum cleaner and sucked everything out of her.

"Get out of here," Inez cried. "I'm not talking to you anymore."

"Obviously, I hit a nerve," Bernie said to

Brandon when they were outside.

"Obviously, you did."

"I guess my dad is right," Bernie said.

"How do you mean?" Brandon asked as he and Bernie retraced their steps.

"He said that Bessie Osgood is at the center of what happened, and I'm starting to think so, too."

CHAPTER 9

Sean carefully seated himself in a chair in front of a long table and laid before him the bag with the View-Master that Felicity Huffer had given Bernie. His idea probably wouldn't come to anything, but he wanted to check it out, anyway.

It would have been easier for him to use his wheelchair in here since getting up and down was a problem for him. It would have been more comfortable, too, but he hated it, so he'd brought Marvin along to help out instead. Which had its own set of problems.

Libby said he didn't use the chair, because he was too vain, but that wasn't it at all. It was that he saw using it as a sign of giving in, and for him, giving in meant giving up. He'd been that way all his life, and he couldn't change now. Maybe that was because his mom had taught him not to take the easy way out. *Ever.*

The chair was a little too deep for him, but he settled back in it as best he could and looked around. The Longely Historical Society was housed in an old Victorian house that had belonged to one of the town's founders. The town board had rescued it from the wrecking ball and had put on a new roof and painted the outside lilac, an act that Sean had never understood, and that had been the extent of the fixing up. The house itself was narrow and cluttered with pictures and objects from the town's past.

Recently, Halloween decorations had been added to the mix. At this time of day, the Longely Historical Society was empty, but then, it usually was. Most people in this town were too busy worrying about whether or not they could afford a Beamer to think much about the past. In fact, he, Marvin, and the librarian, Jeanine Applegate, who was the real reason they were here, were the only people in the place.

"Sit down," Sean hissed at Marvin, who was roaming around like a demented, fidgeting whooping crane. Why he couldn't stay still was quite beyond Sean.

"I just wanted to look at the pictures on the wall," Marvin said.

"You're distracting me."

"But you're not doing anything," Marvin pointed out.

"I'm thinking."

Marvin turned and almost knocked a stack of brochures off one of the shelves.

"And you're going to break something."

Marvin looked hurt, and Sean felt remorseful for a second or two. But it was true; Marvin was a klutz. Plus he was overly sensitive. The kid had to toughen up.

"Did you know that jack-o'-lanterns come from Ireland and that people used to use turnips?" Marvin said.

Now this, Sean thought, *is what my daughter would call a random comment.* "Yes, Marvin, I know," Sean said.

"Because you're Irish?"

"Because Bernie told me."

"That would mean the Irish don't eat roasted pumpkin seeds. That's one of my favorite parts about Halloween."

Sean took a deep breath and let it out. "Marvin."

"Turnips don't have seeds."

"Yes. I know." And with that, Sean reached out and grabbed the newspaper that was sitting there, held it up to his face, and pretended to read the front page. He'd never had that much patience, but now that he was getting older, he had none at all.

God, Marvin talked a lot. There was no disputing that. His driving wasn't great, either, but Libby loved him, and basically, he was a good kid, even if he did make Sean crazy. Back in the Ice Age, when he'd been chief of police, he'd learned from the man he'd served under that you had to work with what you had and bring your men up to a higher level of functioning. That was what being a leader meant.

Sean thought about that for a moment, and then he went back to thinking about what he hoped to accomplish here. Besides talking to Jeanine, who was Amethyst's second or third cousin, he couldn't remember which, he wanted to look at the old pictures of the Peabody School and read any material they had pertaining to the place. He was also hoping that the Longely Historical Society had some materials on Bessie Osgood, although he kind of doubted it.

He threw Jeanine his most charming smile as she came toward him, and she smiled back. Honestly, he couldn't imagine two more different people than Amethyst and Jeanine. Jeanine was sweet and low-keyed, while Amethyst had been . . . What was that word his mother had always used about women she didn't like? He had it . . . Amethyst had been a mantrap. Nothing about her had been real.

"Good to see you, Jeanine," Sean said when she got close enough.

Rather than shake Sean's hand, she nodded, because her hands were full of books and newspaper clippings. Sean noted she was wearing a pleated skirt, a blouse with a rounded collar, and a green cardigan sweater. A large pin of a witch on a broomstick was attached to her collar. He approved of her clothes; they were sensible and pleasant. And they didn't call attention to themselves the way some of the things that his youngest daughter wore did.

Jeanine smiled again. "Good to see you, too, Sean. I'm glad to see you're up and about."

Sean spread his hands out. Since they were no longer shaking, he could do that now. "I'm trying."

"Well, I'm glad you are." Jeanine put the stack she was carrying down in front of him. "Here," she said. "I figure this is what you're interested in."

Sean was amazed. "How do you know what I'm interested in?"

Jeanine laughed. "Well, you're not really into local history, so what else could you be here for but the Amethyst thing."

Sean just stared at her. How had she known, and how had she pulled everything together so fast?

"I'm not a mind reader," Jeanine said, interpreting his silence correctly. "Actually, I did this before you arrived because I was interested myself. When I saw you coming up the walkway, I ran and got what I'd found."

"And did you find anything?"

Jeanine shook her head. "Nothing that I didn't know before. Although I'd forgotten that Bessie Osgood was related to your wife."

Sean shifted his weight around. "Rose never liked to talk about it."

"She was like that."

"Yes, she was."

"Well, if it's any consolation, my family never liked to talk about Amethyst's possible role in Bessie's death," Jeanine said. "They just pretended it was an accident."

"But you didn't think so?"

"No. Absolutely not. And I don't think they thought so, either. They never said anything, but it was just the sense I got."

Sean nodded toward the chair next to him. "Why don't you sit down? Unless you have something else to do, that is."

Jeanine laughed. Sean decided her laugh

was like her clothes. Nice.

"I'm sure my cataloging will wait for me," she said as she folded herself into the chair he'd indicated. She fussed with her pin for a moment, and then she said, "I don't like to talk this way about people, but Amethyst was just bad. She always was. That's why she was in that school, you know. Her mom was afraid of her." Jeanine leaned forward and lowered her voice. "She got mad at her mom one day and killed her cat. Set it on fire, and then she tried to blame my cousin Natalie."

Marvin came and stood behind Sean. "How did everyone know it wasn't Natalie?" he asked.

"Because Natalie loved animals. She was one of those people who always brought strays home with her," said Jeanine.

"Then why did Amethyst pick her?" asked Sean.

"Probably because she thought it would be funny, you know, Natalie being blamed for something like that. She even planted one of Natalie's books at the scene. And she was so convincing. If you didn't know Natalie, you'd really think she'd done something like that."

"Maybe we could talk to Natalie," Sean said.

Jeanine's eyes misted over, and then she blinked, and the tears were gone. "I'm afraid that's not possible. She died in a plane crash a couple of years ago. Amethyst was so nice on the outside, but inside . . ." Jeanine shuddered. "I tried to stay as far away from her as I could when I was growing up. One day she and Inez Colley were baby-sitting me —"

"Wait," Sean interrupted. "Inez was friends with Amethyst?"

"Oh yes," said Jeanine. She wrinkled her brow while she thought. "Along with Zinnia McGuire and Zachery Timberland and Bob Small. They used to sneak into the school at night and visit Amethyst. I think Bessie Osgood saw them, and she was going to tell."

"Are you sure?" said Sean.

"No. I'm not sure about anything. I just remember overhearing my parents talking," replied Jeanine. "Then they saw me outside, listening, and changed the subject."

"Interesting," Sean said. "Maybe one of them killed Bessie."

"Maybe," Jeanine replied.

"I don't suppose you kept in touch?" Sean asked.

"With Amethyst?" asked Jeanine.

Sean nodded.

"Kind of. She called when she needed something." Jeanine fingered her pin. "I spoke to her about four months ago. She wanted to know if I could give her Ed Banks's private phone number."

"The guy who owns Lexus Gardens?" asked Sean.

"Yeah."

Sean remembered that Bernie had tried to get in contact with Ed Banks and had been told by his personal assistant that he didn't talk to people he wasn't familiar with.

"He's not very friendly."

"He's a recluse."

"Like Howard Hughes?" asked Sean.

"Not that bad, but heading in that direction. I wasn't going to give her the number, but then Amethyst called again, and she was so sweet . . . That was her talent, you know. She made you believe you were her best friend, and even though you knew it was a lie, you still wanted to believe her."

"So you gave it to her?" asked Sean.

"Yes, I did."

"I wonder what she wanted it for."

Jeanine shrugged. "Your guess is as good as mine."

"And Zinnia? What about her?"

"She died a while ago," said Jeanine.

Sean raised an eyebrow.

"No, no," Jeanine said. "It was nothing like that. She was in a car accident." She pushed the stack of articles in front of Sean. "And now I'm sure you're anxious to get going on these materials."

Actually, Sean wasn't at all anxious to get going on his reading. He was having a good time talking to Jeanine, but he smiled and thanked her again for the time she'd taken with him.

"Nice lady," Marvin said after she'd gone back to her office.

Sean grunted.

"I don't think she's seeing anyone," Marvin said.

"Now why would you say that?" Sean demanded.

"I don't know," Marvin stammered. "I thought you might be interested."

"Well, I'm not," Sean snapped as he went through the papers that Jeanine had brought him. He separated out all the ones with pictures of the Peabody School. The rest he pushed toward Marvin with the tips of his fingers.

"Read these," Sean ordered.

"What am I looking for?" Marvin asked.

"Anything of interest."

"But how will I know what's of interest to you? I mean, I thought that thing about the turnips being jack-o'-lanterns in Ireland was pretty interesting, and you didn't."

"Just read," Sean hissed. He didn't know why he was suddenly in such a bad mood.

Marvin opened his mouth, closed it again, and began to do what he was told. As soon as he was settled, Sean took all the pictures of the Peabody School out and spread them on the table. Then he began to compare them with the slides from the View-Master. Half an hour later, he wasn't any better off than he had been before. He had his hand on the small of his back and was stretching when Jeanine came back out of her office.

"I haven't seen one of those in years," Jeanine said, pointing to the View-Master.

"Me either," said Sean. He explained where he'd gotten it from.

"So what are you hoping to find?" Jeanine asked.

Sean shook his head. "I have no idea," he confessed. "No idea at all."

"Mind if I take a look?" Jeanine asked.

"Be my guest," said Sean. He watched as she went through the slides.

"I don't get it," she said.

"Neither do I," replied Sean.

"These slides are pictures of the Peabody School," Jeanine noted.

Sean nodded.

"What are they supposed to show?" asked Jeanine.

Sean shook his head. He hated to admit it, but he didn't have a clue. "I thought if I could compare some photos with the slides, it might give me an idea, but it hasn't."

"Maybe you should go talk to Felicity Huffer," Jeanine suggested.

"That's whom I got them from. Or rather my daughter did. Felicity Huffer just told her the answer to our problem is there and to go figure it out for herself."

Jeanine made a face. "I could see her doing that and it having nothing to do with the solution to your problem."

"She could," Sean said, thinking of what she'd been like.

"Age doesn't necessarily make people nicer," said Jeanine.

"That's for sure," Marvin interjected.

Sean glared at him, and he went back to reading the papers he'd been given.

"What do you think the odds of that are?" Sean asked Jeanine.

"I'll tell you what," Jeanine said after a moment had gone by. "Felicity's daughter is on the board of the Longely Historical Society. Maybe she can help us. Would you like me to talk to her?"

Sean nodded.

"All right then," said Jeanine. "And would you mind if I kept the View-Master and looked at the slides again? Maybe something will occur to me."

Sean could feel himself smiling. "That would be lovely," he said.

"Good," Jeanine said. "I'll call you either way." She gathered up the materials and withdrew to her office.

A few minutes later Sean and Marvin were out the door.

"Aren't you going to ask me what I found?" Marvin asked when they were settled in Marvin's black limo.

"What?" Sean asked as he fastened his seat belt. He hated riding in this car. It reminded him of riding in a hearse, but as Libby had said to him when he'd complained, "Beggars can't be choosers."

"I didn't find out anything. All the articles in the papers reported Bessie Osgood's death as an accident."

"That's what I expected," Sean said.

"Why do you say that?"

"Because that's what was in everyone's interest to do. After all, if you report a murder at a private boarding/day school, most people will pull their kids out."

"True," Marvin said.

"Of course, they did, anyway," Sean said.

He and Marvin were silent for a moment. Then Sean said, "Bessie's death pretty much closed the school."

"What happened to the owner?"

"George Marak killed himself. He'd put all the money he had, plus his wife's money, into the place, as well as borrowing from his family and friends. He couldn't stand the disgrace when it became clear that the school was going to have to close, so he shot himself in the garage. The note he left asked his wife to forgive him for the shame he'd brought on her.

"It would have been more considerate if he'd killed himself somewhere else, because she and his son found his body when they came back from grocery shopping. PS: The kid was in the front seat, so he saw everything. The wife never got over it. I dare say the kid didn't, either. The wife died in an auto accident six months later. She'd been drinking and ran her car into a tree. Their kid, poor thing, went to live with a relative in Texas or Wyoming, some place like that."

"That sucks," Marvin said.

"Doesn't it, though." Sean leaned back in his seat. "Like I said, the Peabody School has always been a bad-luck place. And now, if you don't mind, I think I'd like to take a drive up to Lexus Gardens and see if we can talk to Ed Banks and find out what Amethyst wanted from him."

Sean could feel his gut tightening as Marvin zoomed away from the curb without looking or putting his signal light on. He'd faced coked-up guys and guys with loaded rifles in the line of duty, but they weren't as scary as driving with Marvin.

CHAPTER 10

Bernie took in a breath of fresh air as she drove toward Zachery Timberland's office. It was a beautiful late fall afternoon, and she was glad to be outside driving around instead of inside the shop. She glanced at the clock on the dashboard. It was a little after three, and she figured she didn't have to start up to the Peabody School until four-thirty, which should leave her more than enough time to talk to Timberland.

She drove slowly, enjoying the sensation of being in the car, imagining what fun a road trip to Vermont with Brandon would be. She was thinking that fall was her favorite season of the year when her cell phone trilled "Raindrops Keep Falling on My Head." It was her dad's ring. She fished her cell out of her bag and answered it.

"Dad?" she said.

She got static.

"Dad?"

He was talking, but his voice sounded like a jigsaw puzzle — each syllable another piece. She couldn't understand a thing he was saying. She tried calling back. Nothing. She'd just noticed she was down to no bars when her phone went dead. That was when she remembered she'd forgotten to charge it last night. *Drat and double drat,* she thought as she tossed her cell on the seat next to her. She wondered if her dad wanted to tell her something about Zachery Timberland. He was always a big one for armchair quarterbacking. Oh well. Too late now.

She knew Timberland well enough to say hello to. Her only memory of him was the time, last March, she'd met him at Laura's place. She'd shaken his hand, and it had been unpleasantly clammy.

When she'd called around this morning, it turned out that none of her friends knew him either, not surprising when you considered that his family had moved away after the Bessie Osgood incident, and he'd just come back to town a couple of years ago. Couple that with the fact that Timberland had palled around with Amethyst and Inez back then and you had something interesting going on.

And then there was the fact that Timberland was a volunteer at the Haunted House, although according to her dad, he hadn't been scheduled to work there when Amethyst had died, not that that meant anything. He could have easily come and gone without being seen.

When she'd called him, she'd told him she was interested in shopping around for a new insurance policy. It was a plausible story, but she was pretty sure he hadn't believed her. She couldn't say why she thought that but something in his tone of voice when she'd talked to him on the phone had led her to that conclusion. So, if that was the case, and she was almost certain it was, the question became, Why was he talking to her?

He probably had a pretty good idea of what she wanted to talk to him about. Or maybe not. After all, she hadn't known that he'd been friends with Amethyst Applegate until Jeanine had told her dad. Or with Bob Small. Or Inez. Or Zinnia. Which got her thinking about flowers for the dining room at the Peabody School. Maybe she should get some more pots of mums to put on the table. In her view, flowers were like diamonds. You could never have too many.

Bernie sighed as she made a left onto Avondale Place. Libby really hadn't wanted to go back to the Peabody School by herself, and Bernie couldn't really blame her. If what had happened to Libby had happened to her, she'd be thoroughly freaked out, too. Well, not really. Libby always overreacted to this kind of stuff, even though, according to her mom, she had the "gift." Or maybe that was the reason she did it. Bernie was glad she'd never been blessed that way.

Usually, Bernie thought of Halloween in terms of crunching leaves underfoot, excited children, hot mulled cider, and pumpkin spice cupcakes with cream-cheese icing on top. But after what had happened with Amethyst, her thoughts were darker.

Try as she might, she couldn't get Amethyst's head out of her mind. And even though she'd really disliked her, she wasn't sure Amethyst had deserved to die that way. She wasn't sure that anyone did. Although if they did, Amethyst would be up there on her list. She'd made bad things happen wherever she'd gone.

That much was not debatable. And there was a good chance she might have killed someone as well. Looked at in that light, whoever had killed Amethyst had done the world a favor. Not that her father or her sister would agree with that thought. And on that note, Bernie turned into the driveway of the house where the Timberland

Insurance Company was located.

The house was a classic wooden, two-story Colonial, painted a boring shade of beige, with white trim. The two front windows had white blinds pulled halfway down. Bernie parked her car, walked up three steps, rang the doorbell, and walked in. The hallway was a different shade of beige. Obviously, Timberland had beige on his mind. Either that or he'd gotten a deal on the paint.

The receptionist's desk, which was situated in what had been the sitting room of the house, was empty. Judging from the cup that was sitting there, someone had inhabited that desk not too long ago. She was probably beige, too, Bernie reflected. A moment later Zachery Timberland came out. When he looked at her, Bernie decided he resembled a shark. All teeth. She didn't remember so many teeth from the last time she'd seen him.

"So you want to change your insurance policy, do you?" he asked.

Bernie smiled her charming smile. "That's why I'm here."

"Life?"

"No. Automobile. I told you that."

Timberland put his palms outward. "Everyone makes mistakes. Some people make more then others," he said, glancing pointedly in her direction.

Great, Bernie thought as she kept smiling. "I'm sure that's true."

Timberland took a step closer to her. "I know it is."

Bernie remained where she was. She was damned if she was going to move for this guy. She'd been hoping to start with the buying the insurance thing and to gradually work the conversation around to the Peabody School, but things didn't seem to be going that way.

"So," Bernie said, trying again, "can you give me a quote on a policy for my car?"

Timberland's smile got bigger. Bernie decided he'd definitely gotten veneers on his teeth.

"No. But I can give you a quote on a life-insurance policy."

"Really? You think I'm going to need one?"

"Everyone needs one," Timberland said in a bland voice.

"Is that the case?"

"It certainly is."

"So that's not a threat or anything?"

"What a fertile imagination you have. Why would I threaten you?"

"I don't know."

"There you go." Timberland leered at her.

"I like the shoes."

Bernie considered them for a moment. They were high brown suede boots with a thin gold chain threaded through the top. She'd gotten them at deep discount last summer, when she'd been looking for a convection oven on the Lower East Side.

"They do wonders for your ass," Timberland said.

"Nice. You don't want to sell me life insurance, do you?"

"You don't want to buy life insurance, do you?"

"So I guess that makes us even," Bernie observed. "By the way, those veneers on your teeth. You should have them redone. They look like Chiclets."

Bernie was happy to see that Timberland's smile was now slightly smaller.

"You're not here for auto insurance," he said.

"Then what am I here for?"

"To ask me questions about my relationship with Amethyst."

"And why do you suppose that?"

"A little birdie told me."

Somehow Bernie couldn't believe that birdie was Jeanine. Maybe Inez? Most probably Inez.

The corners of Timberland's mouth

140

turned up at Bernie's evident confusion. "But actually, it doesn't matter," he said.

"That you and Amethyst hung out together?" asked Bernie.

"So what if we did back in the day?"

"And that your family moved away right after Bessie Osgood went out the window?"

Timberland smirked. "Again, so what? I'm sure if you check, you'll find that lots of people left around that time."

"So maybe that has something to do with Amethyst's death."

Timberland's smirk grew bigger. "I guess you're behind the times."

"Not me. I'm fashion forward," said Bernie.

Timberland blinked for a minute, then recovered himself. "You mean, you haven't heard?" he asked.

"Heard what?" Bernie replied. Now it was her turn to be puzzled.

"They arrested Bob Small this morning for Amethyst's murder."

Bernie shifted from one leg to the other. She wondered if that was what her dad had been calling her about. It probably was.

"So?" she said. "Your point is?"

"My point is that I want you to keep away from me. You have no legal authority."

"Is that what you brought me here to tell me?"

"As a matter of fact, it is. I brought you here to tell you that I'll have you arrested for stalking if you keep bothering me."

Bernie couldn't help it. She laughed. "You're kidding me, right?"

"Not in the least."

"You could have said no when I called."

"I just saw your name on today's calendar."

"Even so. You could have called and cancelled."

"I wanted to tell you in person."

"How considerate."

"I'm a considerate guy."

"I don't know . . . ," Bernie said.

"That's obvious."

Bernie talked over him. "For someone who is in the clear, you're certainly going to a lot of trouble to tell me to lay off. Why is that?"

Timberland took another step toward her. "You and your sister have a reputation for causing trouble."

"It depends on your definition of *trouble.* And, anyway, what could we do to you? You just told me you had nothing to do with any of this."

Timberland went on as if she hadn't

spoken. "If you're smart, you'll stay out of my way."

"You want to tell me about your daughter?"

Timberland flushed. "You've been warned," he growled.

"I guess you don't like talking about her."

"Get out before I have you arrested." Timberland took his cell off the clip on his belt. "I'm dialing."

"I'm going. I'm going."

Well, that had been a complete waste of time, Bernie thought as she got back in her vehicle. She shook her head in disgust at herself. She'd let him lead the conversation from the get-go. Bad. Bad. Bad. The only thing she did know was that the daughter was a definite sore spot. She sighed and looked at her watch.

She had another hour before she had to meet Libby at the Haunted House. She decided to use it to pick up more potted mums at the garden center. If she recalled, they still had some left. And as long as she was there, she could ask Kathy about Zinnia. They were the same age. Maybe she'd know something about her.

Then if she had any time left over, she'd buy some more napkins. She'd seen some really cute ones with ghosts on them in the dollar store over on Grand Avenue. And maybe they had some other Halloween stuff as well. That was the thing with the dollar store. You never knew what you were going to find. *Kind of like life,* Bernie decided. She shook her head. She was definitely getting sappy in her old age.

Kathy's Garden Shop was located in a mini strip mall three miles off of Longely's main road. The strip mall had been built recently. There was more and more mall sprawl lately, taking up land that, in Bernie's judgment, should have been left alone. After all, how many Home Depots and Staples did you need?

Kathy's Garden Shop was located between a drugstore and a place selling chicken wings, but as Kathy had pointed out to Bernie, the rent was cheap, the utilities were fairly low, and there was plenty of parking. Like Bernie and Libby, Kathy managed to compete with the chains by charm, customer service, and interesting merchandise. So far she'd done pretty well for herself.

When Bernie got out of her car, she was happy to see there were eight pots of mums sitting outside of Kathy's shop.

"You want to do a trade?" Bernie said when she went inside.

Her friend Kathy looked up from behind the register. Today her hair was in cornrows. She had light brown skin and large green eyes. It was a smashing combination.

"What kind of trade?"

"You let me borrow the mums to decorate the tables up at the Haunted House, and I'll give you three apple pies."

"Apple and cranberry and throw in a parsnip pie and you got a deal."

"You are the only person I know, except for me and Libby, that likes parsnip pie."

"That's because you're making my grandmother's recipe."

"No. It's my grandmother's. We've had this discussion before."

Bernie pointed to the display of orange and lemon trees. "Those would look nice in my bedroom."

"And I would sell them to you," Kathy said, "if you didn't have a black thumb."

"Gray thumb."

"Black," Kathy said firmly.

"All right. Black." It was true. Bernie had yet to keep a plant alive. She simply forgot to water them. "By the way, do you remember Zinnia McGuire?"

Kathy put her pen down. "Course, I do. She used to pal around with Zachery Timberland, Bob Small, and Amethyst Applegate. Now there was a nice crew."

"Whatever happened to her?"

"She died in an automobile accident down in Coopersville. Hit-and-run, if I remember correctly. Some guy went right through the stop at Elves and Ash and T-boned her. He must have been going really fast, from what I understand."

Bernie raised an eyebrow. "And no one saw anything?"

"It was three-thirty in the morning. You know what that place is like. It's even worse than Longely. A neighbor called it in. She said the crash woke her up."

"I wonder why Zinnia was there?"

Kathy shrugged. "She was probably doing the typical druggie high school dropout thing."

"Did Zinnia ever say anything?"

"Nope. She died on the way to the hospital. I guess she was in pretty bad shape when the police got there. It's really too bad."

"How's that?"

"Because she was getting her act together. She'd given up the stuff she was doing — the coke and the weed — and was talking about going back to school."

"How long after Bessie Osgood died was she killed?"

146

Kathy thought for a moment. "Maybe one year. Certainly no more than two."

"Interesting," Bernie murmured.

"You don't think one thing had anything to do with the other, do you?" Kathy asked.

"Probably not," Bernie said.

Nevertheless, she filed the fact away in her head for possible use later.

CHAPTER 11

"Damn cell," Sean said as he and Marvin headed toward Lexus Gardens.

Marvin turned his head to look at Sean. "Can't you —"

"Eyes on the road," Sean yelled.

"They are on the road," Marvin said.

"Now they're on the road. Before they weren't. Maybe you shouldn't talk while you're driving."

Marvin didn't say anything. Sean could tell he was sulking. Young people didn't take correction well these days. They should be thankful for the help. But when he'd said that to Libby and Bernie, they'd just rolled their eyes.

After a moment, Sean said, "Things are stressful." Which was as close to an apology as he was going to get.

Marvin stared straight ahead. Another moment went by before he spoke.

"There was no one on the road."

"Maybe there wasn't," Sean allowed, "but that's not the issue. The issue is there could have been."

"I don't get it," Marvin told him.

Sean watched him for a moment and shook his head. Now he was driving like a little old lady, with both hands gripping the steering wheel.

"Bad habits are bad habits," Sean explained. "The object in life is to develop good ones. That way, when a situation comes along, you don't have to think about what to do. You know what to do."

"I suppose," Marvin said.

"You suppose! That's the basis for military training. It stops people from getting killed." Sean nodded at the turn coming up. "You want to take a right here."

"I know," Marvin said. "Contrary to popular opinion, I can drive."

"I never said you couldn't."

This time when Marvin talked, Sean was delighted to see he kept his eyes on the road. He knew he should feel guilty about yelling at the kid, but he didn't, because he'd accomplished his objective. He couldn't forbid Libby to ride around with Marvin, but he could endeavor to make him the best driver possible. And if yelling was what it took, then so be it. Sean could live with that.

"So Banks doesn't know that we're coming?" Marvin asked.

"No. I can't call him, because I can't get any reception here. Maybe it's better that way," Sean said.

"What if he's not in?" Marvin asked.

Sean waved his hand to indicate the countryside. "Then we'll have enjoyed a drive in the country."

Sean was glad to be out riding around. And if Edward Banks wasn't in, they could always speak to him another time. Some people would say that talking to Banks was just a waste of time, but Sean had always found that the more information one could gather, the better. You could never tell what might prove to be important and what wasn't until you got it all together and laid it out on the metaphorical table.

So why had Amethyst wanted to speak to Banks? Banks was a recluse. Sean had heard that his house and gardens were spectacular, but no one Sean knew had seen them. So maybe he'd see them now. That is, if Banks was in and was willing to talk to them. If not, all he and Marvin had wasted was the fifteen-mile drive into the country. Which wasn't a waste, especially not today.

Maybe they'd go home by way of Orchid

150

Farms, and he'd get some apples. Cortlands were always good. And they had unpasteurized cider, something you couldn't get in the grocery stores anymore. Maybe he'd get a gallon for the house and a quart for Jeanine for all the help she'd given him. Yes. That was what he'd do. He was feeling very pleased with himself when Marvin started talking.

"What?" Sean asked.

"I asked if Bernie knows that Bob Small was arrested," Marvin said.

"Probably not," Sean said.

Clyde had phoned to tell him after Bernie had gone, and although he'd tried phoning Bernie, he hadn't gotten through. He hadn't even been able to leave a message, because her mailbox was full. Not that it really mattered.

He'd tell her when he met up with her at the Peabody School. He sat back and took in the scenery while keeping one eye on Marvin's driving. Even if Marvin were the best driver in the world, which he wasn't, Sean had to admit to himself, he wouldn't be able to relax. The truth was he didn't trust anyone to drive except himself.

They got to Lexus Gardens twenty minutes later. The road up to the estate formed a winding ribbon as it went up to the top of the Altamar Hill. Huge evergreens hugged either side of the road, blotting out the light.

"I wouldn't want to drive up and down this road in the winter," Marvin observed as he made another turn.

"Me either," Sean replied. "But he probably doesn't have to. He probably spends his winters in the Caribbean. I mean, I would if I had that kind of money."

"Would you really?" Marvin asked.

"No," Sean said. He hated the heat.

Another one-eighth mile and they were at the estate. The whole thing was enclosed in a stucco wall, with barbed wire on the top.

"I guess he doesn't want any visitors," Marvin said.

"I guess not," Sean agreed. He was surprised there wasn't an ARMED RESPONSE sign tacked up to the wall.

The house and the gardens had been featured in some magazine named *Shelters*. Or something like that. Maybe when Sean gave Jeanine the cider, he'd ask her if she could look that up, too. He directed Marvin to drive up to the gate. There was an intercom mounted on the far wall. Sean told him to lean out the window and push the button. Marvin did. There was a crackling noise.

"Ask if we can come up and talk to him

for a moment," Sean ordered. "Tell him we're involved in a homicide investigation."

"But we're not the police," Marvin protested.

"I'm not saying we are," Sean told him. It just sounded that way.

"If you say so."

"I do," Sean said.

"Okay," Marvin said, and he turned and yelled into the intercom. There was no response. He tried again. Nothing.

Marvin turned back to Sean. "Maybe no one is home."

"Maybe," Sean said. "Try another time."

Marvin did, with the same results.

Sean looked through the gate. The opening offered a narrow perspective. All he could see was a lawn, a large red maple, the front of the house, and a large blow-up statue of a witch bowing up and down. Sean did a double take.

Talk about something being out of place. You expected to see something like that at Wal-Mart, not someplace like here, a place that was known for its taste and elegance. Another odd thing caught his attention. No lights were on in the house, and he didn't see any movement anywhere. Which was strange because a house this size required a staff to run it. Sean gave a mental shrug.

Banks could be off in China, for all he knew.

"It's awfully quiet," Marvin observed.

"It is, isn't it," Sean agreed. All he could hear was the wind murmuring and a flock of geese honking as they flew overhead.

Marvin leaned out and pressed the intercom button again. Just static. "Hello," he cried. "Anyone home?"

"Let's just go," Sean said.

Marvin turned back to Sean. "Maybe he went to the Caribbean, after all."

"He could be anywhere," Sean said. One thing was clear. No one was home. Or if they were, they weren't answering the intercom. "We can stop at the farm stand on our way to the Peabody School."

Marvin nodded and turned around. Later Sean would be sorry that he had made that decision. Later he'd be sorry that he hadn't asked Marvin to try the gate. Later he'd tell himself he was turning into a careless old man. But that was later. Right now he wanted to get to the farm stand before it closed.

"Thank you," Libby said as Mark helped her carry the last of her cartons into the kitchen.

She began unpacking. Mark coughed. Libby looked up. He was standing beside her, shuffling from one well-shod foot to another.

"Yes?" she said.

Mark coughed again. Libby decided he looked uneasy. Somehow she liked him better that way.

"Can I help you with anything?" she asked. She wished he'd come to the point. She had a lot of things she had to do.

"I heard." Mark stopped.

"Heard what?" Libby asked, mystified.

"Er. I heard you saw something the other day." He spoke quickly, running his words together. "Or maybe I should say someone."

Libby knew instantly what he meant. "That's right," she said cautiously as she took the jugs with the waffle batter out of the cardboard box she'd carried them in. "You're talking about Bessie Osgood, aren't you?"

Mark nodded and fidgeted some more.

Libby rested her hand on top of one of the five-quart jugs. "I still can't believe I did."

"You don't believe in that kind of thing?" Mark asked.

"Not at all. I keep thinking she was some kind of optical illusion that someone had created."

"I don't think so," Mark said softly.

155

"Why not?"

"Because I saw her, too," he said a moment later. He held up three fingers.

"Three times?" Libby asked.

Mark nodded. "I don't believe in ghosts, either."

"Neither do I," Libby lied, because in her heart she did. "But here we are."

Mark nodded. "I didn't tell anyone, because I didn't want them to think I'm crazy."

"I'm surprised. I'd think you'd want the publicity."

"I'm a behind-the-scenes kind of guy."

Libby unscrewed the top of the five-quart jug of whole-wheat batter and started pouring it into a pitcher. "I felt so cold," she said.

"I got goose bumps on my arms," Mark said.

"Me too. And I could kind of see a shape."

"Out of the corner of your eye?"

Libby nodded. "I had the impression of a teenage girl. But I don't know why I thought that. I couldn't really see her all that well. I could hardly see her at all. I closed my eyes for a second, and when I opened them again, she was gone."

"That's what happened with me. For some reason, I thought she was wearing a pleated skirt and a white shirt."

"She was so hazy," Libby said.

Mark bobbed his head. "*Hazy* is a good word."

Libby finished filling the pitcher and put the cap back on the jug. She didn't know what to feel: relieved because someone else had seen what she had or dismayed that what she had seen was apparently real.

"Maybe we both saw an optical illusion," she said.

Mark shook his head. "I don't see how anyone could create something like that."

"FX has created some pretty strange stuff in your haunted house."

"Yeah. But Bessie Osgood is on a totally different plane."

Libby had to agree that she was. "Why are we seeing her?"

Mark shook his head. "Maybe because we're here. I don't think anyone else has seen her."

"Curtis and Konrad have a tape of her confessing she killed Amethyst Applegate."

"Them." Mark ran his hand through his hair. "All I could hear was static."

"That's all I could hear, too. The police refused to listen."

"Can you blame them?"

Libby shook her head.

"Did they tell you I offered them one

thousand dollars if they could get her voice on tape? I thought it would be good for the Haunted House. So maybe that's why they're hearing things that no one else can."

"Could be," Libby agreed.

Mark gave Libby a wan smile. "I thought it would be cool to have a real ghost moving around, especially considering that it's Halloween and I'm running a haunted house, but it's really not. In fact, it's kind of upsetting." He looked at his watch. "Gotta go. I have to find a replacement for Bob Small. I thought I had someone, and he pooped out on me." He shook his head again. "Talk about upsetting."

"You mean Bob Small killing Amethyst?"

"What do you think I'm talking about?"

"I thought you might have been referring to finding a replacement."

"Hardly."

"Do you think he did it?" Libby asked.

"I'd like to think he didn't," Mark said. "After all, if it wasn't for me giving him that job, maybe he wouldn't have had the opportunity to do what he did. What is it that they say about the road to hell and good intentions? But I have to assume he did it, and all the tapes in the world aren't going to make things any different."

"I'm not so sure," Libby said. "Chopping

off someone's head doesn't seem like something Bob would do."

"Who do you know who would do something like that?"

"No one," Libby admitted.

"Exactly," Mark said.

"I just can't see him setting something like this up."

"The police think otherwise."

"They've been wrong before."

"Maybe you're right. Maybe I shouldn't be so quick to judge. I have to watch myself with that. It's my besetting sin." He glanced down at his watch. "Oops," he said. "I didn't realize how late it is. You can't believe how crowded we've been since that . . . thing . . . with Amethyst."

"I can believe it," Libby said, thinking of what happened at the shop whenever a crime was committed that they were connected to in some way or other. "That's why I brought extra. I figure we're going to be swamped."

"People are amazing," Mark said. "Who would have thought?"

Then he headed out the door, leaving Libby by herself. She got right to work, but try as she might, she couldn't stop thinking that there was more to Amethyst's death than she was seeing. Maybe her dad would see something that she wasn't. She decided she was glad he was coming. Having him look over the crime scene would make her feel better.

CHAPTER 12

Sean went into the Pit and the Pendulum Room with the same attitude he'd brought to every crime scene he'd processed when he'd been the Longely chief of police. With dispassion. He went in without expectations — at least as far as it was possible for a human being to do that.

The first thing he noticed was that the room was dark enough that it took his eyes a moment to accustom themselves to the low light. According to Mark, everything was the same as it had been the afternoon that Amethyst Applegate died. Sean still couldn't believe that they had opened this up in such a short time. But that was Lucy for you. Always in a hurry. Always overlooking things.

He took in his surroundings. The mirrored walls, the platform, the high table draped in a red cloth, the spotlight on the blade, the speed at which the blade swung back and forth — all worked to focus your attention on one central point. The table. Everyone walking in here would automatically be looking at one thing and one thing only. Whoever had set this up had done an excellent job. He turned to Libby.

"Tell me what you saw."

"I already told you," she protested.

"I know you did, but I want to hear it again," Sean said.

As he looked at his daughters, he thought that neither of them were happy being here. Marvin wasn't, either. But given the circumstances, who could blame them?

"It's simple," Libby said. "We walked in the room, and we saw this table on the platform, with the blade swinging back and forth."

"And then?" Sean prompted.

"And then I took a couple of steps and saw a headless body on the table, and then I took another step, and that's when I saw it."

"Amethyst's head?" asked Sean.

Libby nodded. "It was just sitting there at the top of the stairs. At first, I thought it was part of the exhibit, and then I looked at Mark's face, and I knew it wasn't."

"How did you know?" asked Sean.

"I just did. He was staring at it. He had a

162

strange expression on his face," replied Libby.

"What kind of strange expression?" asked Sean.

"I don't know how to describe it," Libby said.

Sean looked at his other daughter. Bernic shook her head.

"I wasn't paying attention to him. I was mesmerized by the head," said Libby. "And then he went up and tapped it with his foot, and it started rolling. . . ."

"Just like at the Bastille," Bernie said.

"I didn't know whether it was real or not, but then, when it stopped in front of my feet . . ." Libby shuddered.

Sean nodded. "And then?"

"And then I screamed," said Libby.

"Did anyone come in?" asked Sean.

"No," Bernie said, "because we ran out."

"I see," Sean said as he looked around.

"Do you need us for anything else?" Bernie asked after a moment had gone by.

"No," Sean answered absentmindedly. He was already focused on trying to figure out what had happened. "I just want to stay and walk around a little."

"Good," Libby said. "Then we'll finish setting up."

They turned to go, and Marvin started

walking out with them.

"No, Marvin. You stay here," Sean instructed.

"But . . . ," said Marvin.

Sean glared at him.

Marvin's shoulders slumped. "Fine," he said.

"Do me a favor and turn on the lights for me. They're over in the far corner, hidden behind the cloth panel."

Sean watched Marvin fumble around, but after a moment or so, he found the switch. Suddenly, the room was bathed in light.

"It looks different," Marvin remarked.

"It certainly does," Sean agreed.

The mirrors looked dirty; the platform was badly made; the steps looked thrown together. Sean slowly walked over to the control panel that was hidden behind the cloth. From that vantage point, he looked across the wall to where the device that sent out the hologram was situated. A person walked in and tripped a circuit that would trigger a digital camera, which would capture their image and transfer it to a hologram that would make it look as if that person's head were being cut off.

Mark had explained it, but Sean hadn't understood the explanation. Clyde hadn't, either.

What had Clyde said? *There's a whole new world out there, Sean, and I don't want to be part of it.* Sean had had to say that he agreed. He turned to Marvin. "Did you understand Mark's explanation?"

Marvin shook his head. "I was lost after the second sentence."

"Me too," Sean said gloomily. But then Mark had admitted that he really didn't understand how it all worked, either.

"So what do you think happened?" Marvin asked Sean.

Sean rubbed his hands together. He'd come up with two scenarios. In scenario number one, Bob Small snuck in while Amethyst was lying on the table and cut her head off with a piece of fiber-optic laser wire that he'd taken with him into the ceiling. At least that was the weapon the ME had identified as the cause of death. But then why had she been lying on the table? Why had she stayed still for Bob Small to do this? Why had she agreed to meet Bob Small in the first place?

More likely, Amethyst walked into the room, and the killer, who was hiding behind the door, took the wire and wrapped it around her neck. After all, if fiber-optic wire could cut through steel, it would definitely cut through flesh and bone. There wouldn't be any blood, because the high heat of the wire would cauterize the wound. Then the murderer positioned the body the way that Bernie, Libby, and Mark had found it and left. But two questions remained: who killed Amethyst, and why?

"Are you all right?" Marvin asked.

Sean was startled. He realized he must have been staring off into space.

"I'm fine," he said. "Absolutely fine."

"Maybe this place has secret passageways or something like that."

"That's in books."

"But it's possible," Marvin insisted.

"Anything is possible," Sean retorted. In all his thirty odd years on the police force, he'd never come across a secret compartment, much less a secret passageway. "What are you doing?" he asked Marvin as he began tapping on the wall.

"Looking."

Sean was just about to tell him to stop when Mark stuck his head into the room.

"I hope you guys are finishing up, because we're going to open the doors to the Haunted House in ten minutes," he said.

Sean stood up slowly. "Not a problem. By any chance, do you have the original plans for this place?"

"I do, but I won't be able to get them till

the a.m.," replied Mark. "What do you need them for?"

Sean massaged the small of his back. Getting old sucked. "Just checking to see if there's a connection between this room and the main house."

Mark raised an eyebrow. "Like a secret passageway?"

Sean shrugged.

"There isn't one," said Mark.

"How do you know?" Sean asked.

"Because I went over the original plans of this place with the architect last week," said Mark. "We're remodeling this section as soon as the Haunted House closes, and I wanted to make sure we didn't run into any unpleasant surprises. Nothing like not having a wall where you expect to find one or the other way around."

"You must have a lot of rich people bankrolling you," said Sean.

"Well, one or two," Mark allowed. "We've been blessed that way. And now I really have to go. If I had known that I was going to have to be here overseeing everything the whole time the Haunted House was open, I would have hired a manager." And he walked away.

"I'd love to know who his backers are," Sean said.

"Why?"

"Just curiosity."

"Are you going to ask him?"

"Yes, I am," Sean said. "But he doesn't have to answer, and I have a feeling he won't."

Marvin cocked his head, and Sean answered his unspoken question.

"Because he's not going to want me to go annoy them with questions. If I piss them off, there's a good chance he won't get any more money out of them. After all, why do they need this type of aggravation? The answer is: they don't."

"So what are you going to do?"

"I'll think of something," Sean said.

As it turned out, that something came sooner than Sean had expected. Sean and Marvin were crossing the parking lot when the Kurtz twins ran up to them.

Konrad grabbed Sean by the arm. "Have you heard?" he cried. "They've gone and arrested Bob. Poor Bob. You gotta do something."

"I'm trying. Let go of my arm," Sean demanded. "Now." Sean didn't like being touched.

Konrad looked down. "Sorry," he muttered and took a step back. "I forgot."

"Well, don't forget again," growled Sean.

Curtis looked as if he was going to cry. "You have to make them listen to the tape."

"I've tried," said Sean. Which wasn't true, but Sean wasn't in the mood to hear a lecture on the merits of ESV. Or was it EVC? Whatever the hell it was called.

Konrad absentmindedly jiggled his ring of keys. "You have to make them understand."

Sean looked at the keys. *Maybe*, he thought, *this trip wouldn't be a total waste, after all.* "You guys just going to work?"

Curtis nodded.

"Where's Inez?" asked Sean.

"She called in sick. Again," Curtis told him. "Ian is going to fire her ass for sure if she doesn't look out."

"So it's just you two?" asked Sean.

Konrad nodded. "I don't mind. It's easier without her. Quieter."

"Isn't it kind of early for you guys to be cleaning?" asked Sean.

"Oh. We're going to do one of our tapings at the Haunted House," Konrad said. "Mr. Kane called and told us to come in."

Sean was quiet for a moment, and then he said, "Is everyone at the offices gone?"

Curtis answered, "Well, they're usually gone this time of day. No one seems to work very late in there."

Sean was silent for another moment. Then

169

he said, "Are you serious about helping your cousin?"

"Of course, we are," Konrad answered. "Why?"

"Because I'd like to have a look around the offices of the Foundation," replied Sean.

"Are you nuts?" Marvin hissed.

Sean ignored him and watched Konrad and Curtis exchange looks.

"What do you say, boys?" Sean asked.

In answer, Konrad took his keys off the hook that was holding them and gave them to Sean. "We forgot them, and we had to go home to get them," he said.

"But we have them," Curtis protested.

"We're —" Konrad began. Then he stopped. "Forget it," he said to Curtis. "I'll explain in the truck."

"But what about our demonstration?" Curtis protested.

"We'll just be a little late," said Konrad.

"I don't know," Curtis said.

"I do," Konrad replied.

Sean watched while Konrad dragged Curtis away.

"You can't do this," Marvin said when they were gone.

"Why not? Now is the perfect time. Mark is tied up. Figuratively speaking."

"But what if someone is at the Foundation, working?"

"Then we'll say we're sorry and leave."

"I don't think I can do this," Marvin protested.

"Of course, you can," Sean said.

Marvin bit his lip. "I don't know."

"Well, I do."

"Why don't I drive you over and sit in the car and wait?"

"Don't be ridiculous. I need you. And drive around to the side entrance. We can leave the car there. I don't want the police to see it on one of their patrols."

"The police," Marvin cried.

"It'll be fine," Sean said in as soothing a voice as he could manage. "Everything will be just fine."

"No, it won't," Marvin protested.

"Just think of everything you're learning," Sean told him.

Marvin straightened his back. "Breaking and entering is not something I want to learn."

"We're not breaking and entering, because we have the keys. At worst, this could be called unlawful trespass."

"That's wonderful," Marvin said.

Sean decided to take his comment literally. "I think so. It's a misdemeanor. At most, we'd be looking at community service if we get caught."

CHAPTER 13

Libby looked at the woman standing in front of her. She was small and plain and had one of those short, mannish haircuts that women tended to get when they didn't want to bother about their looks anymore.

"Aren't you scared working here?" she asked Libby as Libby placed a slice of pumpkin cheesecake on a paper plate and handed it to her.

"You mean because of the murder?" Libby asked.

"After all, Mark said you saw Amethyst's head rolling down the stairs."

Thanks, Mark, Libby thought. "Frankly," she said to the woman, "I think I'm too tired to be scared."

The woman gave her an odd look and walked away.

But it was true. Things had finally settled down some, and for that, she was eternally grateful. People were no longer standing out in the hallway, waiting to get in. But her back and her feet were killing her. So were her wrists and arms, for that matter. She couldn't imagine how Bernie's feet were feeling. She was wearing pink ballet slippers, which had no support whatsoever. She and Bernie had been making waffles and dishing out desserts since they'd opened the doors, and she was ready to take a break.

Evidently, the combination of the chance to visit a real live murder scene and go through a haunted house at the same time had proved irresistible to the population of Longley and the surrounding towns. This was better than reality TV. When Libby thought about it, she realized this could be reality TV.

They'd sold way more Belgian and chocolate brownie waffles than she or her sister had anticipated. Hopefully, they'd have enough to squeak by until the end of the night, which was another couple of hours away. All she could say was thank heavens she'd prepared extra.

The real winner of the day, though, was the apple compote. People couldn't stop talking about it. Libby had to admit it was pretty darn good. The lemon peel, the touch of rum, and the small amount of apricot jam in it made all the difference.

They were doing very well. The bad part was that they had to go home and get ready for tomorrow. Hopefully, Amber and Googie had done everything they were supposed to do. Otherwise, Libby and Bernie would be up till three in the morning, doing prep work. Sometimes Libby thought of the public as an insatiable mouth that she and Bernie labored to feed. She shook her head to clear that thought from her mind and got back to the business at hand.

"How are we doing with the pumpkin bars?" she asked Bernie.

"We've got two trays, but the apple and the pumpkin pies are gone. We should bake a few more of those for tomorrow. Did you get a look at the fat woman in the latex suit? That was certainly a mistake. Fetish dressing is definitely for thin people. Don't look at me like that. Half the fun of Halloween is commenting on the costumes people wear."

"See. This is why I'm not getting into a costume."

Bernie looked hurt. "I wouldn't let you make a mistake like that."

Libby knew Bernie wouldn't, but she still didn't want to wear a costume. She just felt silly. She just didn't know how to explain that to someone who was dressed as Little Bo Peep ("to balance the energy," Bernie had explained). But at least that was better than the witch and the vampire, Libby thought. Bernie wasn't wearing fake nails today. They had driven Libby crazy. She had been eyeing them the past two nights, waiting for one to fall into the waffle batter.

"How about we just do make-up?" Bernie said.

"I'll think about it."

"Come on," Bernie cajoled.

Libby threw up her hands. She was too tired to argue. "Fine," she said. "I give up."

Bernie grinned. "You won't regret it."

Libby thought she probably would, but at least she'd have a short interval of peace and quiet. She shook her head to clear it and continued to take stock of what they needed.

"We need more cider," she said. "Would you mind going out to the van and getting the rest of it?"

"Why is it still in the van?"

"Because I was too tired to bring it all in."

"Makes sense," Bernie said. "I'll do it now."

Bernie was back two minutes later with a jug in each hand. Libby noticed her sister was frowning.

"Libby," Bernie said, "didn't Dad and

Marvin leave for home?"

Libby kept stocking the square rattan box she used for the napkins. "Yes. At least I thought they did."

"Well, I spotted Marvin's car on the far side of the parking lot. I'm going to call and see what they're up to."

Bernie was reaching for her phone when it rang. She picked it up and checked her caller ID. It was her dad. She listened to him for a moment and hung up.

"They're at the Foundation," she said to Libby.

"The Foundation? What are they doing there?"

"Snooping."

"Snooping?"

"That's what I said," Bernie replied. Sometimes she thought her sister had a hearing problem.

"What are they looking for?"

"They wanted to find out who the Foundation backers are," replied Bernie.

"But why?"

Bernie shook her head. "You got me. But they're going back to Ed Banks's house to talk to him. He's one of the big backers. And guess what?"

"What?" Libby said as she ladled pumpkin batter into one of the waffle machines and closed the top.

"So was Amethyst."

Libby's eyes remained focused on the machine. "She had that kind of money?"

"Evidently, she did."

"Interesting," Libby said as she opened the machine up. "Very interesting indeed."

She was about to say something else when Mark appeared by their side. He'd been so quiet, Libby hadn't heard him approach. She wondered if he'd been standing there long.

"You gals holding up under the on-slaught?" he asked.

"Oh yes," Bernie said, even though she detested being called a gal.

"Is your dad around?" asked Mark.

Bernie shook her head. "Not that I know of."

Mark wrinkled his forehead. "That's odd, because I thought I saw the car he came in off to the side of the parking lot."

"Must have been a different car," Libby lied.

"Marvin and dad went home a while ago," said Bernie, backing her up.

"Absolutely," Libby agreed.

"Well, someone is over there," Mark said. "I think I'll take a walk around and see what's what. Can't have any more bad things happening here, can we? And, by the way, Bernie, I like your costume." He grinned. "I'd be one of your sheep anytime of the week."

"My pleasure," Bernie said.

As soon as Mark turned and started walking away, Bernie grabbed her cell phone and called her dad to tell him what was happening.

"Poor Marvin," she said to Libby when she was done. "He's probably having a heart attack."

Libby grimaced. "I was thinking the same thing myself."

"What's going on?" Marvin asked Sean as Sean clicked off his cell phone.

"I guess you were right," Sean said.

"Right about what?"

"I guess we should have left a little earlier."

"What do you mean?" Marvin asked.

Sean noticed that Marvin's voice was rising in a spiral of panic. "Bernie just told me that Mark is on his way over."

"Oh my God," Marvin said.

"Relax," Sean said. "It'll be fine."

"That's what you said when we walked in here."

"And I meant it."

"But we have to get out of here."

"It's too late."

"What are we going to do?" Marvin wailed.

"Learn from the master," Sean told him. "Now grab my coat, and let's go."

He watched Marvin hurry away. A moment later he was back with Sean's coat. Sean struggled into it; then he and Marvin walked to the door. Sean would have liked to have gone faster, but he couldn't walk at a decent pace anymore. These days he was lucky he could walk at all. He really should have had Marvin bring the wheelchair along. It would have made things so much simpler. They had just gotten to the door and Marvin had reached out to open it when the door swung open and Mark was standing there.

"Hello," Sean said. "What a pleasant surprise."

Mark started to stammer.

"You're probably wondering what we're doing here," Sean said.

"Well —," Mark began, but Sean had already cut him off.

"Trying to find the old plans for the house." Sean smiled.

"But I told you I'd show them to you," Mark protested.

"I know you did, and I'm sorry, but I just

couldn't wait. You know how old men get. Impatient. Like in the song lyrics, 'oh the days dwindle down to a precious few.' "

Mark scowled at him.

"What? You've never heard 'September Song'?" Sean asked. "It's Frank Sinatra. At least I think it's Frank Sinatra. I thought the plans would be in the archives. . . ."

"We don't have archives," Mark said.

"I finally remembered you'd told me that after I went looking for them," said Sean as he rubbed his hands together. "I'm telling you, getting old is a bitch." He smiled at Mark. "Well, as long as you're here, maybe you can get them for us now?"

"No," Mark replied. Sean could tell he was very annoyed and anxious to get away from this garrulous old man in front of him. Which was the whole idea. "I have to go down to the basement to get them. It could take quite some time."

"I'll be back tomorrow afternoon then," Sean told him and started to walk off.

"Wait," Mark said.

Sean stopped and turned.

"How did you get in here?" asked Mark.

"I used my superpowers. No, really. Some people were going out. . . ."

"What people?" A sharp thinker, Mark.

"A woman and a man," said Sean.

"Describe them," Mark ordered.

Sean shrugged and tried to keep from jingling the keys in his pocket that Konrad and Curtis had given him. "I don't know. Ordinary people. I have trouble identifying people now." Sean tried to look contrite. "I'm sorry if I caused a problem," he said.

"You didn't." Mark ran his hand through his hair.

It looked so perfect, Sean wondered if he dyed it. Or went to some fancy spa.

"I just don't want anything to happen to you," Mark added.

"That's so nice. Nothing will," Sean said firmly.

Mark waved his hands in the air. "I'd feel better if you weren't in this place by yourself."

"I'm not here by myself. I have Marvin," replied Sean.

Mark's eyes narrowed slightly. "You know what I mean."

"I do indeed," said Sean. "Tell me, does your insurance kick in if someone gets killed or injured by a ghost, or does that come under the 'act of God' clause?"

Mark smiled. "You're a funny man," he said.

"I like to think so," said Sean.

"Now I know where Bernie gets it from.

I'll have to ask my insurance agent," replied Mark.

"Do you have a good one?" asked Sean.

Mark reached into his pocket, took out a piece of gum, unwrapped it, and popped it in his mouth. "The company we hired to mount the Haunted House show carries lots of liability, but it doesn't cover homicide."

"Tomorrow then?" Sean asked.

"Absolutely," Mark said, with what Sean decided was a tad too much enthusiasm.

"You see," Sean explained to Marvin as they walked to Marvin's car. "You should never explain. You should never run. If you're caught in a situation like this, you walk toward the person and spin them a plausible story."

"I don't think Mark believed you," Marvin said as he opened the door of his car.

"That's the point," Sean said once he was comfortably settled in his seat. "He didn't believe me, but because of the way I was acting, he couldn't call me a liar. Now let's get back to Lexus Gardens."

"But it's late," Marvin protested.

"Precisely. That way there's a better chance that Banks might be in."

CHAPTER 14

"Slow down," Sean yelled at Marvin as they took one of the turns on the road up to Lexus Gardens. "It's too damn dark to be going this fast."

"I'm going twenty miles an hour," Marvin told him.

"Then go fifteen."

It was pitch black out, and even with Marvin using his brights, the turns just leaped out. At night the evergreens on either side of the road reminded Sean of huge saws. Or maybe Halloween was getting to him. In any case, Sean hoped there weren't any deer up this way. There didn't used to be, but these days they were everywhere, eating everything. Clyde called them rodents with long legs.

"I wish I could drive," Sean complained as he scrunched up his eyes so he could see better in the dark.

"I wish you could, too," Marvin said.

"Was that a note of bitterness I detected?" Sean asked.

"No," Marvin stammered. "It's just that —"

"I criticize you?"

"It's more like I never seem to do anything right."

Sean's hand tightened around the door handle as Marvin took a particularly sharp curve.

"Of course, you do," Sean told him. "If you didn't, I wouldn't even bother with you."

"Really?" Marvin said.

Sean could hear Marvin's voice brightening. "Yes, really," Sean replied.

There was a short pause. Then Marvin said, "My father says I can't do anything right."

"Well, he's wrong," Sean said. "Dead wrong. And speaking of dead, don't take your eyes off the road. Aside from the turns, there could be deer wandering about."

Marvin didn't say anything. Sean turned to look at him. He was smiling in a way Sean had never seen him smile before. The two men sat silently for a moment before Marvin spoke.

"What are you going to ask Banks?" Marvin said.

"What the Foundation is about, what Amethyst wanted from him, stuff like that."

"And if he won't answer? It's not as if he has to."

"Oh, he'll answer," Sean said, with assurance. "I'll make him want to."

"How will you make him do that?"

"By letting him know his life will be a lot easier if he talks to me."

"I see," Marvin said. "But what if he doesn't want to? What if you can't convince him?"

"Then we'll find another approach."

Over the years, Sean had found that there was always a way to get the information he needed. It was just a matter of figuring it out. He sat back and watched the road stitch itself up the hill.

"We're almost there," Marvin said.

"I know," Sean replied.

A moment later, the gate appeared before them. It seemed to spring up out of nowhere. The gate was illuminated by two halogen spotlights that bore down on it from above. For a moment, Sean had the ridiculous feeling that any second now border guards would step out from behind the gate and demand to see his passport. *I'm watching too many old movies,* he said to himself.

As they got closer, they could see Banks's house. It was lit up; someone was home, unless the house was on a timer.

"Press the intercom button," Sean instructed Marvin as they stopped in front of the gate.

Marvin got the same results as before.

"Try again," Sean instructed.

As Marvin did, Sean scanned the wall. Now that he was looking more closely, he could see two cameras mounted on either side of the gate. He didn't know whom he was more annoyed with: himself for not seeing the cameras sooner or Banks for not answering.

"Do you want to go?" Marvin asked when no one answered.

"Not yet," Sean replied.

If Banks had answered him, he'd have let the matter go, but ignoring him was something else entirely. Maybe he wasn't the chief of police anymore, but that didn't mean he had to tolerate this type of rudeness. He never had, and he wasn't about to start now.

He looked at the house again. He thought he saw a flicker of movement in the right window. And then he realized he was seeing something else as well. The gate was slightly ajar. Very slightly. Was it like that before?

Sean closed his eyes and tried to remember. He couldn't.

"Are you okay," Marvin asked.

"I'm fine. Do me a favor and get out and see if you can push the gate open."

"But . . . ," Marvin objected.

"Just do it," Sean snapped. This was what he hated. In the old days, preillness, he wouldn't have had to ask. He'd have just gotten out and done it.

He watched Marvin get out of the car. Could he move any slower, Sean wondered.

"Don't slam your door," Sean warned just as Marvin did.

Great, Sean thought. *Now we'll get to see if someone comes out.* But no one did. Maybe they hadn't heard. Maybe no one was at the control panel. Maybe the cameras were just for show. No way to know unless he saw the control room. He turned his attention back to Marvin. Marvin was at the gate now.

"Open it all the way," Sean instructed, after rolling his window down. "We want to drive in." Sean paused. "And, yes, I'm sure," he told Marvin even though Marvin hadn't said anything.

Finally, Marvin began to push. The gate slowly opened. When it was open all the way, he got back in the car. "I expected it to squeak," he said.

Sean just sighed. "Drive in," he said.

"Where?"

"Up to the front of the house."

"I still don't think this is a good idea," Marvin said as he put the car in gear. "In fact, I think it's a terrible idea."

"Everything will be fine," Sean said automatically.

"That's what you said about the Foundation," Marvin protested.

"And it was, wasn't it?"

Sean guessed Marvin couldn't think of a comeback, because he didn't say anything. As they drove in, Sean kept looking around, expecting to see someone, but there was no sign of movement. Most of the windows in the house were lit up, but Sean didn't see any people. He must have imagined he saw someone before.

The lawn seemed like a vast expanse of dark sea. Over to the left, he spotted a garage. He could make out what looked like a Jeep parked in front of it, which really didn't mean a whole lot vis-a-vis whether or not someone was home. People that lived in houses like this one usually had multiple cars.

"Where do you want me to stop?" Marvin asked.

"In front of the house," Sean told him as

189

he reached in his jacket pocket and got out his cigarettes.

"Since when did you start smoking?" Marvin cried.

"I didn't start smoking. I restarted smoking."

"Libby must be really pissed."

"Libby doesn't know, and you're not going to tell her."

"I don't think I can do that."

"Of course, you can. I'm not going to stop, so why upset her?"

Marvin digested this piece of information for a moment and then said, "It's so bad for you."

"Yes, it is, but look at what I have. What difference does it make? Besides, I read recently that smoking may put what I have in remission."

"Really?" Marvin said.

"Yes, really," Sean replied. "Now park in front of the house, and help me out of the car."

Marvin did as he was told. "It's a big house," Marvin said.

Sean took another couple of puffs of his cigarette and threw it down on the grass. "It's enormous."

He stood there for a moment, taking it in. The building was a two-story Greek Revival affair. Because the drapes weren't closed, Sean had the feeling he was looking at a stage set. The furnishings in the rooms gave him the same feeling. Everything was for show. *Banks must live in the other part of the house,* Sean decided. No one's dwelling could be that perfect.

He lifted his hand and rang the bell. He could hear the chime echoing within the house. No one came. He tried again, only this time he left his hand on the buzzer a bit longer. By the third time, his finger was on the buzzer for a full minute. Sean tried the door next. It was locked.

"He's not here. Let's go," Marvin said eagerly.

Obviously, Sean thought, the kid could hardly wait to get out of there. But that wasn't going to happen yet.

"First, let's go around to the side," Sean said as they got back in Marvin's car.

"But why?" Marvin wailed.

"To see if the side door is open. Something's wrong here, and I want to check it out."

Marvin began tapping his fingers on the steering wheel. "Then let's call the police."

"A valid suggestion," Sean told him, "but the moment the police arrive, I'm going to be shut out, and I want to see what I can find out before that happens. We'll call them when I'm done."

"Great," Marvin muttered, putting his car in gear.

Sean pretended he hadn't heard Marvin's last comment as they drove around to the side. After all, the kid was going along with Sean, and that was all that mattered. Marvin parked, and they both got out. He offered Sean his arm in support, but Sean waved him away. Damned if he wasn't going to do this by himself.

The trick was to take slow, careful steps. The dark made seeing the path clearly harder, and he didn't want to stumble and fall. Then Marvin would tell Libby, and she wouldn't let him out of the house at all. Of course, she wouldn't be too happy when she heard about this, anyway. Oh well. There wasn't much he could do about that.

As he walked, he debated about what course of action he was going to take if the side door was locked. After all, there was no reason to think that it wouldn't be. But it wasn't. Sean could see the light spilling out from the space between the door and its frame.

"We should call the police," Marvin repeated.

Sean nodded absentmindedly as he pulled

his jacket sleeve over his hand and pushed the door open.

"Why are you doing that?" Marvin asked.

"So I don't contaminate the crime scene."

"But you don't know it's a crime scene," Marvin pointed out.

"Always assume the worst," Sean told him. "And don't touch anything," he warned.

"I don't think I want to go in," Marvin said.

"Then stay outside," Sean snapped as he took a step inside. God, what a pain in the ass that kid was sometimes.

"I can't. Libby would kill me if anything happened to you."

"And I'm going to kill you if you don't stop talking. I can't concentrate with you chattering away."

"Okay."

Sean watched Marvin get that hangdog look. He felt a small stab of guilt but managed to stifle it.

"I guess no one's here," Marvin said. Then he realized what he'd done and put his hand to his mouth. "Sorry."

"I think that's a fair assumption to make," Sean said. "Given the amount of talking we've been doing, if anyone was here, they'd be pointing their rifles at us by now."

193

Sean looked around. He was in the mud-room. There were four jackets hanging on the wooden pegs and three pairs of boots sitting on bootjacks. A wicker basket full of hats, scarves, and gloves sat on a bench. He took another step and found himself in the kitchen. Marvin was right behind him.

The kitchen was huge. The cooking appliances were at one end, and the family room, complete with a flat-screen TV large enough to cover the entire wall, was at the other end. CNN news was on, but there was no sound. Judging from the size of the stove and the fridge, you could feed a platoon in here and still have room for another couple of dozen people.

The kitchen table had been set for coffee. There was a French press, plates, mugs, and sugar and cream on the table. A platter of pumpkin bars sat in the center. Sean walked over and took a look at the cookies. They looked like A Touch of Heaven's ginger pumpkin bars with ginger icing. Exactly like them. But just to make sure, he picked one up and took a bite.

"What are you doing?" Marvin cried.

"Eating," Sean said. Yup. They were Libby's. No one made them like she did. It was the Jamaican ginger that did it. "You want one?" he asked Marvin. "They're Libby's."

Marvin shook his head. "If you don't mind, I'll pass."

"No appetite?" Sean asked as he ate another one.

"What happened to contaminating the crime scene?"

"I don't think two cookies will make that big a difference in the scheme of things," Sean said, wishing he had some milk to wash them down. There was probably milk in the fridge, but that would be going a little too far.

He wondered who had brought the cookies here. Maybe Amber or Googie would remember, but Sean doubted it. As he dusted the crumbs off his hands, he noticed that the floor by the sink was wet. He walked over. Three or four apples were bobbing in the basin. Very odd. Then he noticed a few brown-red spots on the lip of the basin. Dirt? He looked closer. No. He got that old familiar feeling. He beckoned Marvin over and pointed.

"What do you think?" he asked.

Marvin leaned over and studied the spots. He sucked in his cheeks as he concentrated. Finally, he said, "I think it's blood."

"Me too," Sean agreed.

Marvin straightened up. "Someone could have cut themselves with a knife."

"Yes. They could have."

"But you don't think so."

"No. Do you?"

"No." Marvin pointed to the apples. "What about those?"

"You got me. I'm going to have to think on that for a bit." He motioned for Marvin to follow him. "Come on. Let's see what else we're going to find."

"I think we might be finding Mr. Banks," Marvin said.

"I think you may be right," Sean agreed.

"Which is why we should call the cops."

"Soon," Sean said.

"You're just placating me," Marvin complained.

"Yup," Sean said. "You got me. That's exactly what I'm doing."

Sean looked around once more just to make sure he hadn't missed anything. Then he walked straight ahead, with Marvin on his heels. When he got to the corner, he turned down a hallway.

There were watermarks on the wallpaper every couple of feet or so, as if someone had bumped into it with his shoulder. He kept walking. About two feet farther, he came to a room. From outside the room, he could hear a fan running. The smell told him what he was going to find.

196

"When you're right, you're right," Sean said.

He and Marvin stepped inside. A man was slumped over the toilet. His hands were tied behind him.

"I have a feeling that we've found Banks," Sean said to Marvin.

"Me too," Marvin said.

Banks was wearing casual attire: a pair of jeans, sneakers, a white shirt, and a blue crewneck sweater.

"How long do you think he's been dead?" Sean asked Marvin. That was one good thing about Marvin, Sean decided. He wasn't squeamish about corpses.

Marvin assessed Banks with a practiced eye. "Maybe three or four hours, but Wenzel should be able to narrow it down more closely."

Sean just hoped that they hadn't been standing by the gate when Banks was getting drowned. He watched Marvin take out his cell phone. "Calling the police?" he asked.

"Yes."

"I am a policeman."

"You're a retired policeman."

"It's almost the same thing."

"Not quite." Marvin just looked at him.

"All I'm asking for is fifteen minutes to

see if we can find Banks's records. That's it. I swear."

Marvin didn't say anything.

"Well?" Sean said after a minute had gone by. "Is it a yes or a no?"

Marvin let out a long sigh. Then he said, "I'm only doing this because you're Libby's dad."

"And I can't tell you how much Libby will appreciate this," Sean said.

"That's the point. I'm not sure she will."

Sean waved away Marvin's objections. "Come help me look. The sooner we get started, the sooner we'll be done."

"We'll be arrested. That's what we'll be," Marvin muttered.

Sean ignored him and led the way out.

CHAPTER 15

Bernie watched her dad's friend Clyde settle back in his usual chair in their living room. He reached over and took another one of Libby's ginger pumpkin bars. He took little bites and chewed slowly so he could savor every mouthful.

"Wonderful," he said as he poured more cream in his coffee. "Simply wonderful. And that includes the cream. My wife only has skim milk in the house. It turns coffee the most unappetizing shade of gray." He took a sip and then held up the ginger pumpkin bar. "This is the embodiment of Halloween," he declared. "The color, the bouquet of spices, all suggest late fall to me."

"You've been watching the cooking channel again, haven't you?" Sean asked. This was a man who in his prime consumed cans of cold Dinty Moore stew, and now he was rhapsodizing about flavor bouquets the same way he used to talk about the Playmate of the Month. Old age was a terrible thing.

Clyde glared at him. "So what if I have?"

"Nothing. Nothing at all," replied Sean.

"You're also eating the evidence," Bernie said.

"No. That was what I did last night," Sean said.

Clyde shook his head. "Good thing Lucy didn't catch you."

Sean snorted. "Lucas never appears at crime scenes."

"He did at this one," said Clyde.

"I didn't see him," said Sean.

"That's because he came after you left, and stayed for about a minute and a half."

"Interesting," Sean said as he moved his motorized wheelchair a little more toward the window. It was a little after ten on a Tuesday evening, and the street was empty. But it didn't matter. He enjoyed looking at the Halloween decorations in his neighbors' windows. Black cats, witches, ghosts — all were stuck to the windowpanes. They reminded him of when his daughters were young and they had helped decorate. "That must mean that Banks's murder is important."

Clyde reached over and took a third ginger pumpkin bar. "Well, Banks was rich."

"That would do it," Sean said. "What does

Lucy think the relationship between the two homicides is?"

Clyde took a bite of the ginger pumpkin bar and swallowed. "Oh, the chief doesn't think Amethyst's murder and Banks's murder are related."

Bernie rolled her eyes. "That's absurd."

"He said they had dissimilar styles," Clyde continued. "And the fingerprints don't match. Not that there were many of them at either crime scene. Ergo, it's just coincidence."

Sean took a sip of his tea and put the cup down. "I, myself, have never believed in coincidence."

"Me either," Clyde agreed. "I don't know how the homicides are linked, but they definitely are."

"That's for sure," Sean said. "What are the odds of having two homicides in a town like this in one week and not having them be related?"

"It could be a statistical anomaly," Bernie suggested. Her dad glared at her. "Or maybe Bessie Osgood came back to life and traveled over to Lexus Gardens."

Libby rolled her eyes. "Now, why didn't I think of that?" She pointedly turned to her dad. "What do you think happened?"

Sean took another sip of his tea and put

the cup down. "On the most literal level, I think Ed Banks had a visitor, and that visitor brought some ginger pumpkin bars from our shop as a gift."

"Ed Banks could have bought them himself," Libby pointed out.

"I don't think so," Bernie said. "We pretty much know everyone that comes into our shop, and when I asked, Amber and Googie said no one unfamiliar came in that day. Given the fact that we've never done business with Ed Banks, I think the conclusion is self-evident."

"Which means whoever brought them is one of our customers," Libby observed.

"Unfortunately," Sean said.

"Well, that narrows the field," Bernie said, thinking of the hundreds of men, women, and children who went through the shop each day.

"Maybe we could put out a sign reading WHOEVER BOUGHT COOKIES FOR ED BANKS COME TALK TO US," Libby suggested.

Sean laughed. "That's what I call wishful thinking." He turned to Clyde. "So what do we know about this guy Banks?"

"The most obvious fact is that the guy was a recluse," Clyde said.

Bernie leaned forward. "But he let his

house be photographed. Recluses don't usually do that."

"True," Clyde said. "Maybe he just didn't want to talk to anyone around here."

"Then why buy a house here?" Bernie asked.

Sean waved his hand impatiently. "Let's come back to that question later. What else do we know about him?"

"Really not that much," Clyde replied. "At this point, we know that Banks has no known next of kin. Both parents are deceased. He never married. He didn't seem to have a girlfriend. . . ."

"Maybe he had a boyfriend," Bernie interjected.

"He didn't have anyone that we're aware of," Clyde said, with a touch of asperity.

Bernie shrugged. "It was just a suggestion."

Clyde went on. "Anyway, he was born here, in this town, but his family moved to Hawaii when he was in his teens . . . Evidently, his dad was some kind of expert on sugarcane . . . and he only came back recently. He did hedge funds, which is where he got his money. He has a clean record. No priors. And that's about all we know at this moment."

"Who is claiming the body?" Sean asked.

"A distant relative in Hawaii. She wants the body flown to Oahu as soon as it's released," said Clyde.

"How about the staff?" Sean asked. "Where were they last night?"

"There is no live-in staff," said Clyde.

Libby took a sip of her mulled cider and asked, "He lived in that huge house all by himself?" Her voice was incredulous.

Clyde ate the rest of his ginger pumpkin bar before answering. "Yes, he did. He had a personal assistant that he brought with him. The guy came in six days a week, from nine to six. He had Sundays off."

"Did you talk to him?" asked Sean.

Clyde nodded. "We managed to track him down. Conveniently for him, he's been on vacation in Maui for the last two weeks. According to the hotel manager, he hasn't left the island."

"Did he sound upset when he found out about his boss?" Sean asked.

"Very. They'd been together for a long time. Maybe there's something there, but I don't see it," said Clyde. "More interestingly, however, is the fact that Banks contracted with the same firm that cleans the Foundation to do the cleaning up there."

"Inez?" Sean said.

"It's a definite link," Clyde said, turning

204

to Libby. "How's the pumpkin cheesecake?"

Libby put a piece on a plate and handed it to him. "Try it and see."

Clyde took a bite. "Delicious," he said. "I have to come over to the Haunted House to try your waffles."

"Anytime," Libby said. Then she turned to her dad. "I've been thinking. It must have taken a really big man to hold Banks's head under water like that. And what were the apples about? Are they a symbol of some kind?"

"They could be," Bernie said. "The Celts used bobbing for apples in marriage divination ceremonies. The first person to bite the apple was the first person to get married. It was their version of throwing the bouquet."

"Are you saying that Banks was planning on getting married?" Libby asked her sister.

"No. I'm just sharing a little information with you," replied Bernie.

"I'm sorry. I just don't see the relevance," said Libby.

Sean looked away from the street and settled himself in his wheelchair. He had a pack of cigarettes in his pants pocket, which he would have very much liked to light, but he wasn't going to do it and risk the wrath of his daughters.

"It is relevant, just not in the way that Bernie said," Sean interjected.

Libby shook her head. "I don't understand."

"It tells us what happened," said Sean. He held up his hand as Libby started to speak. "Let's go back to the beginning. Banks and his friend, and I'm putting *friend* in quotes here, had made an appointment. We know this because Banks had already set the table. I think that they sat around and talked for a while, and then his friend probably casually introduced the topic of bobbing for apples. You know, he said something like, 'I bet you can't bob for apples,' or something to that effect, and Banks took him up on the challenge. So while Banks was bending over, his friend slipped a plastic tie out of his pocket and cuffed him. Easy enough to do."

"Then why didn't he drown him right there? Why take him to the bathroom?" Clyde asked.

Sean thought about the blood on the kitchen sink and the marks on the hallway walls. "I'm thinking that Banks got away from him, and they had a scuffle. I figure Banks started running, and his friend finally caught up with him in the hallway, near the bathroom. He managed to get Banks in there and hold his head in the toilet."

"You think the toilet was a metaphor?"

Bernie asked.

Sean laughed. "No. I think the toilet was convenient." He took another sip of his tea. "So Lucy sees no connection at all between these two crimes?" he asked Clyde.

Clyde put his fork down. "If he does, he isn't telling me."

Sean sat and thought for a moment. "It's true we have minimal connections between the two events," he finally said. "We only have Jeanine's word that Amethyst wanted to talk to Banks."

"Okay," Clyde said.

"But why would Jeanine lie?" Libby asked.

"I'm not saying she did. In fact, I don't think she did. I'm just talking it through," Sean said.

"And we don't know if Amethyst actually went up and talked to Banks," Clyde pointed out.

Sean nodded. "Maybe Banks's personal assistant knows."

"I'll find out, but it might take a little while," Clyde told Sean. "When I spoke to him, he was leaving for a sailing trip."

"And even if he did," Sean said, continuing with his train of thought, "we have a very thin line linking Amethyst and Banks. A very thin line. Maybe she wanted to talk to him about some sort of charity affair. Or about opening up a shop of some kind. We really don't know."

Bernie tucked a strand of her hair behind her ear. "I'm getting the impression you agree with Lucy that there is no connection between the two homicides."

Sean leaned back in his wheelchair and folded his hands over his stomach. "No. I think there is. I just think it has to be ferreted out. In order to find it, we need more information."

Clyde finished off his piece of cheesecake and looked at the plate wistfully. He sighed. "I can't eat another thing," he said.

"Not even a sliver?" Libby coaxed.

Clyde shook his head. "You're a very bad person."

"I know," Libby said as she took his plate, cut him a small piece of cheesecake, and handed the plate back to him.

"Tell me," Clyde asked Sean after he'd taken a bite, "do you still think that Bessie Osgood had anything to do with this mess?"

"Without a doubt," Sean said. "All the names that have come up have been linked to her death. I still think that if you find out what happened the night she died, and you'll find out who killed Amethyst and, possibly, Banks."

Clyde leaned forward. "The question is,

why is all of this happening now?"

"That is the question, isn't it?" Sean said.

"There has to have been a precipitating incident," Clyde mused.

Bernie stifled a yawn. "But what?"

"I wish I knew," Sean said, and he went back to watching the street. A little girl decked out in a Hello Kitty outfit skipped by, holding her mother's hand. He smiled, remembering how the girls used to wear their costumes around the house during the week before Halloween.

"You know," Bernie said, "not to change the subject, but Kathy —"

Sean turned away from the window. "Big Kathy?"

Bernie made an impatient gesture. "Garden shop Kathy. My friend Kathy."

"What about her?" asked Sean.

"She told me that Zinnia was killed by a hit-and-run driver a year after Bessie Osgood died," said Bernie.

"I remember that one," Clyde said. He turned to Sean. "Didn't Porter get that guy?"

"Guys," Sean corrected. "Two of them. They'd just robbed the Quick Mart in Oakley when they got McGuire. They said they didn't see her, because she was sitting in the middle of the road. She had enough alcohol in her to embalm an elephant."

"So much for that one," Clyde said.

Everyone was silent for a moment. Then Bernie said, "We still don't know about Timberland's daughter."

Clyde stifled a yawn. "Refresh my memory as to why we care about her."

"Because she might furnish a motive for Timberland's animosity toward Amethyst," said Sean.

"Maybe I can find out," Libby said.

"How?" her dad finally asked.

"Well," Libby stammered, "I know his sister from yoga class."

Bernie's eyebrows shot up. "You're taking a yoga class?"

Libby straightened her shoulders. "As a matter of fact, I am."

"Since when?" asked Bernie.

"Since last week, if you must know. Why?" said Libby.

"I'm just surprised. It doesn't seem like your kind of thing," replied Bernie.

Libby put her hands on her hips. "And why ever not?"

Sean intervened before things got started. "Bernie, maybe you could talk to Inez. She spends a lot of time at R.J.'s, and I can talk to Jeanine and see if she's figured out the View-Master yet."

"I understand Bob Small is going to be out on bail tomorrow," Clyde said.

"Then I suppose one of us should go talk to him as well," Sean said.

"Not me," Clyde said.

"Obviously," Sean shot back.

Clyde stifled another yawn. "Okeydokey. Time to get going." He rose. "After all, another glorious day in Longely's police force awaits me tomorrow morning."

"By the way," Sean called out, "who put up Small's bail?"

"Kane," said Clyde.

"Interesting," said Sean.

"It's not that high," added Clyde.

"Still," said Sean.

"While we're on the subject, I found out some more info on Kane," said Clyde.

Sean leaned forward. "Such as?"

"Nothing that we didn't already know," said Clyde. "He's considered a genius with numbers, which is how he got so rich. He's pretty much a workaholic. No surprise there. He had a minor heart attack a couple of years ago, and his doctors advised him to get a hobby. Hence the Foundation. I also talked to the guys that rigged up the Haunted House show. They said he couldn't even put in a lightbulb without help."

"That's what he said about himself,"

Libby commented.

"Well, it looks as if he was telling the truth," Sean said. "So there you go."

As Clyde headed down the stairs, Sean reflected on how nice it was to be working with him again. That was probably the thing he missed most from his days on the force.

CHAPTER 16

Libby walked into the class, hung up her jacket, and looked around. It was seven-thirty in the morning, and everyone in the class looked disgustingly perky, but then they probably hadn't been up since five making lemon squares and chocolate chip cookies.

And then there were the clothes. Everyone was wearing cute little yoga outfits, the kind that cost a couple of hundred dollars or so, while she was in her old stretched-out sweatpants and T-shirt. It was true she could have gone and bought one of those outfits — nothing was stopping her — but she hated spending money on stuff like that. Okay, that was a lie. What she hated to do was wear stuff like that. Even trying it on was painful. One look in the mirror and she wanted to reach for the cookies — not exactly a productive response given the circumstances.

She was taking this class to tone up, but she didn't know how long she could stand it. The ad had promised results in three sessions. Well, this was her third session, and she had yet to see any results. She surreptitiously pinched the roll of fat on her belly. Yup. It was still there. She felt especially depressed as she scanned the rows of women rolling out their yoga mats. They were all so trim and taut, and she was so . . . so not. Even their mats looked better than hers.

Libby sighed. Everyone was doing their warm-up stretching. Little tinkling bells chimed in the air. There was incense burning on the front table, where the instructor, an impossibly lithe woman wearing adorable yoga pants and a bralike top that showed off a midriff with no fat at all, was talking to someone. A sign that said, BREATHE! BREATHE! was hanging on the wall.

She spotted Timberland's sister in the fourth row and reluctantly headed for her. Why couldn't Ramona be in the back? Why did she have to be up front? God. Libby reminded herself she was here to do a job and that no one was looking at her — yeah, right — as she unrolled her yoga mat and plopped herself next to Ramona.

"Hi," she said.

Ramona smiled. She had perfect blond hair and white, white teeth, and was extremely flexible. "Hi," she said, with her head down almost to her right thigh.

Libby, who couldn't even touch her toes and hadn't been able to since high school, hated her.

"How are things going?" Libby asked. General questions were always best in situations like this, her dad had taught her.

"Good. We're all going to the Haunted House tonight. Which waffles would you recommend?"

"The pumpkin ones are my favorite," Libby replied promptly. "But lots of people like the chocolate ones."

Ramona switched to her left thigh and held the stretch for a moment. "This class makes me feel so alive."

"Me too," Libby lied as she followed Ramona's lead. What it really made her feel was sorer than anything she'd ever done.

A moment later Ramona put her left arm up, bent it toward the middle of her back, and grasped her right arm with it. Libby did likewise. She could hear her shoulder pop. She ignored it. All the same, it wasn't a good sign.

Ramona looked around the room for a

moment, then scooched closer to Libby and whispered, "Did you really find Amethyst's head?"

Libby nodded. She had an idea that this wasn't exactly yoga-class discussion material.

"It must have been horrible," Ramona said.

"It was."

"You know my brother knew her," Ramona continued as she stretched out her other shoulder.

"Yeah. He told me they used to hang out back in the day," Libby lied again.

Ramona set her mouth in a thin line.

Libby waited. Ramona remained silent.

"He didn't seem that sorry," Libby ventured after it became obvious that Ramona wasn't going to say anything else.

Ramona snorted and worked her legs into a lotus position. Libby tried to emulate her and failed. Her calves didn't seem to want to do that.

"I don't think anyone is that sorry about Amethyst," Ramona observed. "Are you?"

"Not really," Libby confessed.

"Exactly my point."

"But I thought she and your brother were friends."

"Zachery thought they were friends, too,"

216

Ramona said.

"So what happened?"

"What happened?" Ramona repeated. She took a deep breath and let it out. "What happened was that Amethyst didn't have any friends. She had people she used, and she had people she was going to use."

"You don't sound like a big fan of hers, either."

"I'm not."

Libby started to lean over to ask Ramona why, but the instructor stared at her, brought her hands together, gave a slight bow, and chirped, *"Namaste."*

"Namaste," the class replied.

Libby took a deep breath. Her questions would have to wait. Class was beginning.

Forty-five minutes later it was over, and Libby was still smarting from having gotten stuck in the lotus position. Life was so unfair. She'd finally managed to get herself into the stupid position, and then she couldn't get herself out of it. She closed her eyes and tried to blot out the memory of her tipping over and falling into Ramona. Someone else might have laughed. Ramona hadn't. What she had done was look very annoyed.

"It will get better in time," the instructor murmured in her ear as Libby walked by her. "You just have to practice, practice, practice. Remember if at first you don't succeed . . ."

Libby nodded. Could you get any more clichéd, she wondered. She didn't feel it necessary to tell the instructor there wasn't going to be a next time. She had four more classes. Maybe Bernie would like to go in her place.

So much for self-improvement, Libby thought as she walked out of the class. Aside from publicly humiliating herself, she'd learned absolutely nothing about Timberland, and now she was behind schedule at the shop. She was standing by her van, eating a piece of dark chocolate and thinking about the costume Bernie wanted her to wear this evening — she was not going as a bowl of Special K! — when she saw Ramona walk to her car. She was talking on her cell and making angry gestures in the air with her free hand. *Okay,* Libby decided. *Maybe I should give this one more try.* After all, what did she have to lose?

Even though Ramona was half turned away from her, as she got closer, Libby could hear Ramona saying, "Listen, Madison, don't do this. No. I don't have an address to send a card. Neither does your dad. And for heaven's sake, don't ask him. He doesn't need any more aggravation. I mean it, Madison."

Libby bit her lip. Madison was the name of Timberland's daughter. Someone had been talking about her recently. As she was trying to remember who it was, she watched Ramona glare at her phone.

"Great," Ramona muttered under her breath as she flipped the phone closed and shoved it in her bag. She gave a little jump as she spotted Libby, but quickly recovered. "Just be happy you don't have kids," she said to Libby. "Even if they aren't yours, they're an epic pain in the ass."

"Can I ask you a question?" Libby inquired.

Ramona looked at her. "That depends on what it is."

This time Libby got right down to it. "It's about why your brother disliked Amethyst."

Ramona put her hand on the door handle of her Caddy Escalade. "Everyone disliked Amethyst. We already discussed that."

"But your brother seems to have a special reason."

Ramona threw Libby what her father would have called a measuring glance and said, "Go ask him."

"You were going to tell me back in class."

"Maybe I've changed my mind."

"Because you think that your brother had a motive to kill Amethyst?"

Ramona composed her mouth into a shocked O, only Libby wasn't buying it. Too much drama. "Heavens no. What a terrible thing to say."

"Then why won't you tell me?"

Ramona shrugged again. "Because it's none of your business."

"True," Libby told her. "It isn't. But the fact that you're not answering me will make other people curious."

"And I should care why?"

Good question. Libby improvised. "The police will care," she said.

"You'll have to do better than that," Ramona said. "The police already arrested Bob Small. They're not interested in me."

"How about if we make a deal," Libby said.

Ramona arched one of her perfectly tweezed eyebrows. "Which would be?"

"You tell me what I want to know, and I'll never come to your yoga class again."

Ramona burst out laughing. "Good. But not good enough." Ramona's phone started ringing again. She took it out, looked at it, and grimaced. "Madison," she said.

And all of a sudden, Libby remembered where she'd heard the name. It was from

Amber, one of the kids that worked in her place.

"She's your niece, isn't she?" Libby said.

Ramona raised her eyebrow again.

"One of the girls who works for us went to school with her," said Libby.

Ramona didn't say anything.

"She was telling me about her. She dropped out of school."

Ramona sighed. "It's not that big of a deal. Lots of kids drop out."

Libby closed her eyes for a moment and concentrated on remembering the details of what Amber had said. "But she was at the head of the class. Number one. Editor of the school newspaper. Varsity track. Student council president. Had been admitted to Yale. People like that don't usually do that type of thing."

"Who knows what kids will do these days?" Ramona said, trying to sound casual and failing, as she opened the door of the Escalade and tossed her yoga mat into the backseat.

"Still, you have to admit it's pretty unusual."

Ramona shrugged.

"Your brother must have had a fit."

"It's true he was very disappointed. Everyone in the family was. He thought she was going to Yale and then on to law school. But what can you do."

"I guess not much," Libby said.

"If she wants to work as a waitress down in the city, that's her business. I'm hoping that eventually she'll come to her senses. And now, if you're through, I have to get back to my house. My cleaning people will be there shortly. . . ."

Libby raised a finger. "Just one more thing. Amber said all this happened because your niece had an affair with an older woman, and she dropped your niece in a particularly not nice way." Judging from Ramona's expression, Libby knew that what Amber had told her was correct. "And," Libby said, making the logical leap, "I'm betting the person she had an affair with was Amethyst."

Ramona blinked.

"It was, wasn't it?"

Libby watched Ramona's hand come up and finger the heart-shaped locket she wore around her neck.

"So what if it was?" Ramona snapped. "That's no reason for my brother to kill her. Other kids end up a lot worse off. If you want someone who had a reason to kill Amethyst, talk to Bob Small or Inez." With that, Ramona got in her vehicle and drove off, missing Libby by inches.

"Maybe it's not a great reason," Libby said to herself as she walked back to her van, "but it's good enough."

Especially these days, when more and more parents are living through their children.

CHAPTER 17

Libby looked at the clock on the kitchen wall. It read twenty minutes past eleven. *Great.* Only an hour and a half behind schedule. She had to get the Rogets' birthday cake done before three, as well as the chicken curry for the Mathers' party, which meant she might not be able to make the two apple pies for the Haunted House, which she hadn't gotten to last night.

Fortunately, she had a couple of lemon tarts in the freezer. They might not be very Halloweeny, but it was the best she could do. And she had made the black cat cookies, so they were ahead there.

She wiped her spatula off and went back to the pumpkin chocolate cake she was icing. This time she'd used a different kind of chocolate, one with a lower butterfat content, and the icing was not as shiny as she would have liked.

She was thinking about complaining to

her supplier, who'd told her the results would be the same, when her dad darted in, came up behind her, scooped up a taste from the bowl with the icing in it, and ate it.

"Stop that," Libby ordered.

Sean grinned. "But it's so good, it's hard to resist."

"I wish it looked better."

"It looks fine," Sean assured his daughter as he finished licking the teaspoon. "And it tastes even better. After all, as your mom used to say, 'The proof is in the eating.' "

"Yeah. But Mom didn't have the Food Channel to contend with."

"True," Sean allowed as he stared wistfully at the icing.

"You can have the bowl when I'm done," Libby told him, and then she told her dad what she'd found out from Ramona.

"Interesting," Sean said. "Maybe that's not the best motive, but it's certainly up there. If someone had done something like that to you, I'd want to kill them."

"Kill who?" Bernie asked as she stepped into the kitchen.

Libby explained.

"I guess it's a motive," Bernie said as she poured herself a cup of coffee and added cream and sugar.

Libby drew her spatula across the icing on top of the cake to even it out. "Amber said Madison's dad was livid when he found out. Timberland wanted to press charges, but his wife told him she'd divorce him if he did. Of course, she left him, anyway."

"And this was how long ago?" Sean asked.

"A couple of years," said Libby.

Sean put the spoon in the sink. "So once more we come to the question, why now?"

"Opportunity?" Bernie said.

Sean shook his head. "That might apply to Bob Small, but not to Timberland. At least not as far as I can see."

"None of this makes any sense," Libby complained.

"We're missing information," Sean said. "We have too much on the one hand and not enough on the other."

Bernie flicked a piece of lint from her turtleneck sweater. "And what about Banks's murder?"

"The one that doesn't have anything to do with Amethyst's?" her dad said.

"Yes. That one," said Bernie.

"We have even less on that one. Except for the fact that Amethyst was going to go see him, we have nothing to link the two events," said Sean.

Libby put her spatula down.

"It's kind of like trying to put together a jigsaw puzzle blindfolded," said Sean.

"Good analogy," Bernie said, and she leaned over and gave her dad a peck on the cheek. "I'm off to check something at the historical society, and then I'm going to see if I can talk to Inez."

"When will you be back?" Libby asked.

"In a couple of hours," said Bernie as she eyed her sister's baggy sweatpants and stretched-out T-shirt. "Is that what you wore to yoga class?"

Libby put her hands on her hips. "So what if it is?"

"I didn't say anything," Bernie mumbled.

"But you were thinking it," said Libby.

"What was I thinking?" Bernie asked.

"That I look like a mess," said Libby.

"You're always so defensive," Bernie protested.

The comment only made Libby more annoyed, because it was true. She was. But Bernie couldn't possibly understand how she felt. She always looked perfect. Then, to make things worse, Bernie reached over and patted her sister on the shoulder. "We'll find you a nice costume for tonight."

Like I'm a little kid, Libby thought resentfully. "I am not going as a bowl of cereal!"

"That was a joke," Bernie insisted.

"It didn't sound like a joke to me," Libby told her.

"Well, it was," said Bernie. She took a sip of her coffee and walked toward the door. "Wish me luck," she called.

As Sean watched her go, he wanted to tell her that he'd changed his mind and she didn't need to go to the historical society, after all. Then he realized that her visit didn't preclude his later in the day. He could ask Jeanine about the stills on the View-Master Bernie had been handed by Felicity Huffer. Somehow he felt better. He was thinking about why that was when a horn beeped outside. His ride was here. It was time to go.

"That must be Marvin," Sean informed his daughter as he put on his rain jacket. "We're off to talk to Bob Small."

Libby reached over and gave her dad two cinnamon spice cupcakes with mocha icing. "For the road," she said.

Sean handed one to Marvin as soon as he got in the car. "Eat it now," he instructed.

The idea of Marvin eating and driving at the same time didn't bear thinking about. When Marvin was done, Sean said, "Bob Small's house."

Marvin turned to him. "And that would be where?"

228

"I thought you were supposed to look up the address."

"I thought you were."

"How would I know where he's living?"

"I thought you knew everything."

Sean glared at Marvin for a moment. A year ago he would never have said something like that. He was definitely getting entirely too comfortable. When Sean judged that he'd conveyed his displeasure, he reached for his cell phone. Ten minutes later, he'd gotten the address from Clyde. As Marvin pulled away from the curb, Sean realized that he'd forgotten to bring the tapes that Konrad and Curtis had brought him. He was annoyed with himself, but not so annoyed that he was going to go back and get them.

According to Clyde, Bob Small was renting a place on the outskirts of Longely, about two blocks away from the train station — which was as slummy an area as Longely possessed. It was damp and chilly in the car, and Sean wished Marvin would put the heat on, but he wasn't going to ask because, one, he was still annoyed with him and, two, that would be admitting he was cold. Instead, he concentrated on the scenery going by. Every other house had a skeleton hanging in the window or a group of tombstones in the yard.

They looked sad in the rain, Sean thought. The day was dark and gloomy, making them appear as if they were in a netherworld. He was still thinking that when they got to Bob Small's house. The word that occurred to him when he saw it was *shack*. It had taken Marvin a moment to find it because it was hidden in the alley behind the dry cleaners. The place was a two-story house covered in asphalt shingles. A blue tarp was tied around the front part of the roof, presumably to fend off leaks. If there had ever been paint on the windowsills and the doors, it had vanished a long time ago.

As Sean studied the place, he couldn't help thinking of Bob's former house. It had been a good-sized Colonial on a half acre of carefully tended lawn, with a swimming pool and a gazebo and a four-car garage. And then there had been the wife and the two kids that had lived in that house, not to mention the two golden retrievers. As Bernie would say, Bob had had the sweet life, and now, because of Amethyst, he had nothing. The woman had cost Bob Small everything that had mattered. If there was a better motive for murder, Sean couldn't think of one.

"What are you thinking?" Marvin asked

as he brought his car to a stop in front of the house.

"I'm thinking that if I had to live here, I would want to kill the person who put me here." Sean nodded at the van parked by the side of the house. "It looks as if the Kurtz boys are here."

"You want to come back another time?" Marvin asked.

Sean shook his head. "No. No. It'll be fine."

"Your call," Marvin said as he turned off his vehicle and pocketed the key. "Tell me, do you believe in Bessie at all?"

Sean laughed. "People keep asking me that, and I keep saying I don't, but I gotta tell you, the way things are progressing, she could just as easily have done this as anyone else. How about you?"

"No ghosts for me."

But there was something about the way Marvin said it that made Sean turn and look at him. "Is there something you're not telling me?" he asked.

"Not at all," Marvin said and got out of the car.

Sean watched Marvin go around the car to help him out. He wasn't convinced that Marvin was telling him the truth, but he decided to let it go for now. At that moment

231

he had to concentrate on getting from the car to the top of the steps. The ground leading to the steps looked uneven, and it was probably more so because of the rain. In addition, the two steps up to Bob Small's apartment were sagging in the middle, and there was no banister to hang on to.

This is what he hated more than anything, he reflected as Marvin helped him out of the car. *Being dependent on someone.* Sometimes things were okay, and other times they weren't, and the hell of it was he never knew what was going to happen. He shook off those thoughts. They were of no use whatsoever. He should take a leaf from Rose's book and look on the bright side of things. Of course, if he could do that, Sean concluded, he wouldn't have been a cop. Cops never looked on the bright side of things. They were paid to be suspicious.

He was just thinking about where to put his foot on the step when the door flew open. "See," Curtis Kurtz said to Bob Small. "I told you, you didn't have to call him. I told you he'd be here." He turned to Sean. "We have more recordings. Bessie lied the last time. Remember she said she did it. Only she didn't. She just said that because she wanted to."

Sean made the second step. "I didn't

know that ghosts lied."

"Ghosts do and feel everything that people do," Curtis told him.

"I didn't realize that. So who did it?" Sean asked as Konrad Kurtz closed the door and took their rain gear.

"She's not telling us yet," Konrad said and hung the rain gear up on two pegs sprouting out of the hall wall. "But don't you worry. We have a few tricks up our sleeve. We'll get it out of her. Also, we have her new recordings. You can hear for yourself."

Sean looked from one brother to the other. "You know, guys," he said, "what I really need is a large coffee and two chocolate glazed doughnuts from Dunkin' Donuts. It'll help me concentrate better."

Sean watched Curtis and Konrad exchange glances.

"That's a ways away," Konrad said.

"Fifteen minutes," Sean said.

"Maybe twenty with construction," Curtis corrected.

"Each way," Konrad added. "That's forty minutes."

Sean smiled. "Which would be the amount of time I need to talk to Bob."

"Oh," said Konrad. "Why didn't you say that?"

"I just did," said Sean.

Curtis frowned. "So you don't want to listen to the tapes?"

"I do," Sean said. "But let's listen to them when you come back."

"Do you really want the coffee?" Konrad asked.

Sean thought for a moment. "If it's not too much trouble, I do. And change the chocolate glazed to maple frosted doughnuts."

"You got it," Konrad said.

As Marvin and Bob gave their orders to Curtis and Konrad, Sean took a quick look around the living room. The place was just as depressing on the inside as it was on the outside. It smelled of old clothes, garbage that needed to be taken out, and rotting wood mixed with a faint undertone of cat urine. Two of the legs on the sofa by the far wall were broken, making the sofa lean alarmingly toward the floor, while the chair next to it had a broken arm. Sean's eyes moved to the print hanging next to the lamp. It was a print of Van Gogh's *Irises*.

"It's the only thing I brought from home," Bob said, following Sean's glance. Then he gestured around the living room. "Nice place, huh?"

Sean couldn't see any place to sit, so he leaned against the wall.

"Lovely," Sean replied. "You should take the other two legs off the sofa."

"I'm thinking about it. Maybe I will one of these days." Bob curled his lips into a bad imitation of a smile. "Yeah. I can't wait to come home every night."

"I wouldn't either."

Out of the corner of his eye, Sean saw Marvin walk into another room. Sean was just about to ask him where he was going when he reappeared, with a kitchen chair. Sean sank into it gratefully. He didn't stand well anymore.

Bob went and sat on the lower end of the sofa, while Marvin leaned against the wall.

"So," Bob said, "how are things going?"

"In relation to your case? Not well," replied Sean.

"How come?" asked Bob.

"Because you have a motive and you had opportunity," said Sean.

"But I didn't do it," Bob protested. "I'm the fall guy."

"That's not what the DA thinks," said Sean.

"My lawyer thinks the case is circumstantial," said Bob.

"Really?"

"Yes. Really."

"He used those actual words?"

"Not exactly," Bob mumbled.

"That's what I thought." In Sean's experience, the DA didn't usually charge people unless he thought he had a good chance of getting a conviction.

"I'm so glad you came around," Bob said. "You've really cheered me up."

"Do I detect a note of sarcasm?"

"Just a touch."

"Listen, all I'm saying is in order to talk to the DA, we have to present him with evidence that someone else did this, or at least outline a plausible scenario, which I haven't come across so far."

"Everyone else's motive is just as good as mine. Look at what happened to Inez, for example. She lost everything, just like me," Bob replied.

"But she wasn't in the room next to Amethyst's."

"She was in the building."

"She was next door," said Sean.

"There's supposed to be a passageway that runs between the buildings."

Sean leaned forward. "Mark says it's been closed off."

"Bessie says it hasn't," said Bob.

Sean managed to bite his tongue.

Bob shifted his weight to try to get more comfortable on the sofa, a feat Sean judged

236

impossible.

"Anyway," Bob continued, "how could I get out of where I was? I couldn't."

"Marvin and I are going to check that out again after we leave here," said Sean.

"We are?" Marvin said.

"Yes, we are," Sean told him before turning his attention back to Bob Small. "Maybe you killed Amethyst before you got into that space."

"I was in that hole in the ceiling for hours," said Bob. "I needed to pee, and I couldn't get down to do that. Go check with Mark."

"Was he there with you all the time?" asked Sean.

"No."

"Then he's not a good alibi for you, and for all I know, you may have had an accomplice," Sean said, even though he doubted it.

"Like who?"

"I don't know. You tell me."

Bob glared at him. "This is ridiculous. Konrad and Curtis said you'd help me," he protested.

"I am," Scan insisted.

"This is your idea of help?"

"Yes." Sean rubbed his forehead with his hand. "I need to cover all the possibilities so I can dispute them. Speaking of which, who sprang for your bail?" It was not that he didn't know; he wanted to hear what Bob had to say.

Bob smiled for the first time. "Mark did."

"Interesting. Did he say how come?" asked Sean.

"Because he didn't think I did it."

"He told Libby he thought you had."

"My cousins went to talk to him and changed his mind. I mean, no one else was going to put up money for me. Ever since I got sentenced to Allenwood, no one in my family, except for Curtis and Konrad and a cousin who works as a manager at Burger King, will talk to me."

Marvin coughed. Sean glanced at him.

"You're lucky," Marvin said to Bob. "Not many people would be so nice."

"I know," Bob replied. "He believes in giving people a second chance. Do you want to hear Curtis and Konrad's new tapes?"

"Won't they be upset if you monkey around with their machine?" Sean asked.

Bob shook his head. "I don't see why. I know how to run it. The tapes are pretty interesting."

"So you could hear voices?" Sean asked.

"Not voices," Bob corrected. "Bessie."

"Really," Sean said.

"Well, you have to listen real hard," Bob allowed, "but she's there." And he got up and went into the other room to get the tapes.

Marvin and Sean looked at each other.

"He's probably delusional," Marvin whispered. "I understand stress can do that to people."

At last, Sean thought, he and Marvin had found a point they could agree on.

"At first you don't hear anything," Bob said as he turned the machine on, "except this noise that reminds me of the metal shop. But then —"

"You worked in a metal shop?" Sean interrupted.

"Yeah. At Allenwood. They taught me how to weld, They've got a really good shop there, with all the latest tools. Why are you asking?"

Sean shrugged. "No particular reason. Just making conversation."

"I wish I liked doing it better. You can make a lot of money," said Bob.

"I hear it's tough," Sean said. "But then if it wasn't, it wouldn't be paying well."

"True," Bob said, and he put a finger on his lips. "Sssh. Here comes Bessie."

Sean leaned forward and listened. All he heard was more static. Not that he was

239

listening that carefully. His mind was pre-occupied with something else.

"That was interesting," Sean said to Marvin when they were sitting in Marvin's vehicle again, eating the doughnuts and sipping the coffee that Curtis and Konrad had brought back.

"Are you talking about the tapes?" Marvin asked as he put the key in the ignition. "Because I didn't hear anything."

"No. I'm talking about the fact that Bob Small worked in a welding shop."

"So?" Marvin asked.

"So that means he probably knows about fiber-optic laser wire. Remember I told you they use it to cut metal."

Sean sat back and closed his eyes. He thought better that way.

CHAPTER 18

Bernie parked the van as close to the front of the historical society as she could get, turned off the ignition, and got out of the vehicle. There was no need to lock it, because no one would possibly want to steal it. As she hurried toward the door, she wondered what she'd been thinking when she decided to wear her suede over-the-knee boots on a day like today. Even though she'd put that waterproofing stuff on them that the salesman had recommended, in her experience, it never worked that well, especially not on suede.

The historical society was nice and warm. *Cozy* was the word that popped into Bernie's head. Jeanine was sitting by the front desk, staring at the seven bags of candy laid out on it.

"You got the good stuff," Bernie observed as she got close enough to see the kind of candy it was.

She still remembered getting two large 3 Musketeers Bars plus a Snickers bar from Mrs. Steinberg's mother when she was in the fourth grade. It had been her best score ever, and despite her mother's warning, she'd eaten all three candy bars when she'd gotten home. Much to her mother's dismay, she hadn't gotten sick, either.

Jeanine looked up at her and grinned. "This is what comes from living in a house where my mom gave out apples each year."

"The kids couldn't have been happy."

"They weren't. We got TP'ed a lot. You think this will be enough?"

"Depends on the weather."

"I just don't want to be stuck eating it all."

Bernie laughed. "The mini bars are the worst."

"Yeah. Every time you go by the bowl, you take just one or two, and by the end of the day, the whole bowl is gone."

"There's always the freezer," Bernie suggested.

"That doesn't help someone with a major sweet tooth."

Bernie thought of Libby. "No. I guess it wouldn't."

"So what brings you here? Did your dad want his View-Master back?"

"No. He's coming for that himself." Was that a smile on Jeanine's face? Bernie wasn't sure. "I'm here because I know you have a whole mass of old letters, and I'm wondering if I could take a quick look through them just to make sure there's nothing pertaining to Bessie Osgood."

"I'm pretty sure there isn't, but I'll make us some tea," Jeanine said. "And then we'll get started."

"You don't have to help," Bernie said.

"I know I don't, but I'd like to." Jeanine gestured around the room. "It's not as if I'm exactly busy."

Five minutes later Jeanine came out, bearing a tray with two bone china teacups, a teapot, sugar and cream, and a plate of gingersnaps.

"Rosenthal," Bernie said, looking at the pattern.

"My mother's," Jeanine said as she poured the tea.

Bernie took a sip. It was Indian. Oolong. The two women sat there for a few minutes, savoring their tea, before Jeanine said, "So how's the case coming?"

Bernie shook her head. "Could be better."

"That's what I figured."

"Did you find anything with the View-Master?"

Now it was Jeanine's turn to shake her head. "If there's anything there, I don't see it. There were just multiple shots from out the second-story windows. It's probably Felicity's idea of a joke."

"Maybe I should go back and ask her," Bernie mused, even though talking to Felicity again was not what she wanted to do. Their last conversation had made Bernie feel as if she was standing in front of Mr. Steiffer's math class, and he was saying to her, "Just look at the board, and tell me the answer. It isn't that difficult." But it was to her.

Jeanine delicately placed her cup on her saucer. "You can't ask her. She's in the hospital."

"With what?"

"She had a stroke. At this point, she can't use the left side of her body or talk."

Bernie let out a long sigh. "My father says getting old sucks."

"It certainly does," Jeanine replied. "Although your dad doesn't seem to be doing too badly in that department."

Bernie gave her a speculative look. "He can be a real pain in the ass sometimes."

"I figured," Jeanine said.

She and Jeanine exchanged a woman-to-woman smile.

"Just so you know," Bernie told her while reaching over and grabbing a gingersnap. She took a bite and let the cookie dissolve on her tongue. "Ready?" she said when she was done eating.

"Ready," Jeanine answered.

The two women stood up and moved to the room where the letters — officially called ephemera — were kept. Unlike the other rooms, this one was bare except for the three- and four-drawer file cabinets that lined the wall. A square wooden table sat in the center of the room.

"The chairs aren't very comfortable," Jeanine noted as she went over to the file cabinet on the left. "But I can't get money to replace them. Everyone wants things done, but they don't want to pay for them." She laughed. "But I'm going to stay off that topic. Otherwise, I'll be talking about it all day. Fortunately," she told Bernie, "I've gone through two of the file cabinets and put them in order, so I know that nothing is misfiled. That leaves us just two to go over." And she opened the top drawer of the farthest file cabinet on her left and pulled out three bulging files. "Here you go," she said as she put them in front of Bernie.

Bernie eyed the files for a moment before gingerly opening up the first folder. "Are they in any particular order?" she asked hopefully.

"Not that I know of," Jeanine said. "Organization wasn't my predecessor's strong point."

"Wonderful," Bernie muttered as she started leafing through the papers.

By the time she was done, her back was aching, her eyes were burning, and she had a headache. She'd found nothing about Bessie Osgood, but she had found a small item from the local newspaper about the closing of the Peabody School.

Bernie sat back in her chair and read it aloud. "Today, George Marak, headmaster of the Peabody School, has announced that it is with profound regret that he and the Board of Directors of the Peabody School have come to the painful decision to close the school by the end of the semester." Bernie looked up. "There's no mention of Marak killing himself."

"That happened a week later."

"Did the paper do a follow-up?"

"I believe they called the suicide an unfortunate accident."

"You could say that." Bernie was silent for a moment. Then she said, "Of course, they called Bessie Osgood's murder an unfortunate accident, too."

"Well, don't forget that in those days people used euphemisms. Suicides were unfortunate accidents, and girls didn't have babies out of wedlock. They went on extended trips to Europe. And married couples slept in separate beds."

Bernie put the article back in the folder. "That place really does have bad karma."

Jeanine stretched. "So it would seem."

"I wonder why the article is here?"

Jeanine shrugged. "I guess someone must have thought it was of interest. I really don't know why. As far as I can see, the things in these cabinets are random pieces of stuff, most of which should be thrown out."

"Then why don't you?"

"Because I'm afraid that the moment I do, it will turn out that I've thrown out some irreplaceable document."

Bernie laughed and got up. "Isn't that always the way."

"Well, it is in my life." Jeanine pointed to the folder. "Here. Take the article with you, and show it to your dad, not that there is anything in it he doesn't already know."

"Are you sure?"

"Of course, I'm sure. That's one piece of paper out of here."

"I'll send my dad over with some cupcakes for you," Bernie told her.

Jeanine patted her hips. "Just what I need."

Bernie tucked the article in her bag, thanked Jeanine for all her help, and walked outside.

It had stopped raining, but the sky was overcast, and the air was cold and damp. Bernie buttoned up her jacket and headed for her vehicle. She'd just gotten behind the wheel when her cell rang. It was Brandon.

"No. I can't do a matinee," she said.

Brandon laughed. "Don't flatter yourself."

"Very nice. See what you get the next time you ask."

"I'm irresistible. You can't say no to me."

"Talk about misplaced ego."

"Seriously, I'm calling because Inez is here, drinking away."

"I'll be right over," Bernie told him.

"And can you be a sweetie and stop on the way and get me some sugarless gum? I'm all out."

"I'll think about it," Bernie said before she clicked off. But, of course, Brandon knew that she would.

Including the stop at the gas station to pick up Brandon's gum, it took Bernie fifteen minutes to get to R.J.'s. The place was uncharacteristically empty, except for Inez, who was hunched over her drink at the bar, in the corner farthest from the door.

"She's been here for the last thirty minutes," Brandon told Bernie sotto voce.

Bernie nodded as she assessed Inez out of the corner of her eye. She wasn't wearing any make-up, which made the bruise on her jaw stand out. From its purplish color, Bernie judged it was two days old at the most.

Then there was Inez's hair. Bernie shook her head as she contemplated it. It was orange, the obvious result of a bad dye job, and to make matters worse, tufts were sticking out in various directions. It looked as if Inez hadn't taken a comb to it in two or three days. How anyone could do that to themselves, Bernie couldn't imagine. The stained denim jacket over the grey sweatshirt Inez was wearing didn't do anything to help the situation.

Bernie turned toward Brandon. "Well," she told him, "she certainly doesn't look in good shape."

"She's not," Brandon said.

"Is she drunk?"

"No. But she's getting there fast. Can I get you anything?"

Bernie grabbed a handful of peanuts and started shelling them. "A Coke will be fine."

A moment later Brandon was back with a Coke. Bernie grabbed it and drifted down to where Inez was sitting.

"Hi," Bernie said as she sat down next to Inez.

Inez glared at her. "What do you want?" she demanded.

Bernie cracked open a peanut and tossed the nut into her mouth. "Are you okay?" she asked after she'd swallowed.

"I'm fine."

"Because it doesn't seem to me as if you are."

Inez stared into her beer for a moment and then took a drink. "Well, I am."

"What happened to your face?"

Inez touched the side of her jaw, realized what she was doing, and quickly put her hand back on the bar. "I fell."

"Are you sure no one hit you?"

Bernie couldn't read the fleeting expression that ran across Inez's face. Was it anger? Sorrow? Pleasure that someone cared enough to ask? All of them? None of them? Bernie didn't know.

Then Inez frowned. "I got drunk, and I fell off the sofa and hit the edge of the coffee table on the way down. Satisfied?"

Bernie took a sip of her Coke. "Not really, but if that's what you say happened, then that's what happened."

"That's what I say happened." Inez took a

gulp of her beer and slammed the glass down on the bar. "Ian is a putz. You know that?"

Bernie ate another peanut and put the shell on top of a napkin. "Why is Ian a putz?"

"Because he fired me."

Bernie didn't say anything.

"I had a doctor's note, too. What am I going to do now?" Inez demanded. "Who's going to hire me?"

"No one if you don't pull yourself together," Bernie told her.

Inez gulped down the rest of her beer and signaled Brandon to bring another one. As he went to get it, a man and a woman came in and sat down near the door. The couple was laughing and joking. Inez looked at them with hungry eyes. After a minute or so, she wrenched her eyes away.

"We used to be like that before Amethyst," Inez said wistfully.

Bernie knew Inez was talking about herself and her husband.

"We were really happy together," Inez added. She watched while Brandon set her Coors down in front of her and moved on to the new customers. She poured it into her glass and took a big swallow. "Really happy. We liked each other."

"Is that why you killed Amethyst?"

Inez wiped her lips off with the back of her hand. "A lot you know. Why would I kill her?"

"Because she destroyed your life? You just said as much."

"Yeah. She did. But I was making her pay."

Interesting, Bernie thought as she took another sip of her Coke. "Is that right? And how were you doing that?"

"You don't believe me?" Inez said.

"Well, it's a little hard to imagine."

"You think she was smarter than I was?"

"Well . . ."

"Even with my drinking, I'm still smarter then she was," Inez growled. "Better looking, too."

"I don't believe it," Bernie said, egging Inez on.

"That I was better looking?"

"No. That's true." Bernie remembered when Inez used to come into the shop.

"I had a better body."

"That's true."

"And I dressed better."

"I'm not disputing that. It's the intelligence part."

Inez looked outraged. "Hey, I have a master's in remote sensing."

"True, but I'm not talking about that kind of intelligence."

Inez gave Bernie a beery, conspiratorial smile. "She was a sneaky little bitch, wasn't she?"

Bernie popped another peanut into her mouth. "In a word, yes."

"But I found out something she didn't want anyone to know."

"Really?" Bernie hoped that she had conveyed just the right amount of disbelief.

"Yes. Really. Amethyst was moving, and she didn't want anyone to know. But I knew."

"How did you know?"

"I heard her talking."

Bernie maintained a skeptical expression.

"It's true. I did," Inez insisted.

"Where? While you were cleaning the bathroom?"

A crafty expression stole over Inez's face. "Never you mind."

Bernie ate another peanut. "In the supermarket? The garden store? Probably not." Bernie contemplated the options some more. "Did you clean her house?"

Inez looked at her in astonishment.

"You cleaned her house? I don't believe it," said Bernie.

"Believe it," Inez snarled.

"Given the circumstances, I find that hard to believe."

"I don't want to talk to you anymore," Inez said and gulped her drink.

"Come on," Bernie told her. "You have to give me credit for this. You have to admit I'm good."

"Yes, you are," answered Brandon.

Bernie was startled. She'd been so engrossed in her conversation with Inez that she hadn't realized Brandon was standing in front of her, with another beer for Inez. She was always amazed at how quietly he moved for a big guy. She smiled at him and turned her attention back to Inez.

"That must have been hard, working for Amethyst. More than hard given the circumstances."

Inez didn't say anything.

"Did you do it so you could get back at her?"

"It's none of your business."

"Actually, I think it is." Bernie took a sip of her Coke and put it down. "So after you tried blackmailing her, I'm guessing Amethyst didn't want you working at her place anymore."

"She had no right to do what she did."

"Are you talking about the fact that she broke up your home, the fact that you

254

worked for her, or the fact that she fired you?"

Inez hunched her shoulders and took another swig from her glass. "A person's got to live, doesn't she?"

"So, what did you hear?" Bernie asked.

A cunning expression stole across Inez's face. "Maybe it wasn't something I heard. Maybe it was something I saw."

"How much did you ask from Amethyst?"

Inez drained the last drop from her glass and put it down. "What difference does it make?" She leaned in toward Bernie. Her mouth twisted itself into a sneer. "You know what she did? She laughed at me. At me. Told me I was a loser and no one would ever believe me."

"So what did you do?" Bernie asked.

"Guess," Inez said.

"Got even?" Bernie said.

Inez laughed.

"What's so funny?" Bernie asked.

"You are," Inez replied, and she got up and started for the door.

"How about if I buy you another drink?" Bernie said.

"You think I'm that easy?" Inez said. "Well, screw you." And she left.

"That went well," Brandon said.

"Didn't it, though." Bernie tapped her

fingers on the bar. "I should have offered her money instead."

"Somehow I don't think that twenty dollars would do it."

"Are you saying I'm cheap?"

"No. I'm saying you're broke."

"Amethyst was a real piece of work," Bernie said thoughtfully.

Brandon grinned. "That would be one way of putting it."

"And the other way?"

"She was a sadistic little bitch."

"These days people would say she had a personality disorder."

"They'd probably say that about Hitler, too."

Bernie chuckled. That was one of the things she loved about Brandon. He always made her laugh.

"You know what?" she said.

Brandon planted his elbows on the bar and supported his face with his hands. "What?" he said.

"I think I'm going to take a quick look around Amethyst's place."

"And the reason being?"

"Because maybe there's something there that we need to know."

"You're thinking about what Inez said."

Bernie nodded.

"The police have probably gone through it already."

"It wouldn't be the first time that they missed something."

"You don't have a key," Brandon pointed out.

"I'll use your credit-card trick."

Brandon rolled his eyes.

"You're just jealous that you can't come," said Bernie.

Brandon snorted. "Right. I really want to get arrested. Just don't call me to bail you out."

Bernie leaned over the bar and kissed him. "That would never even occur to me."

"Right," Brandon repeated.

Bernie flashed him her best smile. "Call me when you're off, and I'll meet you at your place."

"I told you, you'd beg me."

She picked up a peanut and threw it at him. Then she hurried out the door before he could get her back.

CHAPTER 19

Marvin and Sean stood in the room of the Haunted House that had the coffin that came out of the floor. No one was there yet, so it was eerily quiet.

"Should we be here?" Marvin asked Sean.

"No one said we couldn't," Sean replied.

"That's because you didn't ask."

Sean didn't answer. Instead, he stared at the ceiling. It was lower than the ceilings in the other rooms by a good foot or so. Sean was betting it was a dropped ceiling made with two-by-fours and covered over with plaster.

"You should return those keys," Marvin told him.

"I will," said Sean while he continued to study the ceiling.

And he *would* return the keys. He didn't want Konrad and Curtis to get in trouble. He was just going to do it later rather than sooner. Obviously, they didn't need the keys at the moment, or else they would have asked for them by now.

"Do me a favor," he said to Marvin. "Turn on the lights for me. The control switch is by the door, on your left." He paused. "Left," he said to Marvin as Marvin went to the right.

"You mean this way?" Marvin asked.

"Right."

Marvin moved toward the right.

"Left," Sean screamed.

"I did, and you said right."

Sean took several deep breaths. According to Bernie, this was supposed to help him calm down. It didn't. "Go to the left," he said in as even a voice as he could manage. "That's correct," he told Marvin when he had.

"You should be clearer," Marvin told him in an injured voice.

In this case Sean decided that silence was a virtue. So, he watched Marvin grope behind the wall hanging. "Farther in," Sean instructed.

"Got it," Marvin told him.

The lights didn't come on.

"Obviously, you didn't get it," Sean replied.

"I got something," Marvin said.

Sean was just about to tell him to try again

when out of the corner of his eye, he saw something move. He jumped back as what he now realized was a coffin rose out of the floor. Then he remembered what Bernie had told him about the exhibit, and his heart settled back down.

A moment later the skeleton sat up. It had a patch over one eye. "Soon you'll look just like me," the skeleton cackled. "Just like me. Eat, drink, and be merry. We don't have six packs in the graveyard."

"I told you I hit the wrong switch," Marvin said.

"See if you can turn the sound off," Sean said. It was impossible to think with that thing babbling on.

Marvin went back to fumbling with the wall switches. A moment later the skeleton shut up in mid-cackle.

Sean looked at the ceiling. "Marvin, how high would you say that was?"

"About eight feet."

"That would be my guess, too. I want you to do me a favor and stand on the edge of the coffin and see if you can touch the ceiling."

"But . . ."

"You should be used to them."

"That's not the point."

"What is?"

"I just don't want to fall in and break the thing."

"You won't," Sean said, with more confidence than he felt. After all, if it was possible to break something, Marvin usually did. "You can hold on to my shoulder for balance." Also a bad idea, but the best he could come up with given the circumstances.

Marvin put one foot on the coffin, then stepped up with the other.

"Steady?" Sean asked when Marvin was standing on the edge of the coffin.

"I guess," Marvin said.

"Now lift your hand up, and touch the ceiling."

"Satisfied?" Marvin said as he made contact.

Sean nodded as Marvin started to tilt. He stepped away just as Marvin lurched forward and crashed to the floor.

"How tall would you say Bob Small is?" Sean asked Marvin as the younger man picked himself up and dusted himself off.

"Aren't you even going to ask me how I am?" Marvin demanded while he rubbed his elbow.

"No. I'm not asking you, because you're obviously fine," Sean said. "Again. How tall is Bob Small?"

"I think he must be almost six feet. I'm five feet ten, and he's about two inches taller than I am. Why?"

"Do you have a flashlight in your car?"

"No."

"A penlight?"

Marvin shook his head.

"Don't you keep an emergency kit in your car?"

Marvin shook his head again. "I can go out and buy one."

"No. By the time you get back, there'll be people here." Sean thought for a moment. Then he took out his cell phone.

"Who are you calling?" Marvin asked.

"I'm not calling anyone," said Sean. He opened up his cell and shined the light on the ceiling, directly above where Marvin had been standing. "Do you see anything?" he asked.

"It would help if I knew what I was looking for."

"A crack in the ceiling."

"Why do we care?"

"We just do," Sean said. "Now concentrate."

Marvin dutifully put his head back and stared at the ceiling. It all looked like a big expanse of white plaster to him. A moment later he rubbed the back of his neck. "I'm getting muscle spasms."

"Move down a foot, and stop complaining," Sean snapped.

"I'm not complaining. I'm just telling you I have a hyper-mobile neck."

"Keep looking, anyway."

"Is this what you mean?" Marvin asked five minutes later.

Sean followed Marvin's finger. There was what looked like a small indentation in the ceiling. He smiled. Today was going to be a good day, after all. "Yes."

"Good," Marvin said. "Because I don't think I can take much more of this. My neck is killing me. I'll probably have to go see the chiropractor now."

It took a lot of willpower on Sean's side to not say anything, even though he would have liked to. Boy, would he ever. He could just imagine the reaction he would have gotten if he'd said something like that to his dad. He probably would have gotten a kick across the room. But that was what kids were like these days. Whine, whine, whine. How they managed to survive in the world was beyond him. Even though he thought Marvin's dad was an asshole, he was beginning to feel a little more sympathy for him.

Sean plastered what he hoped was a pleasant expression on his face and said, "I just want you to do one more thing for me. I want you to get back on the rim of the coffin and see if you can push the panel forward with your hand."

"What panel?"

"The panel that I think is in the ceiling."

"I'm going to fall if I do this," Marvin told him.

"I'll stand next to you. You can lean on me."

"That's what you told me before."

Sean looked at his watch. They didn't have much time left before people started coming in to prepare for this evening.

"Please," Sean said. "Try. This is really important."

"For real?" Marvin asked.

"Yes. It might help us figure out who killed Amethyst."

Marvin thought about it for a moment. Then he got up on the rim of the coffin and spaced his feet apart. Sean moved in so Marvin could lean against him. Marvin raised his hands and pushed. Nothing happened.

"Try again," Sean urged.

Marvin did. "I think I felt something move."

"Good," Sean said encouragingly. "Just

once more. If it doesn't happen, then I'm wrong."

"Okay," Marvin said.

Sean watched as Marvin rebalanced himself on the rim of the coffin, put his hands up flat against the plaster, and pushed. He could see something moving. Marvin pushed harder. The panel slid back some more.

Sean looked up at the eight inches of space Marvin had created. "There goes Bob Small's alibi," he said.

"Someone else could have done it, too," Marvin said.

"I suppose," Sean agreed. "But it's highly unlikely."

"But it's possible," Marvin insisted.

"It's possible," Sean agreed. "Possible, but not probable." He sighed. "Of course, we won't have proof positive until someone crawls up there and tests my theory out," he added as Marvin turned the switch and the coffin disappeared back into the ground.

"Someone?" squeaked Marvin as he turned off the lights.

"Yes. Someone. Obviously, it can't be me," Sean told him as they walked out of the room, through the Chain-Saw Massacre Room, and out into the corridor that led to the outside. Sean paused to lock the outside door to the Haunted House. Then he pulled on the door to make sure it was locked. Test and retest. That was his motto.

"Obviously," Marvin said to Sean's back.

Sean grunted a reply.

"I'll be back in a sec," Marvin said to Sean, and then he ran to the car, which, on Sean's advice, he'd parked behind the Haunted House. That way no one driving by would see them.

Sean looked at his watch. "Make it fast. People will be here soon," he called.

Marvin broke into a trot. He got to his vehicle, put the key in the ignition, started her up, put the car in reverse, and immediately backed into the tree behind him. God. The more nervous he got, the klutzier he became. He jumped out and looked at the damage. Fortunately, it was just a ding in the bumper. He jumped back in his car, put the car in drive, and zoomed off to get Sean.

"What was that I heard?" Sean asked him.

"Nothing," Marvin lied. "Absolutely nothing."

A moment later they were driving out of there. *And not a moment too soon,* Marvin thought as he glanced at the clock on the dashboard. Another couple of minutes and people would be coming up. Thank God they hadn't gotten caught. If Marvin never saw this place again, he'd be ecstatic. As far as he could see, nothing good had ever happened here.

Maybe his dad was right. Maybe a funeral director was a good thing to be. No surprises in that, or at least not the kind of surprises that raised your blood pressure. All he wanted to do now was sit in the kitchen and talk to Libby and eat a slice of her warm apple pie with her homemade vanilla ice cream.

Instead, he was running around with her dad, doing things that could get both of them arrested. And if that happened, it would be his fault. He'd get blamed for it, because he always got blamed for everything that went wrong. That was just the way things were. Marvin sighed and slowed down for the steep curve coming up.

Maybe after Libby was through working tonight, they could go to R.J.'s and have a beer. It wasn't as good as having Libby's pie, but it would be good enough. He had just finished taking another curve — the road to the Haunted House had more twists and turns than a bad soap opera — when he looked over at Sean and saw Sean looking at him, and somehow he knew exactly what Libby's dad was thinking.

"I don't like heights, and I don't like small spaces," Marvin told him.

"The ceiling isn't that high, and the space isn't that small."

"I'll fall through."

"No, you won't. Ceilings like that, built with drywall and two-by-fours, can support a considerable amount of weight."

"How do you know?"

"Because I've put them up."

Marvin thought for a moment. "What happens if I get stuck?"

"You won't get stuck."

"But what happens if I do?"

"We'll walk away and pretend we never met you."

Marvin snuck a quick peek at Sean. He could never tell whether he was kidding or not.

"I was joking," Sean said. "And you don't have to do this. You've been more than enough help already."

"Then who will?"

Sean shrugged. "Don't worry about it. I'll find someone. If worse comes to worst, I'll do it myself."

Marvin groaned.

"Well, it's the truth," Sean said. "Or maybe I can get one of my daughters to do it."

"Why don't you twist the knife a little deeper?" Marvin asked him.

Sean grinned. "I'm good at guilt, aren't I?"

"Yes, you are."

"It's a talent I inherited from my mother's side of the family."

"Fine," Marvin grumped. "I'll climb up there. But if anything happens to me, it's on your head."

Sean laughed. "I think I can handle that responsibility."

"When is this going to happen?"

"Probably tonight after the Haunted House closes."

"What?" squeaked Marvin.

"Well, I am going to have to give the keys back to Konrad and Curtis. Or we could go over to the Home Depot in Thompsonville and get them duped. That might give us a little more leeway."

"Leeway is good," Marvin said.

"Always," Sean said as he leaned over and turned on the radio. For a moment, both men were quiet as they listened to the music.

"So what do you think happened?" Marvin asked once they hit the main road. "How do you think Bob Small pulled this off?"

Sean sat back in his seat and told Marvin what he thought.

CHAPTER 20

Bernie still couldn't believe that Amethyst had lived in Stanton as she pulled up in front of Amethyst's flat.

"Are you sure she lived there?" she'd asked Bree Nottingham, real estate agent extraordinaire, social arbiter of Longely, and general pain in the butt, when she'd tracked her down yesterday morning. After several false starts, Bernie had finally located her at Kim's Nifty Nails.

Bree had fixed her with a gimlet eye. "Of course, I'm sure," she'd snapped.

She'd been, as was usual these days, dressed in pink from head to toe, up to and including her Prada bag. It was, she'd told Bernie, her signature color. Bernie didn't believe in signature colors — people weren't pens — but she'd never say that to Bree, who threw a fair amount of business their way. Actually, she wouldn't have said it to her face, anyway. However, she did say it to her sister in private on several occasions.

Bree had taken her right hand out of the bowl she was soaking it in and had held it out for the Korean girl to dry before speaking. "I tried to persuade Amethyst to live in town, but she wasn't having any of it," she'd told Bernie.

"But why did she choose Stanton of all places?" Bernie had wondered out loud. "That's so strange. I would imagine her somewhere a lot more upscale."

Bree had frowned. "Think about it."

"Nothing comes to mind," Bernie had said.

"Well, she said" — Bree bracketed the *she said* with her voice — "that she liked the people there." Here Bree had paused meaningfully. "She said they were more authentic."

"Authentic? Please."

Bree had nodded encouragingly, pleased that her point had been made.

Bernie had frowned. "Amethyst didn't care about authentic unless the word applied to diamonds and gold. I mean Stanton is made up of Mexicans and Portuguese. I never saw Amethyst look at anyone who wasn't driving at least a Lexus."

"Exactly." Bree had nodded at the Korean girl, who had begun filing her nails. "And

272

this time I want them straight across," she'd told her. "Straight. You understand?" The girl had bobbed her head and had kept filing. Bree had watched her for a moment to make sure she was doing what she'd asked and then had turned her attention back to Bernie. "My guess is that Amethyst was living there because she could come and go as she pleased, without anyone knowing her business, which would most definitely not be true if she lived in Longely or another community she socialized in."

"Makes sense," Bernie had told Bree.

Bree had nodded. "Of course, it makes sense. The expression 'Don't poop where you eat' comes to mind, which would be especially important to someone of Amethyst's . . ." Bree had paused while she hunted for the right word and had finally said, "To someone of Amethyst's bent. Plus, she kept her overhead low and put her money into what counted — herself. From a business point of view, it was a good decision."

"Not that it helped her," Bernie had pointed out.

"No, it didn't," Bree had acknowledged before changing the subject. "I want you or your sister to call me tomorrow. I'm having a dinner party for fifteen in two weeks, and

I want to discuss the menu. I was thinking we could do something retro, something Julia. You do know Julia, don't you?"

"Of course, I know Julia Child," Bernie had said, incensed. How could someone who loved food not know her? She was an icon.

"Good. Because I was thinking we could build the menu around beef Wellington, the real one, with a Bavarian cream for dessert. Or maybe some sort of crêpes flambé. Yes. Let's do that. Maybe crêpes suzette."

"Sounds great," Bernie had said.

And she'd meant it. She loved traditional French food. She just didn't get a chance to make it anymore, because people were so concerned with their diets and the amount of fat they ingested, but in her mind, there were two kinds of food: regular food and party food. And you should be allowed to eat what you wanted at a party. If you couldn't, what was the point? In fact, when Bernie thought about it, cooking wasn't as much fun as it used to be. Ever since people had started saying things like, "I need protein" instead of "I'd like a nice, fat, juicy steak," things had definitely gone downhill.

On her way to Stanton, Bernie found herself thinking about what kind of first course and appetizers she could serve at

Bree's dinner party. She would keep the appetizers on the light side because the meal was going to be heavy. She'd start the ball rolling with Kirs and a good prosecco. They were always good aperitifs. They had just enough alcohol to loosen people up, but not so much that it dulled their taste buds.

Along with the drinks, she could serve two types of spiced nuts, one with pepper and rosemary, and the other with salt and a dash of anise. People seemed to like those. Then she could serve a selection of olives and tiny toast points with heated goat cheese. That should really be enough. Unless she added cubes of feta cheese marinated in olive oil and garlic.

For the first course, she'd serve a clear beef broth with one or two small circles of baked custard and a dusting of chopped chives floating in it, or she could do a celery rémoulade, which was also very nice, and celeriac was in the market these days. Naturally, they'd have to make the mayo for the rémoulade sauce, but she liked doing that. There was something very meditative about whisking the oil into the egg yolks and watching the emulsion form a light yellow cream. Hellmann's just didn't cut it.

Then, after the beef Wellington, she could serve a salad made up of endive and watercress and arugula in a vinaigrette dressing. The sharpness of the greens would be a nice foil to the richness of the main course. She'd do the crêpes suzette that Bree had requested for dessert, or maybe something like crêpes filled with an apple compote and flambéed with a good apple brandy, which would be a little more seasonal.

Or maybe not. The problem with calvados was that you needed a really good one; otherwise, it tasted like diesel fuel. And, thanks to the dollar's weakness, good bottles of calvados were extremely expensive these days, and since they didn't have any on hand in the shop, Bernie would have to purchase a bottle. So she would forget the apple crêpes and stick with Bree's original suggestion. Unless, of course, Bree was willing to buy a bottle of the stuff, which Bernie was pretty sure she wouldn't be.

Bernie was almost at Stanton by the time she'd worked through the pricing of Bree's menu. Between the labor and the ingredients, this was not going to be a cheap meal, but then a good cut of beef, let alone pâté, never was. She was wondering whether or not Bree would want to pay that much when she caught sight of one of the street names on her map. It was, she realized, time to focus on the task at hand.

CHAPTER 21

Amethyst's home was four blocks away from the commercial district, in an unprepossessing neighborhood of small houses, smaller yards, and older, dented cars. No BMWs here. According to the numbers painted on the wall, Amethyst lived in the bottom part of a two-family house. The sagging fence posts, the paint peeling on the porch stairs, the empty planter boxes, and the absence of holiday decorations of any kind gave the place a forlorn appearance. It looked as if no one had loved in it or taken care of it for a long time.

The question, thought Bernie, was how to get in. Now that she was actually here, she wasn't so sure. It was one thing to joke around with Brandon about it and another thing to actually do it, breaking and entering not having been a course in her high school curriculum.

She parked her car and contemplated her

options. She could go the legal or the illegal route. Both had good things going for them. The legal route involved something like knocking on the upstairs neighbor's door, seeing if they had the key to Amethyst's place, then making up a plausible story so she could get it. However, there was a big problem with that approach. The upstairs apartment was for rent. So that took care of that.

Which left the illegal route. For a moment, she debated the wisdom of what she was about to do, and then she thought, *The hell with it.* What was the worst that could happen? The neighbors could call the cops, and she'd get arrested, her father would kill her, and she'd never hear the end of it from Brandon or her sister. Which, in the scheme of things, wasn't so terrible. It wasn't as if she was going to get shot or anything.

Here goes nothing, she said to herself as she zipped up her jacket and got out of the car. She strode toward Amethyst's door like she had business being there. As she did, another thought popped into her mind. Inez had cleaned for Amethyst, which meant either Inez had a key and had let herself in, Amethyst had let her in, or Amethyst had left the key for Inez somewhere inconspicuous, like under a potted plant or the welcome mat. Bernie decided to go with the third option because it was the easiest, while the other two left her with nothing to do but break a window or open the door with a credit card — something she wasn't good with. Besides, these days everyone had dead bolts, which required a little more finesse. And if option one didn't work, she could always go to option two or three.

Bernie casually strolled around to the back of the house, figuring that if Amethyst had left the key anywhere, it would be there, because there was no place in front to hide a key. There was a slot in the door for the mail and no welcome mat on the porch. If anyone asked what she was doing, she would say she was thinking of renting the upstairs apartment and just wanted to see what things looked like.

Like not much, in her opinion. Maple saplings were pushing up through the cracks in the driveway. Their leaves littered the tarmac. Over by the hurricane fence, black-eyed Susans drooped disconsolately. A sand box sat uncovered. In it, three small, chartreuse, plastic starfish molds sat next to a kiddie-sized pail and shovel. She looked in all of them. No key. Then she addressed the doll whose legs were sticking out of the sand.

Bernie reached over and pulled her out. It was a Barbie. She dusted the sand out of her hair and sat her down next to the pail. Then she picked her back up. Poor Barbie. She deserved better than being left out for cats to pee on. Growing up, Libby had never liked Barbie dolls, but Bernie had been a Barbie fanatic, bugging her mom to buy her every new outfit that came on the market. She'd never liked Ken, though. She'd always thought he was a dork.

Bernie slipped the Barbie into her bag. She'd donate it to Goodwill, because it was obvious that the little girl that had lived upstairs with her parents wasn't coming back. As Bernie continued on, she wondered who they were and if they would know anything about Amethyst. Somehow she doubted it. She also doubted that she'd be able to locate them, but maybe Bree would know who the realtor was who handled this house. Then she or her sister could call up and see if the family had left a forwarding address. It was a long shot, but the way things were going, any long shot was a shot worth pursuing.

Bernie walked up to the back steps and picked up the welcome mat. Nothing. Too obvious. She went back down the steps, and taking care to keep her suede boots out of the dirt, she squatted down in front of what had once been a flower bed but was now a tangle of dead and dying weeds that banked the side of the house.

It seemed like an unlikely place for Amethyst to hide anything, but she ran her hand through the soil, anyway, because you never knew. As her father always said, "Do it right the first time so you don't have to go back and do it again."

After a minute of that, her hands were cold from the dirt. Well, that had definitely been a waste of time, she decided as she stood and brushed the soil off her hands. Not only had she not found anything, she'd ruined her manicure as well. Now she'd have to go back to the salon for a touch-up, something that she didn't have time to do.

This definitely wasn't turning out well. But the key had to be somewhere. Unless, of course, it didn't exist at all, which was a possibility she wasn't prepared to consider yet. Bernie tapped what was left of her nails against the boards of the house, thinking that maybe the key was behind a loose board. She tried prying a couple of boards out. No go.

"Okay, Bernie," she said aloud to herself. "If this key is here, it's in some easy, accessible place. Just look around."

First, she looked at the yard again, but aside from starfish molds and the pail and shovel in the sand box, there was nothing in the yard that could be used to hide a key. No trash cans, no cute little garden gnomes, no faux plastic bunnies. The yard was completely bare. So far she was batting zero for zero, or whatever that expression was. She didn't follow baseball, so she didn't know. Bernie turned and studied the back of the house. She got up on her tiptoes and ran her fingers over the top of the door frame. Then she tried the windows. And that was when she got lucky.

The key was sitting in a magnetic box on the underside of the window to the right. She hit her forehead with the heel of her hand. "You are such an idiot," she said aloud.

Why do I always have to make things so much harder than they really are? Bernie thought as she slid the key in the lock and turned it. The door opened with a creak. Then Bernie replaced the key under the window frame, went inside, and locked the door from the inside. Better safe than sorry, as her dad would say. Well, that wasn't what he'd say in this situation, but she didn't want to think about that.

"Might as well start here," she muttered

to herself, stepping into a small, oblong-shaped kitchen. Since she didn't know what she was looking for, she couldn't afford to skip anything.

The first thing that struck her was that the kitchen probably hadn't been touched since the sixties. The walls were painted a greenish yellow, the counters were green Formica, and the floors were some sort of speckled linoleum. The second thing that struck her was that the counters were applianceless. There wasn't even a microwave on them. Who, except for her family, didn't have a microwave these days?

Bernie started opening cabinets. Most were empty. There was a set of pots that looked as if it had never been used, a paring knife, seven steak knives, five dishes, a couple of mugs, and a box containing a set of glass tumblers. Bernie had had more stuff in her college dorm than Amethyst had had in her kitchen. Bernie continued on. There were a few cleaning supplies under the kitchen sink, and two boxes of cereal, a box of mac and cheese, a box of Bisquick, and a couple of packets of honey roasted peanuts in the kitchen cabinet across from the stove, as well as a bottle of Wild Turkey, a bottle of good French brandy, and a couple of bottles of not-bad Chilean wine.

The refrigerator didn't yield much more. There were two bottles of water and a carton of Diet Coke on the top shelf, a lemon with green fuzz on it on the second shelf, and nothing in the vegetable bins. The freezer revealed a bottle of vodka and a bottle of Aquavit. Obviously, Amethyst hadn't done any entertaining here. Or eaten here.

Bernie turned and opened up the lid of the garbage can. There was nothing in it but a bottle of Diet Coke, a bridal magazine, and a copy of the Longely newspaper. Bernie reached in and fished out the two publications. The paper was dated three weeks ago.

Did that mean that that was the last time Amethyst was here, or did she simply read and dispose of more recent papers elsewhere? Bernie took a quick look at the paper but didn't see anything that linked it to Amethyst in any way. Then she looked at *Modern Bride.* There was no mailing label, so Amethyst had bought it off the newsstand. Unless someone else had purchased it and left it here, which, knowing Amethyst, was a more likely scenario. Nevertheless, Bernie tucked both pieces of printed matter under her arm. Maybe her dad would see something in them that she couldn't.

As she walked into the living room, she was wishing that there was some way of finding out what Inez had found out. *If* she was telling the truth. If this didn't pan out, Bernie decided that she'd appear at Inez's house with a large bottle of booze and some money. Despite what Brandon had said, she could probably spare fifty bucks, and it wasn't as if Inez didn't need the money. Her mother would have disapproved, but Bernie always felt that there were times that justified the expedient approach.

Looking around, Bernie decided the living room wasn't much better than the kitchen. There was a brown leather sofa, two chintz-covered armchairs, a coffee table that looked as if it was made out of particleboard, and a cheapo television set. The furniture looked as if it had come from one of those rental stores, and the television looked as if it was at least ten years old.

What Bernie was really struck by was what wasn't there. No cable box. No provisions for music. No books. No magazines. No pictures on the wall. There didn't seem to be anything personal at all. This apartment looked like it was a place for Amethyst to crash and nothing more. Bernie took another quick glance around and headed for the dining room. She found a bridge table and four chairs set up in the middle of the room, along with a floor lamp with a torn lamp shade.

Bernie wondered what she'd find in the bedrooms as she walked down the hall. The walls were covered with the kind of cabbage-rose wallpaper that had been popular in the thirties and forties. She opened the first door she came to. The room was empty. The only thing in it were the shades on the windows. She walked in and opened the closet door. A strong odor of mothballs came out and slapped her in the face. She peered inside. Nothing but some metal hangers, an orange metal container appropriately marked CAMPHOR, and an old navy blue woman's cardigan.

Bernie closed the closet door, left the room, and opened the next door. A made-up bed sat in the middle of the room. The coverlet was dark green and matched the curtains on the windows and the skirt on the bed. *Amethyst's room,* Bernie thought. Had to be. The nightstands were a light ash, as was the dresser standing in the far corner. An old-fashioned doll, the kind with a china head, leaned against the mirror hung over the dresser.

But what really attracted Bernie's attention was the two photographs hanging on the wall. They were both of preteen girls. Both of them were sitting on beds in what looked like dorm rooms, smiling and waving at the camera. Bernie didn't know how she knew who they were, she just did.

The titles written on the mats confirmed her guess. The girl with the big smile on her face and the slight buckteeth was Bessie Osgood. The second picture was of Zinnia McGuire. Bernie stared at them for a long time. She decided that Bessie looked a little bit like Libby had at that age. Kind of schlumpy. The sort of kid who always got As and did everything her mother told her to.

On the other hand, Zinnia looked as if she was going to get in her fair share of trouble. But, of course, she hadn't had the chance. She and Bessie had both been killed, their deaths officially declared accidents. Why did Amethyst have their pictures hanging on her wall? Were they trophies? Expressions of guilt? Reminders of the good old days? Bernie shook her head. She didn't know, and now, since she couldn't ask Amethyst, she never would.

She turned away and went through the dresser and the closet. The dresser had some underwear — the kind you got at JCPenney on sale — a fake pearl necklace, several

T-shirts in different colors, and a couple of stretched-out black turtlenecks. The closet turned out to be a little fuller, but the clothes and shoes in it were old and worn, things that Bernie judged Amethyst wore around the house. In any case, Bernie had never seen her in anything remotely resembling the stuff in her closet. Now more than ever, it looked as if Amethyst had been living somewhere else.

If she needed any more convincing, the bathroom did it. There were towels hanging on the racks, a shower curtain surrounding the bathtub, and a hamper for dirty clothes. Bernie opened the shower curtain. A nubbin of soap sat in the soap dish, while a bottle of shampoo stood on the side of the tub. Bernie lifted up the shampoo bottle. There was practically nothing left in it. *Interesting,* Bernie thought as she put it down. She opened the medicine cabinet over the sink. There was a bottle of aspirin, an unopened tube of toothpaste, mascara, and a couple of lipsticks. Bernie opened the mascara. It was practically empty. She put it back and opened the lipsticks. One was a horrendous orange — obviously a fashion error — while the other was a cheapo discount brand Bernie had never heard of. If Bernie remembered correctly, the only brand she had ever seen Amethyst use was Chanel.

Bernie put everything back the way it had been. She knew Amethyst. Amethyst had not been a back-to-nature kind of gal. She had used lots of product. Lots of styling gel on her hair, three coats of mascara, eyeliner, eye shadow, blush, not to mention concealer, lip liner, gloss, and lipstick. Basically, she'd applied lipstick like Spackle.

And where were the moisturizers, body lotions, hairbrushes, hair spray, and all the other things women like Amethyst couldn't do without? No blow-dryer. No perfume. One thing was clear. Bree's information was outdated. Amethyst hadn't really been living here at the time of her death. Maybe she had in the past, but she'd moved out. The questions were, when and to where?

Another dead end in a case full of them, Bernie thought. She was closing the medicine-cabinet door when she heard a noise. Bernie froze. It was the sound of the back door opening. Then she heard footsteps and what sounded like a crash.

Bernie peered out from the bathroom. The sounds seemed to be coming from the kitchen. There was another crash, followed by a muffled curse. Bernie crept down the hall. The prudent thing, she knew, would be to hide in one of the bedroom closets and wait till whoever it was left, but then she'd never been prudent.

By now she was at the end of the hallway. She carefully stuck her head out and took a look. No one was in the living room or the dining room. Whoever it was, was in the kitchen. Bernie thought for a moment. If she was very careful, she could get a peek at them. She very slowly inched her way to the door that connected the dining room and the kitchen and looked in.

"You," she cried when she saw who it was.

Bernie was gratified to see Inez jump. It was rare that she was able to invoke that kind of reaction. Inez had Amethyst's bottle of Wild Turkey in one hand and the bottle of vodka in the other, while the two bottles of Chilean wine were tucked under her arm.

"Nice," Bernie said as the bottles dropped out of Inez's hands and fell onto the linoleum.

Inez swayed for a moment, righted herself, and then, with the deliberation of the very drunk, carefully bent over and started picking the bottles up. "She owed me money," she explained. "I'm just taking what's mine."

"It's not yours," Bernie told her. "It belongs to Amethyst's estate."

290

"It's mine," Inez insisted.

"First blackmail and now burglary. You're doing well."

"What about you?"

"What about me?" Bernie repeated coolly.

Inez burped. "You're here, too."

"I was given the key," Bernie told her, marveling at how easily she lied.

Inez clutched the bottles to her chest and burped again.

"I guess I'm going to have to call the police," Bernie continued.

Inez continued clutching the bottles to her chest. Bernie wanted Inez to say something along the lines of "Oh no, you're not" so she in turn could say, "I will unless you tell me what I want to know."

But Inez just held on to the bottles. Bernie sighed. She hated when people didn't "get it." But that was the trouble with alcohol. It just made you stupid.

"Okay," she said. "Tell me what you know, and I won't call them."

Inez peered at her suspiciously. "Like what?" she asked.

Bernie wanted to scream, "What do you think I'm talking about?" but she didn't. Instead, she said, "Remember at the bar you told me you'd heard or seen something that got you fired. What was it?"

Inez's eyes narrowed. She swayed slightly. "Huh?"

"You were trying to blackmail her."

Inez burped. She nodded at the bottles with her chin. "Are you going to make me give these back?"

"Not if you tell me what I want to know."

"It wasn't anything really. I heard Amethyst talking on her cell phone."

"And?" Bernie prodded.

"And she was saying that she couldn't believe it, but it was finally happening."

"What?"

"I don't know. I didn't hear that part."

Bernie looked at Inez.

"Honestly," Inez cried. "She thought I did, but I didn't."

"Then why didn't you tell her that?"

Inez shrugged and clutched the bottles closer to her chest. "Because this was more fun. This way I could get back a little of my own."

"I don't believe you," Bernie told her. "I think I'm going to have to take the bottles back."

"Don't," Inez cried. "It's the truth. I wanted to get back at her. She treated me like dirt. We used to be at dinner parties together, and then she ruined my marriage, and I was working for her. Cleaning out her toilets. She asked for me specifically. Did you know that? That's what Ian said. I told him I didn't want to go, but he said I had to. Otherwise, I wouldn't have a job with him. Amethyst had me working for her just for spite. So I thought I could get a little bit back of my own." Inez stopped talking.

"Only things didn't work out that way."

"No, they didn't," Inez said. "But I'm glad she's dead. I'm only sorry *I* didn't kill her."

"You could have," Bernie pointed out.

"I didn't."

"Someone did."

"It wasn't me."

Bernie raised an eyebrow.

"It wasn't," Inez insisted.

"I don't know. Working for Amethyst. That could have been the thing that threw you over the edge."

"That's why I wanted the money," Inez cried.

"Yeah. But killing her would have been so much more rewarding."

Inez drew herself up. "Think whatever you want," she told Bernie. Then, clutching the bottles to her chest, she stumbled out the door.

A moment later Bernie heard a car engine turn over and realized that Inez shouldn't be behind the wheel of a car. But it was too late. By the time she got outside, Inez was weaving down the road.

CHAPTER 22

Amber had finished loading the last of the cartons with the pies snugly nestled in them into the van as Libby hurried toward the vehicle.

"You have everything in there, right?" Libby asked.

Amber nodded.

"You're sure?"

"Positive."

"The walnuts? The sprinkles?"

"I checked off the list you gave me."

Libby noticed she had a Cheshire cat grin on her face.

"What?" Libby said. "Is it the costume I'm wearing?"

"No. I think you look very nice."

Libby looked down at the blue taffeta number Bernie had convinced her to wear. She couldn't bend without getting stabbed in the side by a piece of plastic. She might as well be wearing her grandmother's corset.

How Bernie managed to work in this kind of getup was beyond her. The only saving grace was that the skirt was long enough, so no one could see her shoes. Thank god she was wearing sneakers. If she had to wear heels, she didn't know what she'd do. The truth was, she felt like an idiot. There was just no way around it.

"Are you sure I don't look ridiculous?" she asked Amber.

"Oh yes."

"Then what are you smiling at?"

"Nothing," Amber told her.

"You're smiling at something."

"You'll find out," Amber told her, and then, before Libby could ask her exactly what it was she was going to find out, Amber turned and headed back in the shop.

Under different circumstances, Libby would have followed her inside, but she wanted to get going, especially since she was going to have to unload the van by herself. Playing detective was all well and good, she decided as she slid behind the wheel of the van, but then she was always left to do the shop stuff while Bernie went off, running here and there.

She wondered how Bernie would like it if their positions were reversed. Not at all, Libby would wager. What she wanted to know was, why did she always have to be the responsible one? It really wasn't fair. She was tired of it. And while she was on the subject, she always did favors for Bernie — like wearing this stupid dress. "It'll just make things more festive," Bernie had said. Why had she listened to her? Especially since by now she knew better. The more she thought about everything, the angrier she got.

By the time she reached the Foundation, she was in a really bad mood, and seeing the fake skeletons dangling from the trees in those stupid cages Mark had rigged up didn't do anything to improve it. It just reminded her that if it hadn't been for Bernie, they wouldn't have taken that tour of the Haunted House, and someone else would have found Amethyst. She was still having nightmares about that. When was the last time Bernie had done something for her? That was what she would have liked to know.

Libby glanced around the dining room she would be serving in. She had never realized how big it was. Cavernous really. So was the kitchen. And quiet. So quiet she could hear the creak of a door shutting somewhere down the hall. Kitchens should be full of people cooking. Otherwise, they were just creepy. Except for A Taste of Heaven's kitchen. That was cozy.

She looked at the clock on the wall. It was five-fifteen, fifteen minutes before the Haunted House officially opened. The volunteers who were manning the show should have been here by now, which should have made her feel better. Of course, the volunteers manning the show had been here the last time, too, and precious lot of good it had done her then. She'd been on one side of the door, and they'd been on the other.

She looked out the window on the far side of the room. It was one of those big jobbies, the kind where both sides open up and you can step outside, only someone had sealed them shut, so you couldn't anymore — not that she would want to now. Raindrops were sliding down the panes. The sky had started darkening just as she had brought her last carton of cider in from the van.

Was something hitting the window? Is that the tapping she was hearing? She walked over to get a better look. There was nothing there except the branches from one of the maples. She walked back. From the looks of the tree branches, the wind was picking up. She just hoped the power didn't go off here.

Sometimes a strong wind did that. That was all she'd need. She should have really brought a flashlight along, just in case.

Libby shook her head to clear it. She took a deep breath. Several, in fact. Ever since she'd had that encounter, or whatever you wanted to call it, with . . . with . . . Libby refused to say her name, because Bernie was right on this score. Naming things called them forth. She didn't like being in this room by herself, which was something she'd never admit to Bernie.

Ever.

Because how could she be nervous if she didn't believe in stuff like that? That was — and here she was using one of Bernie's favorite words — an oxymoron. If she found out, Bernie would never let her forget how she felt. She'd ride her forever about it. It wasn't that Bernie was malicious. It was just that she didn't know when to stop. And things that Libby was sensitive about, Bernie wasn't. It was as simple as that.

The whole thing was ridiculous, anyway, Libby decided. There had to be another explanation for what had happened to her the other day, but for the life of her, Libby didn't know what it could be. She'd put in a lot of time thinking about it, and she still hadn't come up with anything — unless there was a secret passageway that led in here from somewhere else.

But in reality, that explanation didn't work, either. The whole thing, for want of a better word, had happened too fast. The . . . thing . . . okay . . . the manifestation couldn't have disappeared in the blink of an eye. And then there was the fact that Mark had said he'd experienced the same thing that Libby had. Three times. Once was enough for her. And Konrad and Curtis had said the same thing. But they were crazy, so they didn't count.

Libby sighed as she rearranged the vanilla cupcakes with the orange icing on the plate and put them toward the front. Then she took the chocolate cupcakes with chocolate frosting that she'd decorated with orange sprinkles and put them where the vanilla cupcakes had been. After that, she took the lemon squares and put them where the chocolate cupcakes had been.

She knew what she was doing was pointless, but she couldn't help it.

Libby pulled at her skirt. Then she tugged the bodice of her dress up. No matter what she did, her boobs kept popping out. Why, she asked herself again for the second time in as many minutes, had she let Bernie bamboozle her into wearing this? She supposed being a princess was better than being a bowl of cereal, but just barely.

She wasn't happy in costume. Especially in this one. She'd never liked dressing up, not even as a little girl. She was what she was. Anyway, it was too cold in here to be wearing something like this. She wanted to be back in her jeans and shirt. The only thing that helped was the fact that she didn't have those sleeves that trailed down and got into everything. She could just see green satin and waffle batter. It was not a pretty picture. Bernie had said Marvin would like the dress, but Marvin wouldn't even see it. He was off doing heaven knows what with her dad.

And speaking of Bernie, where was she? She should have been here half an hour ago. *Just like her,* Libby thought crossly. *Always late.* She never had any consideration for anyone else. She was reaching for her cell to call Bernie when she felt cold. Chilled to the bone, actually. *I need to put on a sweater,* Libby told herself. Hopefully, she'd left her zip-up fleece in the van. It might not look pretty, but it would definitely do the job. And then she felt something else. Something she remembered from the last time, the sensation of something crawling up and down her skin. She looked down. There

301

were goose bumps on her arms.

"Oh no," she moaned. "Please not again."

She sensed a crackling around her.

"Go away," she pleaded. "Just go away."

The crackling increased. She felt a tickling in her left ear. As if someone was breathing in it. She scrunched her eyes shut. *This is a bad dream,* she told herself. *Nothing more.* When she opened her eyes again, everything would be all right. It would be . . . What was her father's word? *Copacetic.* She closed her eyes tighter. Flashes of light exploded across her retinas. Then, unable to help herself, she opened her eyes again. She saw the room through a wave of energy.

"Help me," a voice said. Only the voice sounded as if it were coming from inside her head.

"I can't help you," Libby cried. Or had she thought it, too? She wasn't sure.

"You have to."

Libby wanted to move, but her legs weren't working properly. Her heart was beating so quickly, she felt light-headed, as if all the air was being sucked out of her lungs.

"Leave me alone," she cried.

"Find me. Find me." Now the voice seemed to be echoing in the air.

I shouldn't have eaten that pint of ice cream

for dinner, Libby told herself. *That's why this is happening to me.* She knew it was ridiculous, but for some reason, she found the thought comforting.

CHAPTER 23

Just when Libby thought she was going to pass out, whatever was holding her let go. Or maybe, she thought as she whirled around, she'd done this to herself. She wasn't really sure. Out of the corner of her eye, she caught a fleeting glimpse of a girl dressed in an oxford shirt and pleated skirt. It was the same girl as before. Dressed the same way, too.

Of course, she was. Like she'd have a change of clothes in the great hereafter, Libby thought. They were probably the clothes she died in. Or were they the clothes she was buried in? Libby was trying to decide when the girl vanished. Poof. Just like that. And there was nothing. Libby felt as if she was going to faint again. She closed her eyes and put her hands to her forehead. She was going crazy. She was having hallucinations. Which meant she was a schizophrenic. Or she had a brain tumor. Libby was trying to decide which was worse when she felt a tap on her shoulder. She screamed and spun around.

"Libby," Bernie said.

Libby looked at her sister and struggled to regain her composure. She had no luck. No luck at all.

"Are you all right?" Bernie asked her.

"I'm fine," Libby told her.

"Because you don't look all right."

"Well, I am."

"Who were you talking to?"

Libby squared her shoulders and tried to stand up straight when what she wanted to do was sit down. Lying down would be even better. She was suddenly exhausted. More than exhausted. Totally fried.

She moistened her lips with her tongue. "I wasn't talking to anyone," she lied.

"But I heard you outside," Bernie protested. "You were yelling at someone to leave you alone. That's why I came running in here."

Was I yelling that loud? Libby wondered. She didn't think she was, but if she was being honest with herself, she'd have to say she didn't remember. She didn't remember Bernie opening the door, either. A definite brain tumor. She'd be dead inside of a month. Two at the most.

"So who was it?" Bernie said when Libby didn't answer. "Who were you yelling at?"

"I wasn't yelling at anyone. You imagined it."

"I see." Bernie looked at Libby carefully, something Libby hated. "You look awfully pale." She reached over and took her hands. "And your hands are freezing."

"That's because I'm freezing in this dress," Libby countered while she pulled her hands out of Bernie's grasp and tucked them under her armpits to warm them up. "I'm going to get pneumonia standing here."

Bernie studied her sister's face some more. Finally, she said, "You saw her, didn't you?"

"I don't know what you're talking about," Libby replied.

"Yes, you do. What did she want?"

"She didn't want anything."

"Then you admit that you saw her."

Libby started walking back to the long tables they'd set up the first evening they'd worked here. "I didn't."

"Why are you lying?"

"I'm not lying."

"I told you. I heard you outside."

Libby turned to her. "I don't want to talk about this anymore. Is that clear?"

"Yes. But this could be important."

Libby started setting up the coffee machines. "This always has to be about you," she told her sister.

"Now you're making no sense whatsoever."

"So, you're telling me that I'm crazy on top of everything else?"

"That's not what I said at all, and you know it."

"And, by the way, I hate this dress," Libby told her. Now seemed as good a time as any to share that thought.

"Then why did you wear it?"

"Because you wanted me to."

Bernie snorted in exasperation. "You could have said no."

Libby shrugged and began measuring out the coffee. She knew that this whole thing with Bernie was about her being scared by — okay, she was going to come out and say it — being scared by Bessie Osgood's ghost. When she got scared, she had a bad habit of covering up by getting angry, and the more upset she became, the further away she pushed people. She closed the coffee bag with a snap and reached for the unleaded stuff. But that was the way she was. She was too old to change now. She knew Bernie was watching her. She wanted to say something to her, but somehow she couldn't bring herself to.

After another moment had gone by, Bernie said, "If that's the way you want to be, fine."

Bernie walked over to the table and began to stack the paper plates. Then she grabbed a couple of wicker baskets and arranged the napkins in one, a lot of napkins, because people tended to grab a handful of them at a time, and the plastic knives, forks, and spoons in the other. She liked that they were black. It had taken her a while to locate them at a reasonable price, but white would have ruined the ambience. Although in lots of countries, white was the color of death. But not here. Libby would come around when she was good and ready, Bernie knew. She just didn't know why Libby was making such a big deal about something like this.

A ghost appeared to you. So a ghost appeared to you. Especially this time of the year. Cultures all over the world recognized that this was the time of the year when the membrane that separated the living from the dead was at its thinnest. That was just the way it was. It was nothing to be ashamed of.

In fact, Bernie was slightly miffed that

Bessie Osgood hadn't appeared to her. Why pick someone who so obviously didn't want to have anything to do with you? The only reason she could come up with was that Libby had been in the room by herself the two times it had happened and Bernie had always been here with Libby.

For the next couple of minutes, the two sisters worked in silence. Finally, Libby looked up at the clock.

"Five minutes till we open," she said.

Bernie grinned. She recognized a peace offer when she saw one. "No one ever gets here before six-thirty or seven," she countered, extending her own olive branch.

Libby nodded. What Bernie said was true. Most people came after dinner. Actually, their busiest time was between seven-thirty and nine. Then they had lines out the door. But before that, things were pretty dead. *Dead* was a bad word. Things were quiet.

"I made extra pumpkin walnut muffins, so we shouldn't run out this time," Libby told Bernie as she began slicing up the pies.

"Good," Bernie replied. "Sorry I was a little late, but I found some interesting things at Amethyst's place."

Libby stopped slicing for a moment. "What were you doing at Amethyst's place?" she asked. As far as she knew, that wasn't in

309

the game plan.

Bernie told her sister about her encounter with Inez at R.J.'s.

"You're kidding me," Libby said when Bernie was done.

Bernie shook her head. "Nope. I'm not."

Libby went back to slicing. "Talk about rubbing salt in the wound, as Mom used to say. Boy, if that isn't a motive for killing someone, I don't know what is."

"I wonder if Inez is telling the truth."

Libby put the apple-cranberry pie aside and began on the apple crumb, which was difficult to cut neatly. "You mean about the whole thing being Amethyst's idea?"

"Yeah. Maybe the whole thing was Inez's idea. Maybe she wanted to work for Amethyst so she could get even."

Libby bisected the pie and then cut the halves into quarters. "Could be," she said thoughtfully.

"There's one way to find out," Bernie said, and she reached for her cell phone and dialed.

Libby continued cutting pies while her sister talked to Ian.

"Well, that was interesting," Bernie said when she hung up. "Evidently, Ian didn't even know that Inez was working for Amethyst. She was doing it off the books."

Libby put the knife down, reached over, took a half-moon cookie off the table, and began to eat it. "So we don't know who suggested what."

"And we probably won't know, either. But we do know that Inez was telling the truth about one thing."

"What's that?"

"That Amethyst was going away," said Bernie. "All of her clothes are gone. There's no product in the bathroom, and she was definitely a Spackle and spray kind of gal."

Libby poured herself a glass of cider to go with the cookie. By their nature, half-moon cookies, even hers, were somewhat dry. She'd never been able to find a recipe that kept their half-moon essence and was moist. It was one of those mysteries that still needed to be solved.

"I wonder where she went."

"Not that far, obviously."

"Or she went and came back," Libby said.

"Interesting." Bernie poured herself a cup of cider and took a sip. "This is really good," she commented. "Cotter should sell this in the stores."

"He can't, because it's unpasteurized. State law."

"But we can use it, right?" Bernie asked.

"Correct." Libby finished slicing the apple

crumb pie and went to put the knife away in its case. "Getting married?" Libby asked as she moved her sister's jacket and bag off the carton the knife belonged in.

Bernie's head shot up. "What do you mean?"

Libby lifted up the *Modern Bride* magazine that had been buried under Bernie's jacket.

"Oh that." Bernie laughed. "I got that from Amethyst's house, along with a newspaper."

Libby looked at the date. It was current. "You know," she said. "What if Amethyst was planning to get married?"

"That's a pretty big jump."

"I agree, but bear with me. You said that Inez overheard Amethyst telling someone it was really going to happen, and she was pretty excited. . . ."

Bernie nodded.

"And then she packed up everything and left. What if what she was excited about was getting married?"

"She could have been moving in with someone," replied Bernie.

"Then why *Modern Bride*?"

"Wishful thinking? A friend getting married?"

"Amethyst didn't have friends, and she never struck me as the kind of woman who engaged in wishful thinking."

Bernie had to admit that was true. "But she came back."

"Maybe things didn't work out," said Libby.

"That's an understatement if ever I heard one."

Libby nibbled on her cuticle for a moment. "Here's another idea. Maybe she went to speak to Ed Banks to see if she could hold the wedding at Lexus Gardens. It would be a great spot."

"And she did know him through the Foundation."

"Do we know that for a fact?" Libby asked.

"No. But it seems that they would have met at a dinner party or something like that."

"Can we find out?"

"We can ask Banks's personal assistant when he hits land," replied Bernie.

Libby brushed a strand of hair out of her eyes. "I don't know. You're saying the person who killed Amethyst killed Ed Banks to keep him from talking? That's a definite stretch."

"It's a link."

"A very weak link," said Libby.

"It's possible, but not probable," both

sisters said together. They laughed.

"Good old dad," Bernie said. She could hear him saying it now.

Libby and Bernie looked at each other.

"This is all supposition, you know," Bernie said.

"But it makes as much sense as anything else," Libby countered. "It makes more sense than having a ghost kill her."

"Bessie lied about that, remember? She just wanted to take credit for it."

Libby took the palm of her free hand and smacked herself on the forehead. "Excuse me. How could I forget?"

"Yeah. Curtis and Konrad are going to come up with the real killer's name now any day." Bernie reached over and took a pumpkin bar, broke it in half, and began to nibble on it. "Maybe Amethyst's husband killed her. You know, she married him under false pretenses, and he realized what he'd gotten himself into."

"An annulment would have been easier."

"But not nearly as satisfying," Bernie pointed out.

Libby laughed. "This is true." She finished her half-moon cookie and wiped the crumbs off her hands. "Do you think we should tell Dad what we're thinking?"

Bernie could just hear her father now. *And*

you think this based on what? A copy of Modern Bride *and something a hostile and unreliable witness, a witness who is a suspect in the homicide case, told you?* "No," she said. "I don't think so. At least not yet."

Libby tugged at the top of her dress again. "We could sort of float it by him."

"It would help if we had positive proof that Amethyst got married."

"I could go down to the town hall and check it out," said Libby.

"Go ahead. But the odds are that if she got married, she didn't get married here."

"True," Libby agreed. "She was fairly secretive."

"Fairly? Fairly?" Bernie opened her eyes so wide, she looked like a Kewpie doll. "She lived in Stanton, for heaven's sake. She didn't want anyone in Longely to know her business."

Libby returned to the subject of Ed Banks. "That's why Lexus Gardens would fit in so nicely."

"So go check."

"I intend to," Libby admitted. "Although if she did get married, knowing Amethyst, she probably did it somewhere like Palm Springs or Miami Beach. . . ."

"Or Paris or Rome."

"Or Morocco," Libby added while she

315

tugged at the top of her dress.

"Here. Let me fix that for you." And Bernie went over and pulled the back of Libby's dress up. "Better?" she asked.

Libby looked at her boobs. They were back where they should be. "Much better. Thank you."

Bernie studied her sister while she tapped her fingers against her chin.

"Are you still thinking about Amethyst?" Libby asked.

"No. I'm thinking that I'm sorry I made you wear this."

"You didn't make me. I could have said no. And, anyway, I think you're right. I think Marvin is going to like this."

"It might even make him jealous," Bernie said. "Which would be a good thing." When Libby didn't say anything, Bernie said, "Trust me on this. I'm the expert."

Libby laughed.

Bernie stuck out her hand. "Friends," she said.

"Friends to the end," Libby answered. They'd been saying that to each other for as long as Libby could remember.

"So," Bernie said. "Now that we're pals again, are you going to tell me what happened before, when you were yelling?"

"I wasn't yelling."

"Okay. Speaking loudly."

"You just don't give up, do you?" Libby said.

"No, I don't. It's the secret to my success."

"Yes, it is," Libby agreed.

And Libby gave her a blow-by-blow of what had occurred, which, if she was being honest with herself, she knew she was going to do all along, because eventually, she always told her sister everything.

CHAPTER 24

Libby looked at the clock on the wall. It was now a little past nine. Half an hour and she and Bernie could pack up and leave. Thank heavens. The traffic had been nonstop. Once the people had started coming in, they had never slowed down. Usually, people came in clumps, so you had a chance to take a break, but she hadn't even had time to run to the bathrooom.

In addition, her back was killing her from standing, and her wrists hurt from making all those waffles. She hoped she wasn't developing carpal tunnel syndrome. That would be all she'd need. Maybe she should go to the store and get those braces. See if those helped.

At least her feet weren't killing her. She didn't know how Bernie managed in her three-inch stilettos. Libby didn't know what she'd do if she couldn't wear her sneakers. If she had to wear Bernie's shoes, she'd be going barefoot and the hell with the health codes. She wanted to go home, get out of her dress, take a bath, and go to bed, but instead, she and Bernie were meeting Brandon and Marvin at R.J.'s.

When she'd protested, Bernie had said to her, "First of all, Marvin hasn't seen your dress, and second of all, it's the least you can do to thank him for driving Dad around all afternoon."

Bernie was right. Marvin was incredibly sweet, and she shouldn't take him for granted, which, she was the first to admit, she had a tendency to do. Still, she hoped it would be an early night.

She surveyed what was left on the table. The one bright note was that they didn't have much to take back to the shop. All the cider was gone, as were the pies and the fruit breads, except for the last piece of banana bread, which she was going to eat right now. They could store what was left of the apple compote in the fridge in the kitchen adjoining the dining room, though she'd have to make more tomorrow morning. The leftover waffle batter had got tossed, as had the coffee. Libby was thinking that she wished she could find a use for the leftover batter — it pained her to throw anything out — when she realized that Bernie was talking to her.

"Maybe there's something about you that's attracting Bessie Osgood," Bernie was saying.

"There's nothing about me that's doing that," Libby said firmly and dove into her bag for a piece of chocolate. She knew what Bernie was going to say, and she didn't want to go there.

Just the thought of what had happened was enough to give her the chills.

"You want a piece of chocolate?" Libby asked her sister. "I've got French made, estate harvested, unblended, eighty percent dark, or good old Hershey's Milk Chocolate Kisses."

"I'll take the Kisses," Bernie told her.

"Me too," Libby said.

You could say all you wanted about the joys of dark chocolate, Libby thought. You could go on and on about the notes of cinnamon and cranberry present in it, you could feel virtuous because dark chocolate was now considered good for you, but in times of stress, nothing worked like Hershey's Kisses. Somehow when they dissolved on your tongue, they took your worries with them. For a little while. But in this case, a little while was good enough.

Definitely good enough, Libby thought as

she hoisted her bag off the floor and began rummaging through it, although what she really needed was a milk-chocolate IV right now.

"What in heaven's name do you have in there?" Bernie asked her.

"Stuff. You know." Libby looked at Bernie's sleek clutch. "Or maybe you don't." And she opened her bag as wide as she could and peered in. "Where is that bag of Kisses?" she muttered. "I know I have it somewhere."

"You have a whole bag?" Bernie asked.

"Well," Libby said defensively, "you never know when a chocolate emergency will arise."

"Like the Hudson River will overflow, and we'll be stranded here for weeks."

"Exactly," Libby said. "Or we get caught in a blizzard." She started removing things. Out came a pocket knife, a wallet, sunglasses, a bottle of aspirin, a bottle of vitamin B complex, a screwdriver. "So that's where it was," Libby said as she put the screwdriver down on the table. "I spent twenty minutes looking for this yesterday." Her eyes widened. A moment later she drew out a brown paper bag. "I know I didn't put this in here." And then she remembered. "Amber."

"Amber what?"

"Amber said she had a surprise for me." Libby felt instantly guilty. Amber was probably waiting for her to call.

"A surprise from Amber is not necessarily a good thing," Bernie observed.

"Don't make me more nervous than I already am," Libby told her. "It's been a bad enough day already."

Bernie snorted. "Such a delicate flower."

"I'm serious. What with everything that's going on, I'm a nervous wreck. I think I need an antianxiety drug."

"No. What you need is to get laid."

"Bernie!" Libby wailed.

"What's wrong with what I said?"

"That's personal."

"No, it's not. It's true. It's true for everyone. You mean, it's not? You mean, you don't feel more relaxed afterwards?"

When Libby didn't answer, Bernie decided to change the subject. This was another topic Libby didn't like to talk about, and they'd had enough arguments for one day.

"What's in there?" Bernie asked, motioning to the brown paper bag with her chin.

"Let's see," Libby said. She gingerly opened the bag and peered inside.

"Well?" Bernie demanded.

"It's the puzzle box Felicity gave you." And Libby lifted it out.

"Why did Amber give it to you?"

Libby shook her head. "Don't know. Dad left it downstairs on the kitchen counter. Maybe Amber wanted to make sure it didn't get lost."

"Why should she care?" Bernie asked.

Libby shrugged her shoulders.

"I'm going to call her," Bernie said, reaching for her cell phone. But her call went straight to voice mail. Amber must have turned off her phone, Bernie decided. So, she left a message to call her and hung up. "She's probably with that yo-yo she's seeing."

"Her taste in men isn't very good, is it?" Libby noted as she spotted a piece of paper in the bottom of the bag. *Probably a sales receipt,* she thought as she took it out.

"No, it's not," Bernie agreed as her sister unfolded the paper.

"It's a note," Libby said. She read it quickly. "It's instructions for opening up the puzzle box. Amber must have figured it out."

"Impressive," Bernie said. She certainly hadn't been able to, and neither had her dad or Clyde.

Libby took the puzzle box and looked at

it. It was a little bigger than the palm of her hand. The top was made of three pieces of dark wood; the bottom, of two. The pieces of wood fit together so neatly that you had to look carefully to see where they were joined. Libby smoothed the paper with the edge of her hand and read the instructions.

"Press on the far left-hand piece once." She did. "Then tap lightly on the far right piece." She did that, too. "Then tap the bottom far right piece of wood, and the box should open." Libby looked up at Bernie. "Here goes." She rapped once, and the top flew open.

Libby and Bernie peered in. Inside the box was a piece of paper folded into a tiny square. Bernie lifted it out and began unfolding it.

"What is it?" Libby asked as Bernie finished opening it.

Bernie flattened the paper out with the side of her hand. The writing was so fine, she was having trouble reading it. She brought the paper closer. "It's a map," she said.

"A map of what?"

"Maybe the old Peabody School. I'm not really sure."

Libby took the paper out of Bernie's hand and studied it. "The ink is brown."

"It's from a fountain pen."

"I know that," said Libby.

"I thought you were asking."

"No. I was commenting."

Bernie took the map out of Libby's hand and refolded it. "We should show this to Dad. He'll probably know."

Libby was about to agree when Bernie's cell rang.

"It's Amber," Bernie mouthed after she'd answered it. "Yes," she said into her cell. "We just opened the box. Yes. No. Libby forgot. Well, it was busy from the time she walked in here. I'm sorry your feelings are hurt. No. She doesn't mean to be insensitive."

"Insensitive?" Libby squeaked. "I'm insensitive?"

"Sssh," Bernie whispered and went back to listening to Amber. "Yes. We were very surprised. And impressed. How did you manage to figure it out?" She nodded as she listened to Amber's explanation.

"What is she saying?" Libby asked.

Bernie held up her hand as a signal for silence and went on talking to Amber. "So you know where the map is pointing to?" Bernie was silent for a few more moments as she listened to Amber talking. "Interesting," she said as she hung up. Then she turned to Libby as she put her cell back in her clutch and folded it over.

"We're meeting her and the twins in front of the Foundation in half an hour," Bernie told her. "By that time, everyone should have cleared out from here."

"They'll be gone in ten minutes."

"There are always stragglers. Anyway, it'll take everyone a little time to get here."

Libby took the bag of chocolate Kisses out of her bag and poured several into the palm of her hand. She had a feeling she was going to need them.

"How does Amber know where to go?" Libby asked.

"She looked at the old plans for the Peabody School. I guess the twins have them," Bernie explained before Libby could inquire.

"How does she know the twins?"

"They live on the same block."

"It figures," Libby said morosely. She could see her bath and her bedtime receding further and further into the distance. "What about Marvin and Brandon?"

"I'll call them now. They can meet us there. We'll go for a drink later."

Libby unwrapped two chocolate Kisses and popped them into her mouth.

"What is the matter with you?" Bernie

demanded.

"I'm tired."

"Aren't you excited to see what we're going to find?"

"Of course," Libby lied.

"No, you're not."

"Have it your way."

Libby popped another two Kisses into her mouth. It was going to be even colder and wetter out there now than it had been when she'd come in, and she was dressed in this stupid dress. She didn't even have a warm coat with her. Bernie had insisted she use her mom's paisley shawl instead. She'd loved it since she was a little girl, and it was definitely more elegant than her black, puffy coat. But sometimes elegance wasn't everything, although she doubted she could convince Bernie of that.

Libby knew what was going to happen. She was going to get pneumonia, and then she wouldn't be able to work and the shop would close and they'd be out on the street. And on top of that, they wouldn't find anything tonight. She, Libby, would die of pneumonia for nothing.

"I don't know," Bernie said.

"You don't know what?" Libby demanded. Her sister was looking at her and shaking her head in that particularly smug, irritating way she had.

"If you're like this now, I don't know what you'll be like when you're fifty."

Since Libby couldn't think of a sufficiently cutting reply, she decided that it was better to say nothing at all.

CHAPTER 25

Bernie and Libby were five minutes early for their rendezvous, but Amber was even earlier. They immediately spotted her in the parking lot right behind the Foundation. Hers was the only car in the lot, but even if it weren't, it would have stood out like a lighthouse beacon.

Wonder Woman was a neon green Beetle with big white flowers on the doors and the words FLOWER POWER printed across the hood. And then there was Amber herself. "Not exactly inconspicuous," Bernie had said to her sister. But she had to admit Amber had style, and that was a good thing. On the other hand, given the circumstances, more circumspection might have been better. Before coming here, Amber had changed out of her work clothes and was now wearing black-and-white striped leggings, motorcycle boots, a red baby-doll dress, and a black leather jacket.

"I like the hair," Libby said to Bernie as Amber came galumphing toward them. Since she'd seen her at the store, Amber had dyed her hair a bright yellow and braided it.

Bernie got out of the van. "Very colorful," she commented.

Libby rubbed her arms and drew the shawl around her as tightly as she could. "At least it's better than the blue she had last month."

"I kinda liked the blue," Bernie confessed. "In fact, I'm thinking of dying my hair that color myself."

"You wouldn't," Libby said.

"Why not?" Bernie asked. "I can always change it if I want to."

But before Libby could answer, Amber had reached them. The metal piercings in her nose and eyebrow gleamed in the glow of the security lights.

"This is so-o-o cool," Amber squealed, reminding Bernie of a five-year-old about to go into an ice-cream store. "I'm so excited."

"I never would have guessed," Libby said dryly. If she didn't get pneumonia from being out in this weather, it would be a miracle.

Bernie kicked her in the shin.

"Ouch," Libby cried.

"Sorry about that," Bernie said. "I must have tripped. Where is everyone?"

Amber pulled on one of her braids. "They're coming," she replied. "Curtis and Konrad had to stop and get some batteries."

"They're recording this?" Libby asked.

Amber gave her a look that clearly said that she was too dumb to live. "Shite, mate. Sodding right they are."

"How silly of me." Libby had thought Amber was through with her Brit period, but evidently she was wrong.

A moment later she heard the sound of engines approaching. Then two cars came roaring out from behind the scrim of tall trees that hid the Foundation and headed for Bernie and Libby's van.

For a second, Libby panicked, because she thought they were security, but then she realized the cars belonged to Brandon and to Konrad and Curtis. They both screeched to a halt at the same time. Marvin and Brandon jumped out of one car, while Konrad and Curtis jumped out of the other.

"The cavalry has arrived," Bernie said to Libby out of the side of her mouth.

"So it would seem," Libby agreed.

"What's a cavalry?" Amber asked.

Suddenly, Bernie felt very old. "I'll explain

later," Bernie told her.

Konrad beamed at everyone. "I'm totally psyched," he said. Then he dove back in his car and came out with a tape deck, which he handed to Curtis. He went back in again and came out with a camera. "Infrared," he explained.

"Cool," Amber repeated.

"Very," Brandon agreed.

Watching Amber, Bernie thought that she now understood the expression "grinning from ear to ear."

Libby looked at Marvin. She could tell from the expression on his face that he had the same misgivings about this that she had, a fact that comforted her, because everyone else seemed to think that what they were doing was fine.

"Nice dress," Marvin told Libby. "I especially like the neckline." And he moved both eyebrows up and down.

Libby grinned; then she caught Bernie's eye and stopped smiling. Okay. So Bernie was right about a few things, mostly men and clothes. She'd grant her that, but she wasn't going to give her the satisfaction of showing it.

"Be right back," Marvin said, and he trotted off to his car.

A few seconds later, he returned with a

jacket under his arm. He handed it to Libby. "Here," he said.

Libby put it on gratefully.

"So," Brandon was asking Amber, "how did you solve the puzzle?"

Amber shrugged as everyone gathered around her to hear the answer. "I just like to fool around with stuff like that, you know." She nodded in Bernie's and Libby's direction. "I asked your dad if I could give it a try, and he told me to go ahead."

Bernie buttoned up the sweater she was wearing over her she-devil costume. "Did you tell him that you'd figured it out?"

"No. I thought it would be neater if we could show him what we found," said Amber.

"If there's anything there," Libby said.

"Why shouldn't there be anything there?" Amber demanded.

"Well, because whatever it is has been . . . in its place . . . for a long time. Things happen," Libby pointed out.

"Like what?" asked Amber.

"Like stuff," Bernie said.

The sound of a car pierced their conversation.

"You know what I think?" Brandon said. "I think we should get on with it before security comes around."

"He's right," Konrad agreed. "Mark wouldn't be happy if he saw us here."

"Don't be stupid," Curtis said. "Of course, he'd be happy —"

Libby interrupted. "So where do we go?" She had no intention of standing there while they argued.

"I'll show you," Amber said, and she danced off in front of them.

Marvin began walking. "It must be nice to be young," he remarked.

"You are young," Libby said as she walked beside him.

Marvin beamed.

"Hey, Konrad," Brandon called.

Konrad turned slightly.

"You expect to get anything with that stuff?" Brandon pointed to the tape deck and the camera.

"Yeah. Absolutely," said Konrad. "It's almost Halloween. Everyone is out. This is the time when the dead come visiting."

"So Halloween is sort of like New Year's Eve for the dead? Party time," Brandon asked.

Curtis laughed. "Yeah. That's exactly right. And this is something about Bessie, so she'll probably be there, too."

Boy, I hope not, Libby thought. She'd had enough of her to last for a long time. Libby gave a short prayer that if Bessie was around, she'd pick on someone else for a change.

"Where are we going?" Libby asked.

Everyone shrugged.

"I'm following Amber," Konrad said.

"Me too," Curtis said.

Somehow that didn't make Libby feel any better. After all, Amber was the person who seriously believed in past-life regression and guided dreaming, and based all of her decisions on the I Ching. But then who was she to talk? She'd seen a ghost. She'd done more than see. She'd talked to it. What did that make her?

"How'd you get the plans?" Bernie asked Curtis.

"Mark gave them to us. He said they might help us get . . . situated vis-à-vis the whole recording situation. Well, they're not really plans. They're more like sketches we made from the plans, because he wouldn't let us take the plans out of the building, which really is okay, because they're really, really large, and they'd be hard to carry around."

"Are your sketches to scale?" Marvin asked.

"What's scale?" Konrad replied.

Marvin looked at Libby and raised an

eyebrow. Libby gave an infinitesimal nod back. Now she was even more dubious about the whole endeavor than she'd been before.

"How much farther?" Bernie asked.

Amber turned around and pointed. "We're almost there."

Bernie looked around. There was nothing she could see that looked anything like what was on the map. "I don't get it," she said.

Amber asked for the map from the puzzle box; then she laid the map and Konrad and Curtis's sketches side by side on the bench next to the Foundation's front door.

"It's simple," she said. "See." She pointed to the right wing. "That's the girls' section, and the left wing is the boys'."

"How do you know this?" Libby demanded. "It doesn't say that on the map."

"I just know," replied Amber.

"How do you *just know?*" asked Libby.

Amber put her hands on her hips and narrowed her eyes. "I dreamt it, okay?"

Libby snorted.

"See," Amber cried. "I knew if I told you, you'd get all weird on me."

"I'm not weird," said Libby.

"But you wouldn't have wanted to come," said Amber.

"You're right," Libby told her. "I wouldn't

have, but we're here now, so let's get it over with." *But not for the reason you think,* she silently added.

Amber hesitated for a moment before pointing up to the second floor. "See the windows?"

Bernie looked up. "And Bessie Osgood stood there?"

"Yes," Amber said. "She liked to watch everyone coming and going."

Libby zipped up Marvin's jacket. It was getting colder by the minute. "And that's where she was pushed from?"

"That happened on the other side." Amber pointed to one of the sketches. "That's where the French doors are."

Bernie leaned in closer. She could vaguely, and she meant vaguely, make out the drawing. "I don't suppose anyone brought a flashlight?" she asked.

Everyone shook their heads.

"Use your cell," Brandon suggested.

Bernie tried, but the light was minimal, certainly not enough to read by. She flipped her cell phone closed and slipped it back in her clutch.

Amber turned around and pointed over to the maple tree about twenty feet away. "In my dream, I saw someone burying something right by the base of that tree."

Konrad and Curtis ran over to where Amber was pointing.

"Here?" Konrad asked.

Amber nodded.

Konrad fumbled with the tape deck for a moment. Then he clicked on the switch. "Are you here, Bessie?" he asked.

Brandon moved next to him. "Is she answering?"

Curtis shot him a dirty look. "We won't know that till we play it back."

"I'm surprised you can hear anything on that tape deck. Where did you get that thing?" said Brandon.

Konrad put his finger to his lips. "Sssh. You'll scare her."

"How can you scare a ghost?" Brandon asked.

"They have feelings just like we do," Curtis said.

Brandon was just about to ask him how he knew that when Amber let out a small shriek. Everyone jumped.

"What is it?" Libby cried.

Amber put her hand up to her mouth. "Shite. I gotta go back to Wonder Woman. I forgot the shovel."

"Wonder Woman?" Marvin asked Libby as Amber dashed away.

"That's her car," Libby explained. She

338

rubbed her arms. Even with Marvin's jacket, she was still cold. "This is silly. I think we should go."

"Go on," Bernie told her. "I'll stay."

Libby sighed. Somehow Bernie telling her to go made it harder to do just that. Go figure. She was still debating with herself what to do when Amber came back with a shovel. Libby looked at it carefully.

"That looks like the one we keep by the shop's back door," Libby observed.

"That's because it is," Amber told her. "I figured you wouldn't mind."

Amber marched over to the tree and started digging. Spadefuls of dirt began to fly. Bernie stepped back to avoid getting hit.

"Maybe you should slow down," Bernie told her as a hole began to appear.

Amber wiped some dirt off her cheek. "Why?"

"Well, whatever is down there might be fragile . . . ," said Bernie.

Amber finished the sentence. "And I don't want to damage it."

"Exactly," Brandon said. "Here. Let me do this." And he knelt down next to where she'd been digging and began to scoop the dirt away with his hands while Amber peered over his shoulder.

Everyone moved in closer.

Brandon looked up. "People," he said, "you have to move back. You're blocking whatever light there is."

Everyone moved back half an inch except for Amber. She knelt next to Brandon and began scooping the dirt out with her hands as well.

"Found something," Amber cried after sixty seconds had gone by. Then she corrected herself. "Sorry. It's a tree root."

Brandon grunted and kept digging.

"Maybe your dream is wrong," Libby said to Amber. "Have you ever considered that?"

"I doubt it," Amber replied. "I doubt it very much."

"But how do you know?" asked Libby.

"I just do. That's all. Don't you dream?" said Amber.

"Not like that," Libby lied, trying not to think of her recent dreams.

"It must be cool to have precognition," Bernie observed.

"Pre . . . what?" Amber asked.

Bernie was about to explain when she saw Brandon stiffen. *Like a hunting dog catching a scent,* she thought. "Did you find something?" she asked.

"I think so," Brandon replied.

Everyone leaned forward to watch Brandon as he began clearing the dirt away.

Amber helped. Their movements became faster. No one spoke, not even Konrad or Curtis. Libby could see their breaths drifting upward in the air. The only sound was the whoosh of the tape deck.

"I think it's a box," Amber said.

Brandon lifted it out.

"It's definitely a box," Bernie said.

Amber got up and brushed the dirt off her leggings. "Wow," she said. "This is just like a movie. You know, like the *Curse of the Maya* or something like that. We open the box and the evil spirit comes out and we all die slow, lingering deaths. Wouldn't that be cool?"

"Not really," Brandon said as he straightened up and carried the box over to the bench in front of the Foundation.

"But it would be exciting," Amber said.

"Only in the movies," Brandon replied as he laid the box down.

"It looks like an old-fashioned cash box," Marvin noted. "My dad still has one of those in his drawer. He keeps his stamps in it."

"That's exactly what it is," said Brandon as he flipped up the latch that held the box closed. He was surprised that it opened as easily as it did. He'd expected he'd need a small crowbar and a can of WD-40 because it would be rusted shut. But it wasn't.

Later, when Bernie recalled the event, she would say, "It was almost as if Bessie wanted us to open it," but right now she was too excited to focus on anything but Brandon opening the box. She leaned in as he opened the lid. A smallish something lay wrapped in a paisley scarf.

"I guess we're still standing," Marvin said. "So much for the curse."

Amber picked a leaf off the hem of her dress. "Well, there could still be one. Only we won't know about it for a month or so."

Amber was about to say more when Libby pointed. "That scarf looks just like the shawl I'm wearing," she cried out.

Bernie looked up at her mom's shawl, which was draped over the jacket Libby was wearing, and then back at the scarf in the box. "You're right. It does," she said.

Libby frowned. "That's very weird."

"It was probably a popular pattern back then," Bernie said as she turned her attention back to Brandon while he slowly untied the knots that were holding the scarf together.

There were three of them.

"Three is a magic number," Amber told everyone.

"We know," Bernie said as Brandon untied

the last of the knots. Then he carefully opened up the scarf.

A small leather journal lay in the center.

Bernie reached over and took it out of Brandon's hand. It smelled of earth and mold. The brown leather cover was blank. She unwound the cord that bound the book together and gently opened the cover and read the title page. It was printed in a neat hand.

"This is Bessie Osgood's journal," Bernie read. Underneath the title, in larger letters, Bessie had written "Keep Out" and had underlined the sentence three times.

"Wow," Libby said to Amber. "Maybe you were right, after all."

And then it occurred to Libby that maybe this was what Bessie Osgood had meant when she'd asked Libby to find her. She certainly hoped it was, because then Bessie would leave her alone. Even if Libby hadn't found the diary, she was present when it was found. That had to count for something, right?

Bernie put her hand out. "I felt a raindrop."

"Me too," Konrad said.

Libby looked up. The sky was even darker than it had been. She could see the clouds overhead. A raindrop fell on her forehead and ran down her cheek.

"It's going to pour," she predicted.

A second later there was a clap of thunder, and the sky opened up. Everyone ran for their cars.

CHAPTER 26

Sean sighed as he looked at the tiles he'd just been about to put down on the Scrabble board. The word would have been a twenty-five pointer.

"Saved by the kids," he told Clyde as his daughters, their boyfriends, Amber, Konrad, and Curtis came trooping into the living room. He didn't know what this was about, but it was definitely something big, although getting a twenty-five-point word with three letters was pretty big, too.

Clyde snorted and finished the cream-cheese brownie he was eating. "You'll use any excuse to keep from losing, won't you? I bet you arranged this whole thing."

Sean leaned forward and tapped the board with his index finger. "Believe what you want if it makes you feel better," he told Clyde as Bernie came over and handed him a leather-bound journal.

He ran his hand over the cover while

everyone crowded around him. They were close enough so that he could smell the damp and the night air on their clothes, which was way too close for him.

"What is this?" he asked Bernie. "You look like the cat that swallowed the canary."

"It's Bessie's journal," Bernie said. "We just dug it up."

"Literally?" asked Sean.

"Yes," Brandon said and showed Sean his hands. There was dirt underneath his fingernails.

Sean raised an eyebrow. "Did you now?" he asked Bernie. "Why don't you fill me in."

Bernie told him about the puzzle box, the map, and how they dug up the journal.

"You didn't ask me to come?" Sean said.

Bernie gave an apologetic shrug. "We didn't want to disturb your game."

Right, Sean thought as he turned to Amber, who was looking a little worried about what he was going to say. They just hadn't wanted the old man along. Too much trouble.

But Sean didn't say that, because that would have been whining. Instead, he told Amber she'd done a good job. But then he went and ruined it all by telling her that she should have come and told him first.

"But I . . . ," Amber protested.

346

Sean held up his hand. "No need to explain, and I really am very impressed. I couldn't open the box, and heaven only knows I tried."

Two dots of color appeared on Amber's cheeks. She plucked at one of her braids. "It wasn't anything."

"No, it was," Bernie told her.

Sean watched as Amber looked down at the floor and dug a little hole in the carpet fibers with her toe. "Is anything the matter?" he asked.

Amber paused for a moment.

"Tell us," Sean urged.

Amber looked down and picked a wet leaf off her legging. She hesitated for another moment, and then she blurted, "The truth is, I didn't figure it out. I got the solution off the Web site of the people who made the puzzle box. I guess I should have told you before, but I kind of liked you thinking I was this really smart person, and I figured that this way you'd let me come along."

"Hey," Bernie said. "You are really smart."

Amber studied the toes of her boots. "No, I'm not. Everyone says that."

"You were smart enough to go online. That was more than any of us did. And we wouldn't have hired you if we didn't think you were intelligent."

Amber brightened. "Really?" she asked.

"Really," Libby replied.

Amber was about to say something else when Sean interrupted. "Ladies, enough already with the confidence building." He wanted to say "bullshit" but managed to restrain himself. "I want to know what the journal says."

"We don't know," Bernie said.

"What do you mean you don't know?" Clyde and Sean both said at the same time.

"Just what I said," Bernie snapped.

"You haven't read it?" Sean asked. He couldn't believe it. That would have been the first thing he would have done.

"No, Dad," Libby told him. "We haven't. We wanted to wait till we could read it with you. We figured since you weren't there when we found it, you'd want to be there when we read it."

Sean ducked his head so no one would see how touched he was by the gesture. "That's ridiculous," he barked. "You shouldn't have waited for me."

Bernie grinned. "I figured that's what you would say."

Never could fool her, Sean thought as he handed the journal back to Bernie.

"Why don't you read it out loud?" Sean suggested.

"Good plan," Konrad said. "Then we can play our tapes, too. I bet we got some really good stuff, like maybe Bessie telling us how mad she is that we're reading her journal."

Not if I can help it, Sean thought as Marvin said, "Super."

Sean glared at Marvin, but Marvin was too busy brushing the water out of his hair to notice.

"That's what I'm worried about," Amber cried out. "Maybe we should have an exorcism."

"We'll see," Libby said as she guided Marvin to the sofa.

"Because I know an exorcist," Amber said. "I can call him if you like."

Libby stole a look at her dad. He didn't look happy. She couldn't imagine what he'd look like if they actually got an exorcist up here. He'd probably shoot him.

"Maybe later," Libby told Amber.

Then Libby sat down next to her father, while Bernie sat in the armchair, and Brandon perched himself on one of its arms. Instead of sitting on one of the wooden spindle-back chairs, Amber plopped herself on the floor, and after a moment Konrad and Curtis sat down next to her.

"This is pretty exciting," Marvin said. "I wonder what we're going to find."

"The treasure map to the Templar's gold. I'm kidding," Sean said quickly before Marvin could say anything else. He nodded toward Bernie. "Okay. Let's see what this baby has to tell us."

Everyone leaned forward as Bernie opened the book and began to read.

CHAPTER 27

"Dear Diary," Bernie began. "Mommy gave this to me because she said it would make things easier. I can put down everything that I would say to her. That way I won't be lonely. I don't want to go to the Peabody School, but Mommy says that Rose says that's a better place for me. She says I'm smart, and I should go to college and do all that stuff that she never had a chance to do. I think I'm going to miss everyone, but Mommy says I'll make lots of new friends. She says that everyone there is really excited I'm coming. I'm taking my teddy with me just in case."

Bernie stopped reading and looked up at her dad. "Do you think Rose is Mom?" she asked.

"Definitely," Sean said immediately. Had to be. It would be too big a coincidence otherwise.

Libby thought back to the scarf the journal

had been wrapped in. "I wonder if Mom gave Bessie that scarf?"

Clyde put down the brownie he'd been eating. "What scarf?"

"This scarf," said Libby as she leaned over and took a scarf out of her backpack. "It has the same pattern as one of Mom's shawls."

Clyde turned to Sean. "Any idea on that?"

Sean shook his head. "I worked a lot in those days. Rose took care of the social end of stuff."

"Did you ever meet Bessie Osgood?" asked Clyde.

"I met her mother once," said Sean. "I remember Rose and she were having tea. But that was about it. I was coming back after pulling a fifteen-hour shift." He turned to Clyde. "The Anson robbery."

Clyde nodded. "I remember."

"I went straight up to bed," said Sean.

"No wonder Mom never talked about Bessie," Bernie mused.

Libby sneezed. She was definitely going to get sick. "I don't get what you're saying."

Bernie sighed. "I'm saying that considering what happened, I bet she felt guilty about being the one that convinced her mother to send her there."

Libby bit her cuticle. "Well, I certainly

would have."

"Me too," Bernie allowed.

Sean nodded at Bernie. "Read some more."

Bernie turned back to the book. "The next entry is dated four days later. *Dear Diary, I want to go home.*" Bernie looked up. "The word *home* is underlined four times."

She went back to reading. "No one here is very nice. The food sucks. We've had macaroni and cheese, pineapple, and peanuts four nights in a row. For dessert, we had Jell-O. I asked for ice cream, and the lady in charge of the food said that was a special occasion thing. At home I can have ice cream every night!

"I called Mom, and she promised to bring me some lasagna and my favorite brownies. The ones she makes with walnuts and tiny marshmallows on top. The only good thing is I like my classes. I get to write stories in English, and we have a class in Greek mythology. I started reading the stories already. The assignment sheet said we should read the first one, but I went ahead and read the first four.

"My roommate says I'm stupid. But I think she's pretty dumb. She never studies or anything. I guess she doesn't want to be here, either. Amethyst says her mom made her come, too, so that means we have something in common. But I don't think so. She was really mean to the cleaning lady when she came in to wash the floor this afternoon, during free time. I tried to tell her not to do that, but she wouldn't listen to me. I should have told her my mom cleans houses. I don't know why I didn't." Bernie looked up. "I didn't realize they roomed together," she said.

Sean ate the last of his brownie. "Me either. Go on," he said.

Bernie continued on to the next page. "Not much here," she said. "Bessie's mom dropped by with some homemade brownies and promised she'd be back in two days. They're reading *Macbeth* in English class, which Bessie loves. She's already memorized act one, scene one."

"I remember doing that," Libby said.

"Me too," replied Bernie. "I guess nothing much has changed. Anyway, she really doesn't like her math teacher, and she has to write a report for social studies on the Revolutionary War. And she says, 'Teddy is feeling very, very sad.' Poor thing. But she doesn't say why."

Marvin flicked a drop of water off his sleeve. "I think I can guess."

Bernie moved her finger down to the bottom of the page. "Listen. This is interesting. She says, 'The kids say there are shadow people here.' "

"Shadow people?" Libby echoed.

"That's another name for ghosts," Konrad said.

Bernie continued. "I think I might have seen one, because I saw a lady walking down the hall. She was dressed in funny clothes. The lady that lives in the corner room said not to worry, that it's fine, and that she won't hurt me. I haven't told anyone else, because I don't want them to think I'm crazy."

"She probably saw Esmeralda," suggested Curtis.

"Bad enough to be in boarding school, let alone a haunted one," Libby commented.

"I don't know," Bernie commented. "It could be kind of cool."

"I'm not so sure about the boarding school part," Amber said.

Libby watched enviously as Amber straightened her legs out, leaned over and grasped her shoes with her hands, pulled her body down to her knees for a moment, then let go.

"When my mom was sick, I had to go to my aunt's for a month when I was in high school," Amber said. "It sucked."

Sean made a hurry-it-along motion with his hand to Bernie. "Does Bessie say anything else about Amethyst?"

Bernie started leafing through the pages. "Here's something. I went home for the weekend. I didn't want to leave, so Mom made my favorite cupcakes — white cupcakes with white buttercream frosting and sprinkles on top — to take with me. I put them in my cubby and went to give Mr. Marak, he's the headmaster, the envelope my mom gave me. When I came back, Amethyst and her retarded friends were eating the cupcakes.

"I told her that wasn't nice, and she started to laugh. I started crying, and she told me she could do whatever she wanted, because no one cares about me. I hate her. Hate her. Hate her. I called my mom and told her, and she said to forget it. She said she'd bake me some new ones.

"I said I didn't want to stay here anymore, and she said she'd speak to Mr. Marak about getting me another roommate, but I know that's not going to happen, because I heard him say to someone that they were full up. I started crying on the phone and then Mom started crying and that made me feel worse. She said I'd have to make the best of things for now and that I could come home for good if I wanted at Christmas."

Bernie looked up. "I wonder what was happening with her mom?"

Sean thought for a moment. "If I'm not mistaken, I think her dad lost his job. He worked for the power company. And he went to California to help someone he knew put up a house, which meant Bessie's mom had to do more cleaning jobs. Did Bessie say anything to anyone about this?"

Bernie shook her head. "If she did, it doesn't say so here. Here she says she read *The Catcher in the Rye.*" Bernie's finger stopped moving. "Oh dear. Something happened to teddy."

"What?" Marvin asked.

"He disappeared," said Bernie. "Bessie says Amethyst told her the shadow woman took it, but she doesn't believe her. . . ."

"Go, Bessie," Brandon cried.

"She thinks Amethyst did it, but she can't prove it," said Bernie. "She says she cried for hours, but she doesn't want to tell her mom, because she doesn't want to upset her even more. Also, she thinks she's fat, and all the other girls are making fun of her because of her clothes. She says, 'Amethyst said I'm fat like a pig and that if I had a circle pin, I would have to wear it on the right side, because no boys want anything to do with me.' "

"That's terrible," Libby protested, thinking back to her own high school days. No one had said anything like that, but she'd always felt that they'd thought it.

"Don't kids at boarding schools have to wear uniforms or something?" Brandon asked.

"Evidently not here," Bernie told him. "And, anyway, you're missing the point."

"No, I'm not," Brandon said. "I'm just asking a question."

"You know," Konrad interjected, "Bessie said something on tape about how she wanted a white blouse with a Peter Pan collar and a pleated skirt, and how the girls were being mean to her. You want to hear?"

"I think we need to finish reading the diary first," Sean told him. "We don't want to mix our media."

Curtis frowned. "What does that mean?"

Sean nodded to Bernie. "She'll explain."

"It means," Bernie said as she marked her place in Bessie's journal with her thumb, "that we're going to do one thing at a time, and when we're done with this, we'll listen to the tape." She looked up and caught her father's eye. "Tomorrow. Tomorrow we'll listen. We'll be too tired tonight to give it the attention it deserves." She went back to reading the journal before Konrad and Curtis could protest.

"Okay. More trouble with Amethyst. She stole Bessie's favorite pair of socks. They were pink and gray, and her mom had knitted them for her. But she got an A on her math test. She guesses the math teacher isn't so bad. She loves her mythology course and is excited that she's going to take Latin next semester. Her teacher rcad one of her stories in class and told her she should submit it to the school magazine, which she's going to do. So she's doing well academically, but she still hasn't made any friends, and she really wants to go home."

Bernie turned the page. "Here's something." And she cleared her voice and began to read. "We have dance lessons tomorrow in the gym. They're going to teach us all the steps because we have a mixer in two weeks. I don't want to go, because no one is going to want to dance with me, because I'm fat. Amethyst says I'm too clumsy to learn how to dance, anyway. I told the housemother I don't want to go, but she said I had to. Everyone has to. I told her I couldn't learn the steps, and she told me that was ridiculous. Then I told her that no one would dance with me, and she said that that was just plain silly. Lots of the boys liked me, and anyway, everyone had to dance with everyone else. It was the rules. I'm going to run away."

Bernie stopped reading. "We never had dance lessons."

"I hated the dances," Marvin said. "My hands used to get all sweaty. It was embarrassing."

Brandon stood up and stretched. "Well, I liked them. I used to sneak out and have a smoke with Daisy Dixon."

"Just a smoke?" Bernie demanded.

Brandon grinned. "No."

"That's what I thought," said Bernie.

Sean cleared his throat. Everyone turned toward him. "Can we get back to the journal please?"

"No problem," Bernie said and resumed reading. By now the wind had picked up, and the rain was splattering the windows. "Let's see." She started running her finger down the pages as she scanned them. "More stuff about classes. She's doing well in everything. More complaints about Amethyst and her friends."

"Do we know who they are?" Clyde asked.

Bernie shook her head. "So far she hasn't mentioned them by name."

"Pity," Clyde murmured as Bernie went back to the journal.

"Here's another entry about the shadow lady. She says, 'I saw her in the east wing near the kitchen. I'm never going to sneak food again.' That would certainly cut down on midnight snacking," Bernie noted as she went on. "Okay." She continued turning pages. "Same old. Same old. Aha." She stopped. "This is something new."

Bernie continued reading. "Dear Diary, We had our first dancing lesson today. I knew I was going to hate it. All the other girls had pretty skirts and blouses on, and I just had my old stuff. Mrs. Richards practically had to push me into the room. And then I kept tripping over my own feet. Why do I have to learn to dance, anyway? No one is ever going to ask me. But the worst was when we had to dance with the boys. We formed two lines, and everyone had to rotate every five minutes or so. All the boys looked unhappy when they had to dance with me."

"Poor thing," Libby murmured.

"And then," Bernie continued, "I danced with the headmaster's son, Ken. He said he had heard a lot about me and that he had wanted to meet me. I thought he was just being polite, but when the dance ended, he said he'd meet me tomorrow by the maple tree outside the girls' wing. He had something he wanted to show me."

"Boy," Brandon interjected. "If that isn't a classic line, I don't know what is."

"Be quiet," Bernie said to him. Then she coughed to clear her voice and went on. "I couldn't sleep all night long. It's probably nothing. His father probably told him to be nice to me. I mean, he's so cute, so why should he pay attention to me?

"But I couldn't help it, I put on my plaid gray kilt and my good red V-necked sweater and my Sunday loafers and my last pair of clean white kneesocks, anyway. I even used a little bit of Amethyst's rouge on my cheeks. I hope she doesn't find out, but I don't see how she could, because it was just a little dab. Then I tried to get both sides of my hair to turn under the way the cool girls do, but one side kept flipping up. Good grief!

"I got there five minutes early even though I wanted to get there five minutes late. My mom says it's always best to make the boys wait. Ken wasn't there. I felt so silly standing there that I was going to leave, but then I looked up and saw Ken walking toward me. He was holding something out to me. A book. 'I thought you'd like this,' he said. It was a book of mythology, only this one was about the Celtic people.

"He said they had lots of stuff about Halloween in there, because that's where it came from. I was so happy, I didn't even say thank you. 'Don't you like it?' Ken asked. I told him I loved it, that that was the best thing anyone had ever given me, and he smiled. He has a great smile. It turns out he likes books, too. He even likes fairy tales, which is fairly weird, but he's going to give me some of the old ones. He says they're different. Also, he said he can help me when I start Latin. We're going to go for a walk tomorrow after dinner. I can hardly wait."

"Looks like things are picking up for our Bessie," Marvin said.

Bernie grunted as she kept reading. "Okay. Nothing about Amethyst or being homesick or schoolwork on the next five pages. They're all about Ken. She says, 'Ken gave me a book about Arthur and the Knights of the Round Table today. Ken and I went for a walk, and we found some bright red leaves on the ground. Ken and I held hands. Ken is the cutest guy in the whole school.' Here's one page with Bessie Marak written all over it. Here's another page with little hearts and the initials KM & BO written in them. Looks like our girl is in love. Okay. Here's something. She says, 'Ken kissed me.' "

363

"At last we're getting to the good stuff," Brandon said.

Bernie clucked. "Don't you ever think about anything besides sex?"

"No. Not really. What does she say about it?" said Brandon.

"This. 'Dear Diary, This is the first time I've ever done anything like this except with my cousin Jerome when I was six. I was really worried that Ken's braces and my braces would lock, but they didn't. We kissed for a long time. It was lots better than I thought it would be. We only quit because we heard someone coming. I'm meeting him tomorrow night in the kitchen, and I don't care about the shadow woman, even if she is creepy. I can't believe I made out. I never thought it would happen to me!!!!' " Bernie paused. "That was a four-exclamation sentence," she noted.

"Then Bessie goes on and says, 'Amethyst was up when I came back to my room. She was smiling at me, which she never does. Talk about creepy. Anyway, she told me that she thought that Ken was real cute, and that I was very lucky to have a boyfriend like that, and maybe we could all go out together some time. I didn't want to get her angry, so I told her that was a neat idea, even though I don't think it is. I think it's a very bad idea. Then she smiled at me again. I wish I had teddy.' "

"Trouble in paradise," Libby commented.

"There always is," Bernie observed, thinking back to some of her run–ins with women like Amethyst.

"Go on," Clyde urged. "Tell us what happened."

Bernie shook her head to clear it and continued. "Bessie's next entry takes place the next day. It starts: 'We met in the kitchen. It was really spooky. Lots of shadows, but Ken said I'm just imagining things. He says the shadow people are lots of bunk, so I shouldn't be worried. I'm trying to do what he says, but I keep thinking I'm hearing somebody talking in my ear. I think she's jealous that I'm going to be kissing Ken and she can't kiss anyone. Or maybe shadow people do kiss, and we just don't know it. We did lots of kissing, anyway. Ken says he's going to get me a circle pin, and we're going to go steady. That would be really neat.' "

Bernie looked up. "However, the next day she says, 'I saw Amethyst talking to Ken at lunch. He was laughing. When I asked him what was so funny, he shrugged his shoulders and said she'd told him a joke and that he didn't think she was as bad as he'd heard she was. I told him she was awful, and he said I was being silly and walked away. When I got back to my room, Amethyst was smirking at me. I told her to leave Ken alone, and she said, good grief, it was a free country, and that she was just talking to him. What was wrong with that? Maybe I'm being silly, but I don't like this at all.' "

"I'd say her instincts are pretty good," Sean commented.

Libby's stomach rumbled. "Sorry," she said, mortified.

Her dad laughed. "I think we could all use a little something to eat."

"Cookies would be nice," Clyde suggested.

"More than nice," Konrad observed. "Especially the gingersnaps."

That was the nice thing about baking, Libby thought. It made people happy.

For the next fifteen minutes, everyone helped themselves to the plates of chocolate chip cookies, gingersnaps, and molasses cookies, and to the decaffeinated tea and coffee that Libby and Amber brought up. Bernie got up, got a bottle of brandy from the bottom shelf of the cabinet, poured a little in her coffee, then passed the bottle around.

Konrad raised his cup. "A toast to Bessie,"

he cried.

"To Bessie," everyone repeated, and they clinked their cups and drank.

"To proving my cousin innocent," Curtis said.

Everyone drank to that, too, but this time the response was less enthusiastic. Bernie poured another slug of brandy into her cup and passed the bottle around again. Then she took a sip, opened the journal back up to the page she'd marked, and began to speak.

"Okay," she said. "The next page has more hearts with Ken's and Bessie's initials in them, except down at the bottom, where Bessie's written Amethyst's name and she's drawn a hatchet through it. See?" Bernie passed the book around.

"Not a happy camper," Clyde commented as he looked at the page.

"That's because she knows what's coming," Amber said, "and she doesn't know what to do about it."

Bernie nodded her agreement as Libby handed the journal back to her. Bernie took another sip of her coffee and picked up where she had left off. "Dear Diary, I hate Amethyst. She says she wants to borrow the book on Norse mythology that Ken gave me. She says it's so interesting, and maybe she and I can discuss it some time. I told her I didn't want to lend it to her, and I guess she told Ken, because when I met him in the kitchen, he asked me why I wouldn't give it to her. I tried to explain, but he said I was just being silly. He said she was just misunderstood, and that she had a really bad mother and lots of problems at home, and I had to be understanding, so I told him about the cupcakes, but he said that just proved his point. We spent all this time talking about Amethyst and almost no time kissing, and when we did kiss, it wasn't very good. I could tell his mind wasn't on what he was doing."

Bernie turned the page. "The next day we have, 'I think Ken likes Amethyst better than me. Yesterday I followed them. They didn't see me, because I hid behind the bushes. And they walked down the path that Ken and I walked down. They were both laughing and talking. Amethyst doesn't even like him. He's not her type. And she has lots of boyfriends. She just wants him because I like him. It's so unfair.'

"New entry. 'Tonight I was supposed to meet Ken and take a walk. I got all dressed up and everything. I even set my hair in the rollers Mom brought me. Then he called on the house phone and told me he was sorry, but he couldn't make it. Amethyst was really upset about her social studies test that was coming up — she didn't understand the chapter — and he had to stay in and help her. I'm so mad I don't know what to do. Amethyst smirked at me when she came in.

" 'My mom says I should just ignore them both. That I'm just playing into Amethyst's hands by doing what I'm doing, and that boys don't like girls that run after them. Then she said that I'm much too young to be in a relationship, anyway, and that I'm at the Peabody School so I can better myself. She just doesn't understand!!!!' That's another four-exclamation sentence."

Bernie turned the page and read, "When I got back this afternoon, Amethyst had her friends in our room. They were laughing and drinking and smoking out the window. I think one of them was smoking weed. One of them was even sitting on my bed. I told them they couldn't do that, and they all laughed some more and said they could do whatever they want.

"I was so mad I stomped out of the room, but on the way, I think I saw something on Amethyst's dresser that said Social Studies final. I'm not sure, but I think I did. I'm going to check when we go to dinner. I was right. I did see it. Oh my God. I bet she stole it. Or maybe Ken gave it to her. That would be too horrible to contemplate. I don't know what I'm going to do! I wish teddy was here."

"Then what?" Marvin asked as Bernie paused to eat a part of her chocolate chip cookie.

Bernie wiped her hands on a napkin before continuing and perused the page. "Let's see. We have more angst. No more hearts and initials. No more Bessie Marak. Instead, we have, 'Last night Amethyst came in and told me she and Ken kissed in the kitchen, and that they'd done other things too, things that Ken really liked. I started to cry, and she laughed and said he had told her that he went with me because he felt sorry for me because no one else would because I was so fat, and that he doesn't like me at all, and he thinks I smell bad, and all the kids are making fun of me.' " Bernie stopped reading for a moment and looked up. "You know, judging by the picture of her hanging on the wall in Amethyst's apartment, Bessie wasn't fat at all. She looked good."

"Yeah," Amber interjected. "But she didn't know that. I bet Ken didn't even say those things. I bet Amethyst made them up."

"Possibly," Bernie said. "No. Make that

probably. Poor Bessie." Her finger tapped the bottom of the page. "Her last entry on this page is, 'I called Mom and told her I wanted to come home now, and she said I couldn't, not until Christmas. I told her I had to and she should come and get me right now, and she told me that I had to learn to stand on my own two feet and take care of my own problems, and that I'd thank her later for doing this. Then she hung up. I don't know what I'm going to do.' "

Bernie paused. "The next entry takes place two days later, which is the night before Halloween," she said. "Here Bessie writes, 'I've thought and thought, and I know what I'm going to do. I'm going to tell the headmaster all about Amethyst. I'm going to tell him about her drinking and smoking and sneaking out and not being in class and about the test and about how I think she stole teddy. Then they'll kick her out, and things will be like they were before. I already told Ken, and I guess he told Amethyst, because she said I'd better not. I told her I would.

" 'Then she said I wouldn't dare. I told her I would do it tomorrow. She was trying on her costume for tomorrow night — she's going as Lucy — and she turned to me and said, "No, you won't." Then she went back to looking at herself in the mirror. I don't know why I'm scared. I'm just being silly. There's nothing else she can do to me. She's already ruined my life, because I'll never get over Ken.' "

"She's not going to have the chance," Amber said.

"What does she write next?" Sean asked.

Bernie thumbed through the pages. "Nothing. She wrote her last entry the evening before Halloween. She died the next day."

Everyone fell silent.

CHAPTER 28

Libby looked at the clock on the wall. It was a little after eleven, and from the way things were going, she wouldn't get to sleep for quite a long while. She'd been up since six in the morning and had wanted to be in bed an hour ago. The good news was that Konrad, Curtis, and Amber had finally left, which gave everyone a little more breathing space, not to mention giving her ears a rest.

"I'm glad we don't have to listen to the tape again," Libby said. Once was enough. Twice was definitely way too much.

"I can't imagine why," Bernie retorted. "I love hearing static at ear-piercing levels, don't you?"

"Oh yes," Marvin said. "And I'm sure Amber's mom will feel the same."

"Yes, she's going to be very welcoming," said Bernie. She could see Amber's mom's prune face now. There was no way that Konrad and Curtis and the tape deck were going to get into Amber's house at eleven o'clock at night.

Clyde reached for another chocolate chip cookie. "A definite case of the emperor's new clothes, if you ask me."

"Well," Libby said, stifling a yawn, "Amber claims she heard Bessie saying, 'That's private. Don't read my journal.' "

Bernie snorted as she slipped off her boots and lined them up next to the sofa. "First of all, she wouldn't have said *journal.* She would have said *diary.* And secondly, you'd think she'd want us to read it."

Marvin leaned forward and snagged another cookie from the platter on the coffee table. "She probably thinks it makes her look bad."

Libby turned and stared at Marvin.

Two dots of color appeared on Marvin's cheeks. "That's what she'd be feeling if she existed," he stammered.

"But she doesn't," Sean said. "She did, but she doesn't now. Otherwise, we might as well consult the Ouija board. It would be faster."

"My dad has one of those in the attic. I can get it if you want," said Marvin.

"I'm kidding, Marvin," said Sean.

Sean patted the pocket in his pants where his cigarettes were hiding. He would give anything to have one now. They'd always helped him think. Picked him up and clarified his thoughts. In the old days, he'd tell Rose he was going to answer an emergency call, and then he'd drive a little ways, park on one of the town's side streets, light up, and stare into nothingness. He'd always gotten his best ideas that way. Now, of course, that was impossible, because one or another of the girls was always hovering over him. *At least,* he thought, *I'm well enough now, so I can walk down the stairs if I hold the banister and use a cane.* Remission was a beautiful thing, and he was going to do as much as he could for as long as he could.

"What's the matter, Dad?" Libby asked.

Sean looked at her. "Why should anything be the matter?"

"Well, you were sighing. I just thought you might need something," replied Libby.

"I'm fine," Sean lied. *Drat those cigarettes.* Okay. He knew they were really bad for him, but that didn't help. He could taste them. "I was just thinking about poor Bessie and wondering who buried the journal."

"I guess she couldn't have," Marvin observed.

Sean moved his wheelchair so he could be nearer to the cookies. He particularly liked the lace oatmeal ones. They'd been his wife's specialty. At one time they'd been popular, but to his knowledge, his daughters' shop was the only place that made them anymore, mostly as a favor to him, he suspected.

"No. I don't think Bessie could have," Sean remarked. "Dead people don't usually do things like that."

Brandon grabbed another cookie and took Amber's place on the floor. "So who do you think did, Mr. Simmons?"

"My first guess would be Felicity Huffer. I think she found the journal and read it and didn't know what to do with it, so she buried it and drew herself a map so she wouldn't forget where it was."

Bernie rubbed her feet. She loved the boots she'd been wearing, but if she wore them for too long, they pinched her toes and gave her blisters. "When I spoke to her, she did say she couldn't tell anyone what had happened, because she was afraid she'd lose her job. She said that Amethyst's parents exerted a lot of influence at the school."

Marvin sneezed. "There's nothing that incriminating in the journal."

"There's enough stuff in there to get Amethyst thrown out of school," Bernie countered.

"Yeah," Marvin replied. "That's true. But I'm talking in the criminal sense."

"Well," Clyde said as he wiped cookie crumbs off his leg and into his cupped hand and dumped them in the saucer in front of him, "I'm not so sure about that. If I had what I thought was an accidental death or a suicide and I read that journal, it would definitely get me thinking in a different direction."

Marvin sneezed again. Whenever he got wet, he got sick. "Then why not just destroy it?" he asked. "That would have been lots easier."

"Felicity's conscience probably wouldn't let her," Clyde responded. "This way she could always tell herself that when the time was right, she'd show the journal."

"Which she did," Bernie said. "Never mind that it's a little late to do any good."

"Of course, there's another possibility," Sean said. "Someone else could have buried it. Like Amethyst or Ken Marak."

"And Felicity saw them do it and drew the map," Brandon said.

Sean nodded. "Exactly."

Clyde said, "This is all very fascinating in the academic sense, and Bessie's journal is very sad, but I don't think it helps us any."

Bernie looked at her dad. "What do you

377

say, Dad?"

"My gut tells me there's something here," said Sean. He pointed to Bessie's journal, which was now resting on the coffee table, next to the cookies. "I just don't know what."

"I don't see anything that fits with what we already know," said Clyde.

"Clyde, you don't know that for a fact," Sean objected.

"I think I do," Clyde insisted. "The only facts we know for certain are that we have three people with pretty good motives for killing Amethyst, and each one of them had access to the place where she died. We know that the person that killed her had to have had some facility with tools or been some place where they'd seen a fiber-optic laser cutter at work, which actually isn't much of a lead, because they're used at construction sites and in body shops. But most importantly, we know that Amethyst wanted to use Lexus Gardens as the site for a wedding ceremony. Now whether —"

"Excuse me," Libby interrupted. "How do we know this?"

"I finally got hold of Banks's personal assistant," said Clyde.

"Why didn't you tell us?" Bernie demanded.

"We were going to," her dad said, "but you guys came running in here, and we never got the chance."

"Wow," Bernie said. "Married. The ceremony had to be for her."

"That's what I figured," Clyde said. "By the way, Banks refused the request. He didn't want a ceremony, a reception, or anything at his place. He really did like to keep to himself."

"And this ties in with his death how?" Libby asked.

"It's a stretch," Sean hypothesized, "but the only connection I can see is that Ed Banks was killed because the person who killed her didn't want it known that Amethyst was getting married."

"That's a big stretch," Libby said.

"It's a huge stretch," Sean agreed.

"Which leaves us in the same position we were in before, with Bob Small as our primary suspect," Clyde said.

"Well, Amethyst certainly wouldn't be marrying him," Bernie said. "He has no money."

"Neither does Inez," Brandon observed.

"Inez is a woman," Marvin said.

Brandon just looked at him. "Really? I hadn't noticed. For your information, Inez goes with whatever moves."

Marvin blushed again.

"Which leaves Zachery," Bernie said.

"But he hated her," Libby protested.

"What better reason to marry and kill her?" Bernie asked.

"Someone would have to be really cold-blooded to do that," Brandon said.

"Maybe he is. I've known some psychopaths in my time. They act like everyone else until you get to know them real well," said Bernie. She screwed up her face while she thought. "I think I should go have another talk with him."

"Why? We'd know if they got married," Libby said. "We would have heard."

"Not if it was a secret," Sean said. "Not if they went away and got married somewhere else."

"But we would have heard that they were living together," Bernie objected.

"Maybe they weren't," Marvin said. "Maybe they were living in separate residences."

"Then why bother marrying?" Libby asked. "That makes no sense whatsoever."

"It makes as much sense as everything else about this case does," said Bernie as she picked up her cup and put it down again. "Here's another thought. What if Amethyst was getting married to Ed Banks? What if they got married? Then killing him makes a lot more sense. It means that someone needed to kill them both."

Clyde snorted. "How do you come up with that?"

"What, exactly, did you ask Banks's personal assistant?" Bernie inquired.

"First, I asked him if Amethyst Applegate had talked to his employer, and he said she had," said Clyde. "Then I asked him how he knew, and he said she'd come up to the estate, at which point I asked him what the conversation had been about. He said he heard his employer saying that he didn't want the reception held here, and then Banks shut the door, and he couldn't hear anything else."

Bernie leaned forward and pointed a finger at Clyde. "So Banks and Amethyst could have been talking about holding a reception for their wedding on the estate grounds. I mean, it is a possibility."

"I guess if you put it that way, then yes," Clyde conceded.

"Would there be a record of the wedding in the town hall or somewhere like that?" Brandon asked.

"For the fourth time, not if they didn't get married here," Sean said. "If we're following Bernie's scenario, then it's just as likely that they hopped on a plane to Reno or Vegas, got hitched, and flew back the next day. What do you think, Clyde?"

"I think Bernie should have been a lawyer, that's what I think," said Clyde.

Bernie stood up and took a mock bow.

"But I'm still sticking with what I said before, and all the fancy logic in the world can't convince me otherwise," Clyde told her. "What do you think, Libby?"

"I'm too tired to think," replied Libby.

"Me, too," Marvin said.

Libby turned and looked at him. His eyes were like slits. She was just about to tell him he should go home when her father beat her to it.

"Get some sleep," Sean said to Marvin. "We have a busy day tomorrow, and we need to start bright and early."

Clyde stood up, too. "That goes for me, too."

Libby and Bernie walked everyone down the stairs and said good night. After Bernie locked up, she turned to Libby and said, "This is going to sound crazy, but I'm thinking about having a little work done."

"Work done?" Libby echoed. "What kind of work?"

"Cosmetic surgery kind of work."

"Are you nuts?" Libby asked.

"But see" — Bernie pointed to her fore-head — "I'm beginning to get lines here." She pointed to the area between her nose and chin. "And here. And look at the circles under my eyes."

"You are nuts," Libby told her.

"Look closer."

Libby did. "I still don't see anything."

"That's because the light down here is bad."

"You're having surgery?"

"Well, I'm hoping Botox will take care of everything for awhile. And, anyway, it's not surgery. It's maintenance."

"I don't care what you call it. It's still injecting a deadly toxin into your body."

"It's not a big deal. Millions of people do it, and I think there's something new on the market. That's why I have a consult tomor-row morning."

"Tomorrow morning?" Libby cried. "Why tomorrow morning?"

"Because they had a cancellation. Other-wise, I'd have to wait four months."

"Maybe you should. It'll give you time to think about it."

"I've been thinking about it for almost a year," said Bernie.

"You never mentioned it to me."

Bernie shrugged. "That's because I knew

what you'd say."

"Do you know how busy we're going to be?"

"It's always about you."

Libby rolled her eyes. "I have an idea," she said. "Why don't we grow a little botulinum here, and you can do it yourself."

Bernie ignored her. "I've got the first appointment. It's at eight. I'll be in and out of there in half an hour at the most, and then, if there's time, I'm going to drop in on Zachery, and if not, I'll come right back to the shop."

"Have you told Dad about what you're going to do?"

"I'm not doing anything. I'm going for a consult," said Bernie.

"Fine, Miss Have-To-Say-It-Exactly-Right. Let me rephrase. Have you told him about what you're thinking of doing?"

Bernie snorted. "What, are you crazy? He doesn't even like it when I change my hairstyle."

"I bet Brandon won't be too pleased, either."

"He's not going to know. No one is." Bernie fixed her eyes on Libby. "And you're not going to tell them, either. Right?"

Libby studied the hallway light fixture.

"Promise me you won't say anything,"

said Bernie.

Libby folded her arms over her chest. "I mean it."

"I know you do."

"Well?" Bernie said after a moment had gone by.

"Fine," Libby said sullenly. "I swear. Satisfied?"

"Sister swear."

Libby groaned. Sister swear was an unbreakable oath, the most serious oath there was between them. She might have known Bernie was going to pull this out of the proverbial hat.

"I mean it," Bernie said.

"All right," Libby said. "I sister swear it. But I think you're making a big mistake."

Bernie gave her a hug. "I know."

Their dad barely looked up when Bernie and Libby came upstairs. He was too engrossed in reading Bessie's journal.

"Do you want me to put the Scrabble game away for you?" Libby asked him.

Sean shook his head. "No. Leave it. I'm not done with it yet."

"Some more tea?" asked Libby.

"No, Libby. I'm fine, honestly," said Sean.

Bernie leaned over him. "Are you getting any ideas?"

Sean looked up at her and smiled. "Actually, I am."

"You want to tell us what they are?" asked Libby.

"Not yet. Maybe tomorrow," said Sean. He went back to reading.

Libby and Bernie stood there and watched him. After a moment, they both gave him good-night pecks on his cheeks and went off to sleep. Even Bernie was tired. The whole thing with finding Bessie's journal must have taken more out of her than she thought.

CHAPTER 29

Isn't this just the way? Libby thought bitterly as she stared at the clock on her nightstand. She desperately needed to go to sleep. She was so tired, she couldn't keep her eyes open, but now that she was in bed, she couldn't fall asleep. All she could do was stare at the numbers on the clock face: 2:30, 2:31, 2:33. She was now down to three hours of sleep before she had to get up. At this rate, she might as well get up and go downstairs and start baking. At least she'd be getting something done.

She pulled the comforter up and re-arranged her pillow. Maybe she needed to get a new pillow. Then she turned over and stared out the bedroom window. The rain was smearing everything. The street lights outside looked blurry, and the houses across the street had disappeared behind a watery film. A branch of the maple tree she and Bernie used to climb up when they were young had twisted itself into a face.

Funny. Why hadn't she noticed that before? It had a mouth and eyes. And a nose of sorts. Nostrils, actually. She blinked. It must be a trick of the light. Then she blinked again, because she recognized the face. It was Bessie's. Bessie was tapping at her window. The strange thing was, she wasn't even scared. She was just annoyed. Very odd.

"Go away," Libby told her. "Go bother someone else for a change. I've had enough."

Bessie looked as if she were going to cry. "But I like you."

"Well, I don't like you."

Bessie stamped her foot. "You are so mean."

Then, before Libby could answer, Bessie was floating above her, around her. She was everywhere Libby looked. Something wet was falling on Libby's face. Bessie's tears. They were coming faster and faster. She was getting soaked. She felt as if her bed was floating. She looked down. Water was filling her room. It was carrying the bed up toward the ceiling. She was going to drown.

"I'm sorry," Libby cried. "I didn't mean it. I'm tired."

"You swear?"

"I swear," Libby said. At least it wasn't sister swearing. All at once the bed fell, and she was on the floor again.

"We found your journal," she told Bessie. "We dug it up. Isn't that what you wanted to happen? Don't you want everyone to know what's going on?"

Suddenly, Libby found herself back at the Peabody School. The windows were decorated with cutout witches and pumpkins. Jack-o'-lanterns hung from the trees. Paper skeletons danced on the doors, while students in werewolf masks stalked the hallways. It was the night before Halloween, and she was watching Bessie talk to Ken.

"I don't understand," Bessie was saying. "I don't understand why you're doing this."

"I'm not doing anything," Ken said.

Libby could tell from the way Ken was standing that he was clearly impatient with Bessie. Somehow Libby knew that this discussion had been going on for a half an hour and that Ken was more than ready to leave. And with every word that Bessie said, his interest faded a little bit more.

"But you are," Bessie insisted. "You're helping Amethyst cheat."

"I didn't know she was going to take the test," Ken insisted.

"Then tell your dad."

"I can't."

"Why not?" asked Bessie.

"Because I can't, that's why."

"You can't, because you like her."

"I don't like her at all."

"Yes, you do."

Just let it go, Libby wanted to tell Bessie. *Just walk away. He still likes you. He likes you better than Amethyst, even though he doesn't know it yet. He'll come back to you.* But Libby couldn't get the words out of her mouth.

"I'm going to tell your dad," Bessie declared.

"Bessie, don't," Ken pleaded.

"I am," Bessie said.

Why does Ken look so familiar? Libby wondered as she watched letters come out of Bessie's mouth and form themselves into words above her head. *Just like in the cartoons,* Libby thought. She was trying to read them, but the rain kept on getting in her eyes. Now the letters had turned into Scrabble tiles and had fallen to the ground. They were forming themselves into two words. A name? A place? Whatever it was, it was important. It was more than important. It was crucial. Libby leaned over to get a better look, and suddenly, she was falling, down, down, down. The ground was coming up fast, but she was still trying to see the words. Then, just before she hit the ground, a name flashed through her mind.

Libby woke up with a start. She was covered in sweat, and her heart was hammering so hard, she couldn't catch her breath. It took her a second to realize she was in her bedroom. She sat up.

"It was a dream," Libby said out loud. "Just a dream."

But it hadn't felt like that at all. It had felt real. This was what she got for going along with Amber's nutty schemes and eating too much ice cream. Whenever stuff like this had happened in the past, her mom had always told her it was because of something she'd eaten before bedtime.

She wanted to believe that now, but even then she had known it wasn't true. Despite what her mom had said, these dreams were different. And Libby thought that her mom had known it, too. She just hadn't wanted to talk about it, the way she hadn't wanted to talk about other stuff. Libby still remembered when she'd had the dream about her grandmother dying right before she did, and she'd gone and told her mom. After the funeral, her mom had told her not to say anything to anybody about stuff like that.

"People will think you're weird," her mom

had warned her. And even though Libby had only been nine at the time, she'd understood that her mom had meant "more weird," and she'd never told another living soul about her dreams — except for Bernie — ever again. Eventually, they'd stopped happening. This was the first one she'd had in a long time, and now that she'd had it, she remembered why she'd hated those dreams. They totally freaked her out.

Libby pulled her comforter, which wasn't supplying much comfort, over her head and told herself to go back to sleep. Instead, she spent the rest of the night tossing and turning and trying to remember the name the Scrabble tiles had formed just before she fell, but the name kept skittering away from her, hiding in the recesses of her mind.

CHAPTER 30

"And I thought I had circles under my eyes," Bernie said when she saw Libby the next morning. Libby grunted. She was on her third cup of coffee. Usually, she had just one, but this morning was a notable exception.

"Maybe you should go as a bag lady tonight," Bernie suggested. "You know, bags under the eyes, bags —"

"Ha-ha. I get it. You don't have to explain. You're really going to do this?" Libby asked.

"This" was the cosmetic surgery consult. Bernie looked fine to her. She looked more than fine. The truth was Libby would have killed to look like her sister. Bernie had gotten the good nose, the high cheekbones, and the clear complexion.

Bernie nodded. "You betcha."

Libby took another sip of her coffee. Under other circumstances, she would have tried to talk Bernie out of going, but she was too preoccupied with last night's dream to bother arguing that cosmetic surgery was dangerous and a total waste of money.

"Good luck," Libby said and turned back to survey the to-do list she had tacked up on the fridge.

When Bernie told Libby she was going to pay a visit to Zachery Timberland after her appointment, Libby merely nodded, because she was trying to figure out, as Julia Child would have said, the order of battle for the day.

"Are you sure you're all right?" Bernie asked her. Given everything that had to get done, her sister should be in a frenzy by now.

Libby kept her eyes glued to the list on the fridge. "Why are you asking?"

"Well, ordinarily, I'd think you'd tell me to come right back to the shop. After all, we're going to be pretty busy today."

Libby turned and faced her. She had a grim look on her face. "Why?" she said. "Just because it's Halloween night, and we have that dratted Haunted House to deal with, not to mention three large pickup orders between four- and five-thirty, and we're already behind because the chicken hasn't been prepped, and we need to do the onions and the peppers, not to mention hollowing out the pumpkins for the pumpkin and apple soup, as well as all the muffins, pies, cookies, and cakes that still have to be made?"

"Something like that. I'll call Amber and Googie."

"I already have," Libby informed her. "They'll be here in half an hour."

Bernie reached for a semi-stale pumpkin bar, one of several that they'd forgotten to put away last night, broke off a piece, and ate it.

"You know," she said. "I think I like these better this way. They have more texture. We might even be able to incorporate them into the brownie bars."

Libby grunted. Bernie hated when her sister got this way.

"Well," Bernie continued, trying to be positive, "at least everything will be over tonight."

"Will it?" Libby asked. "I don't see how."

"Why won't it be?" Bernie replied, and then she realized what Libby was really talking about. "You mean the case?"

Libby nodded. "Yes. What were you talking about?"

"Our catering gig."

Libby reached over and grabbed one of the pumpkin bars and nibbled on it. "Not bad," she conceded. "As for the Haunted House, if I never see that place again, it will be too soon for me."

Bernie looked at her carefully. Something was definitely going on behind those bangs and glasses. "Did something happen last night after I went to bed?"

Libby shook her head. "Like what?"

"I don't know."

"Then why are you asking?"

"Because you seem kinda weird this morning."

Libby put her hands on her hips. "So now I'm weird? Thanks a lot. That's certainly helpful."

Bernie gave an exasperated sigh. "You know what I mean."

"No, I don't."

"I mean weird as in off, as in something is bothering you."

"Well, I'm fine."

"Are you sure?" Bernie asked her, noting that Libby was looking at everything but her.

"Positive. Aren't you going to be late for your appointment? Can't keep the plastic surgeon waiting, can we."

"It's a consult." Bernie ate the rest of the pumpkin bar while she thought. Something was definitely wrong. "You didn't have a fight with Marvin, did you?"

"Marvin and I are fine." Libby reached for another pumpkin bar and practically inhaled it.

Bernie studied her some more.

"Stop looking at me," Libby told her.

Bernie snapped her fingers. "I know. You had one of your dreams, didn't you?"

Libby blushed.

Bernie scrutinized her for a moment longer. "You did, didn't you?"

"No, I didn't."

"It's not a bad thing," Bernie said gently.

"Maybe the dreams aren't bad to you," Libby flung back. "But that's easy for you to say because you're not the one that has them. You might feel differently if you did." She turned back and began studying her list with a great deal of intensity.

"So you're against miscegenation?" asked Bernie.

Libby turned back to her. "What are you talking about?"

"You believe there shouldn't be any mixing."

"Mixing?"

"You know. The dead should stay in their world, and the living should stay in theirs."

Libby burst out laughing. "I guess I do."

"So you're a deathist."

"Deathist?"

"Deathist. Like a racist. You're prejudiced against dead people."

Libby laughed harder. "You're nuts," she said when she could talk again.

"I know."

When Bernie went out the door, Libby was still laughing, which somehow made Bernie feel better.

It was so ironic, Bernie thought as she slid into her car. Libby had a gift that some people would give anything to possess, and she refused to have anything to do with it. But wasn't that the way it always was. Bernie, for example, usually wanted men that were totally wrong for her, while she was uninterested in those that were suitable. Fortunately, Brandon was turning out to be the exception to that rule. The operative words here were *turning out,* because, if truth be told, she still didn't entirely trust him yet.

Bernie sighed as she turned on the ignition. It was going to be a long day, and she didn't enjoy starting it this way, but you had to go with what you could get in the appointment department. The drive over to the doc's office took five minutes. Since she was booked for the first appointment of the day, her behind hadn't even had a chance to hit the expensive leather-covered seats, the ones that she'd seen in an architectural magazine and that cost five thousand dollars each, before she was called in. Fifteen minutes later, she left, armed with a price list and an extensively illustrated brochure that described all the procedures Dr. Cornelius Love did.

"Is that your real name?" Bernie had asked when she'd walked into his office.

Dr. Love had laughed and turned the conversation back to her, which probably meant that it wasn't. Having that last name in school would have been . . . well, it would have been awful. She was still thinking about Dr. Love as she thumbed through the brochure. The words that came to mind as she did were "yuck" and "blech," although "gross" was fitting as well. Bernie didn't consider herself squeamish, but looking at the color photographs made her want to throw up.

Maybe Libby's right, Bernie thought as she put her car in drive and headed over to Zachery Timberland's house. *Maybe I should forget about this.* On the other hand, those lines on her forehead and the folds between her nose and her chin were only going to get worse. It was better to do little maintenance jobs over time than to do a face-lift when she got to fifty. Those really did look awful unless they were done by someone very, very good, and even then you couldn't be sure. Look what had happened to Joan Rivers.

And the doc was kinda cute — not that that was a good reason to choose him to do this. But it certainly wouldn't hurt. God. Why did everything have to be so complicated? Maybe she'd try microdermabrasion first, and if that didn't get rid of the lines, she'd go the Botox route. Who knew? By then they might have even come out with a new product.

With that settled, she gradually started thinking about Bessie's journal again and about Amethyst and whether or not she'd gotten married. She was definitely playing a long shot here, but she was running out of ideas.

She had half a mind to turn around and go back to the shop and start making the dough for the pies, but the way things were going, Bob Small was going to go to jail for Amethyst's murder for sure — unless she, Libby, or their dad came up with something. And if her dad did what he wanted to do — which was to demonstrate that Marvin could crawl in and out of the ceiling in the Haunted House — that would be another nail in Bob Small's metaphorical coffin. But fortunately, she'd pretty much convinced her dad to leave things alone. For the moment.

What she'd said was, "Why help Lucy?" And her dad had agreed. Marvin had been incredibly relieved. And she was happy, too, because the more she knew about Bob Small, the more unlikely it seemed to her that Bob had killed Amethyst. Like Libby, she just couldn't imagine him doing something like that. Shooting someone in a fit of rage, yes; but something that took lots of advanced planning, no.

Bob Small seemed so clueless, which, of course, was why he'd gone to jail in the first place. If he wasn't clueless, he would have been able to see through Amethyst. Or, to be perfectly accurate, he wasn't so much clueless as thinking with his dick — but maybe that was the same thing.

This case was like a huge, tangled skein of wool. Every time she, Libby, or her dad thought they were making headway, they ended up in the same place they had been before. Which was why she was going to Zachery Timberland's house at 8:35 in the morning. He probably wasn't even there. He most likely was on his way to his office. But it was worth a try. As her father always said, "When in doubt, do something. Don't sit around like a lump."

Maybe her visit would shake Zachery up a little. Hopefully. She'd read a statistic somewhere that most homicides were solved within the first seventy-two hours, or they were not solved at all. Well, they'd certainly gone past the seventy-two-hour limit, that was for sure. And with that in mind, Bernie turned onto Smith Street and took that straight to Zachery Timberland's house.

He lived in an odd little cul-de-sac off of Meadview Drive. The street wasn't marked, because someone had driven into the street sign last year, and the town had never replaced it. You really had to know it was there to be able to find it.

At one time the cul-de-sac had been the site of a proposed development. Five houses were supposed to have been built on the site, but the builder had gone bankrupt after he'd put up Zachery's. Since Zachery had already purchased his, he was stuck because no one wanted to buy him out. Other developers had bid on the site, but for one reason or another, none of the deals had gone through, so Zachery's house sat in lone splendor on what was now an extremely large vacant lot.

Despite the DO NOT LITTER. VIOLA-

TORS WILL BE FINED TWO HUNDRED DOLLARS sign, piles of leaves, Styrofoam peanuts, and crumpled-up pages of newspaper littered the grass. Three kitchen chairs sat over to the far left, waiting to be claimed by the winter. A little farther on, someone else had disposed of two bags of trash, which were now spilling their guts out onto the ground.

Bernie shivered. You could do whatever you wanted here, and no one would ever know. It was not a comforting thought. Even if she had a couple of big dogs, she wouldn't want to be living here, Bernie decided as she turned onto Dewdrop Lane. It was too spooky. She preferred to live close to people rather than to be isolated. She shook her head. Halloween was getting to her. More to the point, she realized, was the fact that there were no neighbors she could talk to.

She was relieved to see that there were two cars in the driveway of the Timberland residence. The first one, she knew, belonged to Timberland, because she'd seen it parked behind his office. She wondered to whom the second vehicle belonged as she pulled in behind it, got out of her car, and marched toward the front door. *This is going to be interesting,* she thought while she rang the bell.

The house itself was a nondescript, generic Colonial, the housing equivalent of a pair of Wal-Mart blue jeans. It was rendered even more so because everything on it was painted beige except for the dark brown front door. *Just like his office,* Bernie thought. Either the man had a severely limited color palette, or he'd gotten a real good deal on the paint.

At least the foundation plantings weren't beige. But they were tightly pruned, and the driveway was immaculate. The word *constipated* came to mind. She rubbed her arms while she waited for someone to come to the door. It had turned out to be way colder than the weatherman had predicted. The kids were going to have to wear jackets over their costumes tonight when they went trick-or-treating.

She was remembering how much she'd hated that when she heard Timberland say, "Coming." A moment later the door swung open. Bernie could see he was not a thing of beauty in the morning. He had stubble on his chin. His belly was hanging out of his sweatpants, and he had man boobs, a fact his suits had managed to hide. Her mom had always said it was amazing what a decent tailor could do, and she'd been right. Zachery Timberland had a very good one.

"You," he said when he saw her. "What do you want?"

Then, before Bernie could reply, she heard another voice. It was a young woman. Probably his girlfriend from the sound of it. Bernie cursed under her breath. It looked as if this trip was going to be a waste of time, after all.

"Who is it?" the unknown woman trilled.

"No one," Timberland shot back.

"No one? How rude," Bernie countered. "I'm sure your company wouldn't like to hear how you treated a potential customer."

"Oh sure," Timberland sneered. "You're just so excited about the prospect of buying insurance from me that you had to come straight to my house."

"And who's to say that isn't the case?"

"And I'm the queen of Sheba."

"I didn't know you were a woman. But now that I look more closely, I can see the beginning of boobs. How are the hormones working out?"

Timberland looked down at his chest, realized what he was doing, and looked back at Bernie. He brought his lips back into something that was supposed to resemble a smile. "You need to be taught some manners."

Bernie opened her mouth to reply, but

before she could, Timberland's guest came into view. "Honey, what do you mean no one?" she asked.

Bernie estimated that she was about half Timberland's age. She had long blond hair, which she'd put up in a ponytail, and the kind of glowing, flawless skin that Bernie now realized came from dermabrasion, as well as a killer body. The loose pajama bottoms decorated with pictures of cows emphasized her slender hips, and the forest green cami covered breasts that stood at attention without any visible means of support.

Boob job. Got to be, Bernie thought as she turned her eyes away, but not before the young woman saw her looking.

The young woman smiled. She had perfect, white, even teeth. She pointed at her chest. "He bought my boobs for me," she chirped, motioning to Timberland with a toss of her head. "I think the surgeon did a very nice job, don't you? I was going to go down to Mexico to have them done, but Zachy insisted I go somewhere first rate."

Bernie raised an eyebrow. "Zachy?" she repeated.

Timberland glared at her.

"Well," the young woman continued, undaunted, "if you ever need a little pick-me-up, call and I'll give you my surgeon's name. His office is on Park Avenue."

"Sadie," Timberland wailed.

Sadie made a little moue with her lips. "It's not like it's a secret or anything." Then, as Bernie watched, she came up next to Timberland and patted him on the shoulder. "The poor thing is grumpy in the morning without his coffee," she confided. She stood on her tiptoes and gave Timberland a peck on his cheek. "But," she said to Bernie, "he is cute, so I forgive him."

Beauty is definitely in the eyes of the beholder, Bernie thought as she watched Timberland open his mouth and close it again. Bernie could see he was delighted with Sadie's attention on the one hand and mortified on the other.

Sadie extended her hand to Bernie. "Hi," she said. "I'm Sadie Palogski. But then you already know that."

"Sadie's a nice, old-fashioned name," said Bernie.

"I think so. Of course, it's not my real name," said Sadie. "My real name is Scarlett. My mom is a huge *Gone With the Wind* fan. But Scarlett is really lame. All those hoop skirts and that fainting." She wrinkled her nose. "And I don't even like the color."

"I can see why you'd prefer Sadie," Bernie told her.

"I'm going to court to change it," Sadie declared. "Of course, my mom's pissed, but she'll get over it. She always does."

Timberland interrupted. "What do you want?" he asked Bernie.

Bernie smiled. After watching Sadie and Timberland together, she'd decided to tell the truth. She had nothing to lose. Plus, she was curious to see what Sadie's reaction was going to be.

Bernie turned to Timberland. "I came to see if you had married Amethyst."

Timberland just stared at her.

"I guess not," Bernie said.

It took another minute before Timberland recovered himself. "You're kidding, right? That's the stupidest thing I've ever heard."

"Her being married or married to you?" Bernie asked.

"Both," said Timberland.

Bernie turned to Sadie, who had burst out laughing. Laughing was not a reaction she had expected. "Pretty silly, huh?"

"Well, yeah," Sadie said. "How did you ever get that idea?"

"Just sprung into my head," replied Bernie.

"I mean Zach would never marry her, not after what she did with his daughter, and she really wasn't too fond of him," said Sadie. She looked at Timberland. "Well, it's true. She wasn't. She told me you were a real asshole."

"So obviously, you knew her," said Bernie.

"I knew who she was, and we said hello, but that was about it. I didn't *know her,* if you get my meaning," said Sadie. She looked at Bernie, and Bernie nodded to show that she understood. "I ran into her down in the City when I was getting my consult at this really cool lingerie shop down in SoHo. It has the best things." She mentioned the name of the store, one Bernie knew from reading the fashion magazines. "She told me she was getting married."

Bernie leaned forward. "Really?"

Sadie nodded.

"When?" asked Bernie.

"Pretty soon. She was very excited. I've never seen her so excited," said Sadie. "And she was buying all this cool new underwear. Lace bras. Thongs. The whole bit. She showed me her diamond. Five carats." Sadie gave Timberland a meaningful look.

Timberland, I hope you have lots of money, Bernie found herself thinking, *because you're going to need every cent of it with this one.* The thought pleased her.

"So, Sadie," Bernie said. "Did she happen to mention who she was marrying?"

"Yeah, she did. But I've forgotten the name," said Sadie. "I was kinda half listening because I was looking at some really hot teddies at the time. I didn't want to be rude, but I didn't have lots of time, because I was going to have to make the four thirty-seven back to Longely."

Bernie took a deep breath and told herself to stay calm. "Do you remember anything?"

"Well, it was her old boyfriend. She'd just met up with him again," said Sadie.

"Anything else?" asked Bernie.

"Actually, it was more than an old boyfriend. It was the first boy she'd ever kissed," replied Sadie. "Isn't that sweet?"

"Very," Bernie said. "By any chance was his name Ken Marak?"

Sadie clapped her hands together. "That's it," she squealed. "How did you know?"

"I'm psychic," Bernie replied.

When she was back in her vehicle, Bernie got out her cell and hit her dad's speed-dial number. He didn't pick up. Bernie wondered what the point of having a cell was if you always forgot to take it with you. She tried Libby next.

"You're not calling to tell me you want

another two hours, are you, Bernie?" Libby said when she answered.

"You could at least say hello. And no, I'm not," Bernie replied. "I'm calling to tell you something much more interesting."

CHAPTER 31

The dining room at the Haunted House was draftier than usual, Libby decided as she listened to what her sister was saying. Even with wool socks on her feet, they were beginning to feel like Popsicles.

Libby looked up from the cookies she was arranging on a platter. "I think you're nuts," she said to Bernie when she'd finally paused to take a breath. "One hundred percent certifiable."

Bernie dipped the knife she was using to cut the pumpkin cheesecake in a bowl of water, dried it with a towel, and went back to cutting. "No, I'm not."

"Talk about cobbled together," Libby said as she put the platter she'd just finished next to the chocolate cupcakes with orange frosting. "You don't have a lick of proof. This is all speculation and hearsay."

"How can you say that given your dream?"

"That's why I'm saying it. This is like saying that Konrad and Curtis's tapes are real."

"Maybe they are. And, anyway, it's not just the dream. It's the plastic surgery. . . ."

"More speculation . . ."

"But it works in conjunction with everything else," said Bernie.

Libby sighed and started arranging the cinnamon spiced shortbread cookies on a second platter. It was enough already. She and Bernie had been going at it since this morning. She didn't want to talk about it anymore. At least she thought she didn't, but before she knew it, words were spilling out of her mouth again.

"I really am sorry I told you about my dream. I should have kept my mouth shut."

"You shouldn't be sorry," replied Bernie.

"Well, I most definitely am."

Libby shut her eyes for a moment and opened them again. Nope. Everything was still the same. If she could only keep her mouth shut, half of her problems would be solved. When Bernie had called her on her way back from Timberland's house, she'd been in the middle of writing "Happy Halloween" in a nice cursive script on a chocolate frosted yellow cake.

She'd been admiring the *n* she'd just made and thinking that her fourth-grade teacher would have been proud of her — she'd always had the best handwriting in the class — when all of a sudden it had hit her. Maybe writing "Happy Halloween" had jogged her memory, or maybe it had been hearing the name Ken Marak, or maybe it had been having them both happen at the same time — Who knew? — but she had suddenly seen the letter *n* that had been in her dream. The *a* had appeared next. Then she'd seen the rest of the tiles.

She'd been so excited that when Bernie had walked in the kitchen, she'd blurted the name out before she could stop herself. She should have kept quiet because, as she could have predicted, Bernie had come up with this incredibly stupid, half-baked idea, which Libby had been trying to argue her out of ever since.

Bernie dipped the knife blade back in the water and wiped it off again. That was the problem with cheesecake, Libby thought. It was hard to make good, clean cuts, especially when the cheesecake was at room temperature. Cheesecakes were much easier to slice when they were cold, but she hadn't wanted to take the chance of cutting them in the shop and having them fall apart.

"Okay, Libby," she said. "Then give me a better explanation." "I can't," Libby said. "But that doesn't mean there isn't one, and that isn't the point."

"It certainly is." Bernie made her final cut on the cheesecake, wiped the blade off again, and went on to the pies. They were much easier to slice. The only trick here was to make all the slices even. "Dad agrees with me. He said my explanation was possible."

"Dad is just saying that to humor you."

"No, Libby. He's not."

"Yes, Bernadine. He is."

"Don't call me that."

"Sorry," Libby said, but Bernie could see that she didn't look remotely contrite.

"What about Bob Small?" Bernie asked her sister.

"What about him?"

"Don't you care what happens to him?" asked Bernie. Libby looked indignant. "Of course, I do."

"You're not acting that way."

"Now that is a rotten thing to say."

"No, it's the truth. If we don't do something, he's going to go to jail for a long, long time for this."

"Not necessarily," said Libby.

Bernie banged the knife down on the table and turned to face her sister. "Yes, necessarily."

"Something could come up," Libby countered.

Bernie put her hands on her hips. "Like what?" she demanded.

Libby remained silent.

"Exactly my point," Bernie said. "You can't think of anything, can you? And even if some small scintilla —"

"Excuse me. What does *scintilla* mean?"

"It means a little bit, a shred."

"So why don't you say that?" asked Libby.

"I just did. Anyway, even if a bit of evidence does come to light, no one is going to follow it up or, for that matter, go looking for new leads, and you know it as well as I do. Don't deny it."

"I wasn't going to. It is true," Libby conceded.

That was one point Libby couldn't argue. She knew from her father how the prosecutor's office worked. How could she not? She'd seen them in action. When they had someone they liked for a crime, they didn't go running around, looking for alternate explanations. They stuck with what they had. "They're like pit bulls," her dad used to say. "Once they hang on, you can't get them to let go."

Libby knew that it was the defense attorney's job to sniff out new leads, but a good defense lawyer cost lots of money, a commodity Bob was notably lacking. And who was he going to borrow it from? His wife? His business partner? Not too likely. The Simmons family was all he had.

Libby started filling up the pitchers with waffle batter. "Fine. I admit that it seems as if Bob is the fall guy for Amethyst's murder. Happy?"

Bernie brushed a crumb off the table and onto the floor. "Yes, as a matter of fact, I am. At least we're in agreement about that. He's like a custom-made suit. If you'd ordered him up, he couldn't fit this job any better."

"And Ed Banks?" Libby asked. "What about him? How does he fit into this mess?"

"Simple. He was collateral damage. Killing him was merely a matter of tying up a loose end."

Libby stopped to wipe a blob of batter off the rim of the pitcher she'd just filled. "But once again," she continued, "we come down to the inconvenient fact that you have no proof for any of this."

Bernie snagged one of the extra lemon cupcakes with a ginger glaze and took a bite. If she had to say so herself, it was pretty good. "I know," she said.

"And there's no way of getting any."

"That's not true. It's more a question of Bob Small not having the money," Bernie replied. "If he did, we could hire someone to go through the records, but since we don't have a state where the marriage occurred, much less a town, it would be pretty expensive. That's why I've come up with my plan, such as it is."

"Such as it is, is right."

"I wouldn't say that. I do my schtick and stand back and see what the reaction is. It's called stirring the pot."

"I don't think Dad would approve," said Libby.

"That's why we're not telling him."

"I still think we should."

"No, we shouldn't," Bernie insisted. "You know what he's like. He'd be down here in a flash, even if he had to crawl on his hands and knees to get here."

Libby couldn't argue that point, either. When it came to her and her sister, her dad was incredibly overprotective. Always had been and always would be. Bernie finished the cupcake, crumpled up the paper wrapper, and threw it in the trash.

"Okay," Libby agreed. "But what happens if you don't get any reaction?"

"Then we'll come up with something else."

"But then he'll know you suspect him, and he'll move away." Something else occurred to Libby. "What happens if he takes out a gun and shoots you?"

Bernie stopped for a moment.

"Obviously," Libby said, "you haven't considered that possibility."

"Why are you always so negative?"

"I'm not negative," Libby said, forcing the words out between gritted teeth. "I'm realistic. And you haven't answered me."

"He won't," Bernie said.

"That's your answer? He won't?"

"That's right," Bernie said.

"And why not? Because you wear cute shoes? Because you're carrying a Prada bag?"

"Ha-ha. For starters, I don't think he has a gun. If he did, he would have used it on Banks and Amethyst. It would have been a hell of a lot easier than what he did do."

"So he won't use a gun. He'll use a knife. This man has murdered two people," said Libby.

"Yeah. But he did it for revenge."

"Excuse me. According to you, he didn't kill Banks for revenge. He killed him to keep him from talking."

This, Bernie was forced to admit, was true. She clicked her tongue against her teeth while she thought. "I'll tell you what," she finally said. "How about if I talk to him

419

where there are lots of people about? In five more minutes, this place is going to become extremely crowded. Is that okay with you?"

Libby nodded reluctantly. It was better than nothing.

"And if worse comes to worst, Konrad and Curtis can step in."

"Now that's reassuring," Libby mumbled.

"I think they'll be okay. They're going to be pretending they're taping, so if things get funky, I'll signal them and they'll come over."

Libby bit on the inside of her cheek. She attempted to think of some more objections and couldn't. She'd pretty much covered them all.

"Bernie, I still think this is nuts."

"Well, it's not the best plan I've ever come up with," Bernie said. "But then again, it's not the worst. Basically, it's the only thing I can think of to do. I mean, we do have to do something. We can't just stand there and do nothing."

"You're right," Libby said softly. "We do."

"If this doesn't work, at least we will have tried."

Libby nodded. There didn't seem to be anything more to say. She surveyed the table. They were almost ready for customers. All she had to do was put out the napkins, knives, spoons, and forks, and they'd be good to go.

"I almost feel sorry for him," Libby mused. "Amethyst probably deserved what she got."

"I'm sure she did. However, laying the blame on Bob Small isn't very nice."

"No," Libby said. "I suppose it isn't."

"Nor was killing Banks. So are we ready?" Bernie asked.

"Ready as we'll ever be. Just be careful."

"I'm always careful," Bernie retorted.

Libby snorted. Now that was a big fat lie if she'd ever heard one.

"Well, I am," Bernie flung over her shoulder as she marched out the door.

Libby wondered if her sister was feeling nervous, because she was certainly feeling nervous for her.

CHAPTER 32

Bernie fought her way through the crowd of people waiting to go into the Haunted House. It used to be that only kids dressed up at Halloween, but that wasn't true anymore. Today everyone did.

Bernie looked around the hallway. It was like being at a masked ball. There were witches and goblins and ogres, X-Men, Pillsbury Doughboys, Harry Potters, and Voldemorts. There were people in rhinestone and feathered masks, people with bright purple wigs and false noses, and people who had dressed up like Bush, not to mention all the women in bustiers.

Bernie looked down at what she was wearing. It was really pretty lame. Some people wouldn't even think it was a costume. It wasn't sexy or ironic or clever or cute. She wasn't a superhero or a famous person, although why anyone would want to be Paris Hilton for an evening totally eluded

Bernie. In fact, she was pretty sure no one would know who she was supposed to be except her target, and she wasn't too sure about that. Maybe she wouldn't get the big response she was hoping for, after all. Oh well. She guessed she'd find out soon enough.

Bernie had modeled her clothes on the picture of Bessie hanging on the wall in Amethyst's apartment. She was wearing penny loafers, kneesocks, a pleated skirt, a white oxford shirt, and a cardigan, all of which she'd managed to find in the vintage clothes shop three blocks down from A Little Taste of Heaven. She'd gotten the tortoiseshell frames she was wearing from a costume store, ditto the brown, straight-haired wig.

She stood off to one side and scanned the crowd. She could see Konrad and Curtis fiddling with their tape deck near the restrooms. She gave them a slight nod, and they waved back. She sighed. Obviously, they weren't totally clear on the concept of being inconspicuous, but there was nothing she could do about it now. Going over and talking to them would only make matters worse.

After shaking her head at them, she started studying the crowd in earnest. She knew the person she was looking for had to be here somewhere. She looked around the room. Nope, wasn't here. Maybe he was in costume. She scanned everyone's face again. Still nothing. And then, a few minutes later, she saw her target. No. She locked on her target. She liked that phrase better. Much more military. He'd just come in from the dining room and was standing in front of one of the doors that led to the back portion of the house, the portion that hid the scary stuff.

Bernie reflexively patted her shirt pocket. The mini tape recorder she'd bought this morning was in there. That was the nice thing about cardigans and oxford shirts. They hid stuff, unlike her Dolce & Gabbana black Lycra shirt. She figured that as soon as she got close to her target, she'd turn the tape recorder on.

Hopefully, it would work better than that huge thing Konrad and Curtis were using, and she'd get an admission of some kind that she could hear. The guy at the shop had said that the model she'd bought would pick up anything, and it had seemed to work pretty well when she tried it out in the shop. But you never knew with this kind of stuff. Just when you needed them the most, things like this tended to poop out.

Not that a tape recording was admissible evidence. In fact, it was illegal to tape-record someone without their knowledge; you could get arrested for it. Bernie wasn't worried about that. All she wanted to get was some sort of admission that she could hand over to Bob's court-appointed lawyer. Hopefully, he would then get the ball rolling on this stuff.

She clicked on the machine, plastered her best smile on her face, and started walking toward him. He was watching a couple dressed as Humpty Dumpty and All the King's Men, so he didn't see or hear Bernie approach.

Here we go, she said to herself. Then she took a deep breath and tapped Mark Kane on the shoulder. He jumped and spun around.

"Hi, Ken," she said. "How's life treating you these days?"

All the color drained from his face. He opened his mouth and closed it again.

Bernie motioned to her clothes with a nod of her chin. "Like what I'm wearing? I think Bessie would be pleased, don't you? I modeled myself after the picture of her that Amethyst had in her bedroom. Curious that, don't you think? I don't know what to make of it. Do you?"

Kane didn't answer. He was still gulping air. Finally, after another moment had passed, he got hold of himself and spoke.

"I don't know what you're talking about," he said. "My name is Mark Kane."

Bernie's smiled widened. "That's your current name, but before that, your name was Ken Marak. You're the headmaster's son and Bessie Osgood's first true love."

"I've always been Mark Kane."

Later, Bernie would tell Brandon that it was the way he looked at her when he said his name and the emphasis he put on the two words that made her realize what they really meant.

She put her hand to her mouth. "Oh my God." It had been in front of her all the time, and she hadn't seen it. "Mark Kane. Of course. It's an anagram for Ken Marak, isn't it?"

Kane bit his lip.

Bernie realized something else. "Mark Kane. Mark of Cain. They're homophones. You feel that guilty about having taken up with Amethyst all those years ago?" Bernie scrutinized his face. "You do, don't you? No. It's more than that. You were involved in her death, weren't you?"

Kane shook his head.

"Yes, you were. I can see it on your face. Did you tell Amethyst that Bessie was going to go to your dad? Or did you see Amethyst push Bessie out of the window?" For a moment, Bernie thought Kane was going to faint. "You did, didn't you? And you didn't do anything."

"Get out of here," Kane growled. "You're nuts."

"I don't think so," Bernie replied.

"People told me you were crazy, and they're right. You are."

Bernie watched as he turned and tried the door. It didn't open. He pulled harder. It didn't budge.

"Looks as if it's locked from the inside," Bernie observed pleasantly.

Kane ignored her and started walking down the hall. Bernie kept by his side. When she looked around, she could see that Curtis and Konrad were following her.

"Why did you kill Amethyst?" she asked Kane. "Was it revenge because she killed Bessie?"

"I don't know what you're talking about," Kane snarled as he shoved his way between a couple dressed in look-alike Cowardly Lion costumes.

"Hey, fella," the guy cried. "Watch where you're going, will you?"

Kane didn't respond. People shouted, "Hey!" and "You can't do that!" and "Get in line like everyone else!" as Bernie followed Kane through the crowd milling around in front of the entrance to the Haunted House rooms.

"We found Bessie's diary, you know," said Bernie.

"I don't care," Kane hissed.

"You were her first love."

By now they were in the Chain-Saw Massacre Room, with about five other people. The sound of the woman screaming was joined by the sounds of the people in the room going, "Oh my god, that's terrible."

"You shared her first kiss with her," Bernie said as a girl grabbed on to her boyfriend and shrieked.

Another woman glared at Bernie. "Will you shut up and let us enjoy ourselves!" she hissed.

Bernie was just about to tell her to get a life when Kane spun around. Even in the dark Bernie could see that his normal affable expression had been replaced by fear and anguish.

"If I knew who this Bessie Osgood was, I might care," Kane said.

"Oh, you know all right. You gave her a book on Celtic mythology. You introduced her to old fairy tales."

Kane hurried across the room and opened the next door. The skeleton in the casket was cackling and pointing his finger at people. Kane pushed through the crowd to get to the door after that. A woman dressed as the Statue of Liberty told him to watch where he was going.

"I'll get the manager and have you thrown out," she threatened.

"You do that. I am the manager. In fact, I'm the owner of this place," Kane yelled. He turned to open the next door. Bernie watched his hand freeze on the handle as he realized what was on the other side.

"Are you sure you want to go in there?" she asked. "Amethyst's ghost might be waiting for you."

"I don't believe in ghosts," Kane told her. But his hand wavered on the knob, and after a few seconds, he turned and went back the way he had come. By now he was practically running. "Get out of the way," he cried as he plowed through the crowd coming in the opposite direction.

Bernie followed him out the door and into the hallway. He looked around for a second and headed outside. As she followed, she tried not to think about the promise she'd made Libby about staying where the people were. Given the circumstances, what other option did she have? The temperature had fallen, and she could see her breath in the air. Bernie rubbed her arms as she followed Kane across to the other house. Her four-ply cashmere sweater was warm, but it wasn't warm enough. She looked back. Konrad and Curtis were nowhere to be seen. She should go back, but she knew she wasn't going to.

"How did you get Amethyst to marry you?" she asked Kane.

He froze for a second, then turned to face Bernie.

"I know you did," she told him. "We can prove it."

"How?" Kane asked. His voice was hoarse.

"Amethyst told somebody, and she told my dad," Bernie lied.

"Who told you? I don't believe it."

"I'm not telling you."

"Because there is nobody," Kane hissed.

"No. I'm not telling you, because I don't want you killing them the way you killed Ed Banks."

"I didn't kill him," Kane protested.

"You most certainly did. I talked to Amber, and she remembers you buying some ginger pumpkin bars that day. You made a big deal of it by telling her you were taking them to a friend and you wanted the best ones possible."

Kane turned and took a step toward her.

"So if I did everything that you say, how come you're here talking to me? Aren't you afraid I'm going to kill you, too?"

"Not really."

"And why is that? Could it possibly be because I'm not a killer?"

"Oh no. You are," Bernie told him. "There's no doubt about that. I might not be able to prove it, but it's true." And suddenly Bernie knew. She knew that what Kane wanted was a sympathetic ear. Someone to tell him he'd done the right thing. Someone to "get him," as the expression went. "And she deserved it," Bernie continued. "She deserved everything she got."

Kane didn't say anything.

Bernie went on. "She did. She was an awful person. She brought a lot of pain and misery to a lot of people. She wrecked lives. She certainly destroyed yours. Your dad killing himself, your mom having that accident."

Kane turned his face so Bernie couldn't see the expression on it. Then he spoke. "Running a school was his dream. He'd borrowed all this money from my mom and her family, and from his family, and their friends. Then, when that thing with Bessie happened and everyone started taking their children out of the school, Dad, well, Dad couldn't stand it. He was so ashamed. He couldn't face everyone. And he . . . I found him, you know."

"No, I didn't know that."

"We'd just turned the corner, too. We were starting to make money. And then Amethyst pushed . . ." Kane stopped abruptly. "Are you recording this?" he said.

Something told Bernie not to lie. She took the mini tape recorder out of her pocket and handed it to him. "I was, but I'm not anymore."

Kane's hand closed over the tape recorder.

Bernie brushed away a snowflake that had fallen on her sleeve. "You must have been planning this for a long time. You changed your name. You got plastic surgery in case Amethyst recognized you. Did she?"

"Not at first. But I think she might have later. But she would have liked that. She was a game player."

"Only this time she lost," Bernie said.

Kane gave a stiff little bow. "So it would appear."

Bernie waved her hand in the direction of the Peabody School. "And, of course, you spent all this money fixing the place up, but you have it, don't you? I looked you up on the Web. You were one of the partners in the J and K Hedge Fund. You guys made —"

"Billions," Kane said.

"So I guess you figured you could do pretty much what you wanted."

"I never said that. You did."

Bernie nodded her head in assent. "Where did you go after your mother died?" she asked.

"I went out to Dallas to live with some relatives there."

"That must have been very hard."

"No. They were nice."

"That's not what I meant."

"I know what you meant." Kane looked at the mini tape recorder in his hand. "They were nice. But all the time I was there, I just wanted to go home."

"And you finally did."

Kane nodded. "I'm sorry about Banks. I never meant for that to happen. I didn't even know Amethyst had asked him about using his garden." Kane shrugged. "And when I heard . . . I don't know. Something just came over me."

"And you did what you thought had to be done."

"I suppose you could put it that way."

By now they were near the Foundation.

"Damn," Kane said. "The idiot twins."

Bernie turned and followed his gaze. Konrad and Curtis were running toward them.

"Stop," Konrad screamed. "Stay where you are. We've got a gun."

Bernie cursed as she saw the rifle Konrad was carrying. Kane hesitated for two seconds before he took off and ran toward the Foundation. A couple of seconds after that, he opened the front door and entered the building.

"What are you doing?" Bernie yelled at Konrad and Curtis as they rushed by her.

"We're making sure the son of a bitch doesn't get away," Konrad cried.

Bernie ran after them. "He won't."

"Damn right, he won't," Konrad said.

Bernie grabbed on to the back of Konrad's jacket and pulled. Konrad spun around.

"I want you to stay here and guard the front door while I go up and bring him down," Bernie said.

"We can't —"

Bernie cut him off. "You most certainly can." She ran off before Konrad could say anything else. She made it to the front door before Konrad and Curtis could and locked it.

A second later Konrad was pounding on the door. "Hey," he yelled. "Let us in."

Bernie didn't waste time replying.

"Kane," she called.

There was no reply, but she heard footsteps to the left of her. She took off after them. She was running down a long, dark hallway. The footsteps were fainter now.

"Kane, stop," she yelled. "We need to talk."

Now she heard nothing. She came to a standstill. She was sweating now. *Damn the twins,* she thought as she caught her breath. Then she heard a key in a lock.

"We're coming to get you, Kane," Curtis called.

"Great," Bernie muttered to herself.

She'd forgotten they had keys to this place. *Lovely.* The way things were going they'd probably shoot her by accident. *Friggin' morons.* Then she heard something ahead of her again. She strained to listen. Footsteps. Kane's. They were coming from up ahead and over to the right. Bernie followed the sound. She could hear the twins behind her. She ran faster. Now she was in the front hallway. She looked up. Kane was running up the stairs.

"Wait," she cried.

But Kane just ran faster. She took the steps two at a time. They were now on the second floor, on the side where the French doors were. Kane kept on running. Suddenly, Bernie thought she saw something rectangular — a book maybe? — moving across the floor. She knew Kane wouldn't see it, and he didn't. He tripped. She watched him try and retain his balance. He teetered, swaying back and forth, frantically trying to regain his balance, and then he crashed through the glass and fell to the ground below.

"Now we're even-steven," Bernie could have sworn she heard a voice say. Then she saw Bessie smiling at her. "See you later, alligator," Bessie said. And she was gone.

Bernie was still staring at where Bessie had been when Konrad and Curtis reached her.

CHAPTER 33

Bernie looked at the clock on the kitchen wall. It was a little after one in the morning. Halloween was over for another year. Thank goodness. This one had been a little too intense to suit her. Costumes were one thing, but real live ghosts were another. She thought she knew how Libby felt when she had those dreams. They didn't leave you with a pleasant experience, that was for sure.

She sighed and poured some milk into a copper pan and put it on the stove to warm up. She was thinking that the kitchen always calmed her down when she heard Libby coming down the stairs.

Libby tapped her on the shoulder. "How's the hot chocolate coming?" she asked.

Bernie got out six mugs and proceeded to spoon one tablespoon of cocoa powder and two tablespoons of sugar into each of them. "It's coming."

"Marvin and Clyde want marshmallows

in theirs. Brandon and Dad want whipped cream and cinnamon instead, and so do I."

"Is that why you came down?" asked Bernie.

"No. I was just wondering if you wanted to tell me what really happened," said Libby.

"I just did up there."

Libby looked at her.

Bernie hunched up her shoulders. "Well, I did."

"I told you my dream, remember?"

Bernie sighed and checked the flame under the milk. She didn't want it to boil over.

"This is just so weird."

"If you're saying that, it must be good."

"And I can't even be sure. I think I imagined the whole thing."

"Kane's tripping and falling?" asked Libby.

"But that's the thing. I could have sworn I saw something move across the floor. By itself," said Bernie.

The milk started to bubble. Bernie took it off the flame and poured a tiny bit into each mug. Then she mixed together the ingredients in each mug until they formed a paste, after which she poured the rest of the milk in.

"And?" Libby prompted.

Bernie took out a tray and began to put the mugs on it. "I think Bessie did it."

"Did what?"

"Moved it. Made it move. I ran up the stairs and looked. Kane had tripped over an old book that was lying on the floor. A book of Celtic mythology."

"Maybe someone left it there?" Libby suggested.

"Maybe," Bernie said. "But I don't think so. It had no business being there. And here's the clincher. I opened it up. There was an inscription: *To Bessie from Ken. I hope you find this as interesting as I do.*"

Libby stayed silent.

"Exactly," Bernie said as she got the whipped cream out of the fridge. She put two big dollops in four of the mugs and added a sprinkle of cinnamon on top.

"There's more, isn't there?" Libby said after a moment had gone by.

"I saw her. I heard her. She told me, 'Now we're even-steven.' "

"Even-steven meaning she and Kane?"

"Correct," Bernie said.

"But I thought Amethyst pushed her."

"She did, but I think Bessie blamed Ken. After all, if he hadn't gotten involved with Amethyst . . ."

Libby finished the sentence for her. "This

never would have happened."

"Exactly," Bernie said. "And she was smiling. And then she said, 'See you later, alligator.' "

Libby got out the bag of marshmallows and placed three each in the two remaining mugs. "She said that to me, too."

"You think I should tell the guys?" Bernie asked.

Libby put the bag of marshmallows back. "I think you should stick to the 'he tripped and fell out the window" story and leave the rest of it alone."

"I think so, too." Bernie put the whipped cream back in the fridge.

"But I believe you," Libby said.

Bernie grinned. "You do?"

"Yeah. I do. It makes sense in a weird kind of way. But no one else will." Libby took a Tupperware container full of gingersnaps down from the shelf and began putting them out on a plate.

"I guess Bessie finally got her payback," Bernie said.

"So it would seem," Libby agreed as she finished arranging the cookies. "What is it they say about a woman abused?"

"What they say is, 'Hell hath no fury like a woman scorned.' "

"But she wasn't a woman," Libby objected. "She was a teenager."

"Even worse," Bernie said, thinking back to when she was that age. Then she picked up the tray, and she and Libby went upstairs to join the guys.

EPILOGUE

Ken looked at Bessie. "How could you do that?" he demanded.

She blinked. "Do what?"

"Kill me of course."

He didn't know how he knew he was dead. He just did.

"Oh that." Bessie shrugged. "You were going to die anyway. At least this way you're here with me."

"But you made me fall."

"You deserved it. You hurt my feelings."

Ken looked around. He was standing a little way from where he'd gone out the window. He glanced down at himself. He was now wearing the same clothes he had worn at the school. What was that line from one of the Grateful Dead's songs? *What a long strange trip it's been?* Then a horrible idea occurred to him.

"Is Amethyst here too?"

Bessie pouted. "You don't even want to

talk to me. All you're interested in is her."

"No. I didn't mean it like that."

"It certainly sounds that way to me."

"Honestly, that's not why I'm asking."

Bessie looked at him for a moment. Then she said, "No. She's not here."

"Good." Ken heaved a sigh of relief. "Is anyone else here?"

"Like who?"

He thought back to when he used to live at the school. "Like Esmeralda."

Bessie giggled. "Nope. It's just us. Isn't that super?"

Ken thought for a moment. Then he took Bessie's hand and gave it a squeeze.

"Yes, it is," he said to her. "It really is."

RECIPES

I always think of Halloween food as fall food — food made out of apples and pumpkins, pears and cranberries; food seasoned with ginger and cinnamon and cloves; food that says, "Come in and pull up a chair." Here are a few offerings. Two of them are Mexican in origin and are served up in celebration of Mexico's Day of the Dead and the other comes from the niece of a good friend of mine.

MARIA'S PUMPKIN BARS

4 eggs
1 2/3 cups sugar
1 cup vegetable oil
2 cups (16 ounces) canned pumpkin
2 cups flour
2 teaspoons baking powder
2 teaspoons cinnamon
1 teaspoon baking soda

1 teaspoon salt

Icing
8 tablespoons (1 stick) softened butter
Two 8-ounce packages cream cheese
1 tablespoon vanilla
2 to 3 cups powdered sugar
1 tablespoon milk

Beat all the icing ingredients together in a medium mixing bowl until smooth and creamy. Add more powdered sugar if the icing is too runny. Put aside.

Beat the eggs, sugar, oil, and canned pumpkin in a large mixing bowl. Add the flour and all the other ingredients. Mix well and pour the batter into a greased 10 x 15-inch pan. Bake at 350 degrees for 25 to 30 minutes. Let cool. Apply the icing. Cut in one- to two-inch squares. Keep in the refrigerator.

Here are two recipes that Mexicans serve on the Day of the Dead.

Pan de Muerto (BREAD OF THE DEAD)
1/2 cup butter
1/2 cup milk
1/2 cup water
5 to 5 1/2 cups flour
2 (1/4-ounce) packages active dry yeast

1 teaspoon salt
1 tablespoon whole aniseed
1/2 cup sugar
4 eggs

Glaze
1/2 cup sugar
1/3 cup fresh orange juice
2 tablespoons orange zest

Bring the sugar, the orange juice, and the orange zest to a boil in a small saucepan over medium heat. Boil for 2 minutes. Set the glaze aside.

In a saucepan over medium flame, heat the butter, milk, and water until they are warm to the touch. Do not boil.

Measure out 1 1/2 cups of the flour, and set the rest aside. In a large mixing bowl, combine the 1 1/2 cups of flour, yeast, salt, aniseed, and sugar. Beat in the warm liquid until well combined. Add the eggs, and beat in another cup of flour. Continue beating in more flour until the dough is soft but not sticky. Knead the dough on a floured board until smooth and elastic.

Lightly grease a large bowl, and place the dough in it, cover with plastic wrap, and let rise in a warm place until the dough is double in bulk, about 1 1/2 hours. Punch the dough down, and shape it into loaves resembling skulls, skeletons, or bones. Let the loaves rise for an hour.

Bake the loaves in a preheated 350°F oven for 40 minutes. Remove the loaves from the oven, and paint on the glaze with a pastry brush.

CALABAZA EN TACHA

This Mexican recipe uses pumpkin in an unusual way. The dessert is very sweet, and a little goes a long way.

1 4- to 5-pound pumpkin (Pie pumpkins are best for this.)
2 pounds raw or brown sugar
8 cinnamon sticks
Juice of 1 orange
4 cups water

With a sharp, heavy knife, cut the pumpkin into 3 inch squares or triangles. Remove the seeds and strings. Cut a diamond design into the pulp.

Put the sugar in a large pot with the cinnamon sticks, orange juice, and water. Boil until the sugar has dissolved.

Place a layer of pumpkin, pulp side down, in the syrup. Place a second layer of pumpkin on top of the first layer, pulp side up.

Cover and simmer. Check every 10 minutes or so. When the pumpkin is ready, the tops of the pumpkin pieces will look glazed and the pulp will be soft and golden brown.

Let the pumpkin cool. Serve the pumpkin with the syrup.

The next three recipes are my favorites. One is for a cranberry walnut bread, one is for a cranberry cake, and the last one is for a ginger cake. Enjoy all of them.

CRANBERRY WALNUT BREAD

This bread couldn't be simpler to make. It makes one relatively small loaf.

1/2 cup butter
1 cup brown sugar
1 egg
2 1/4 cups flour
1 teaspoon baking soda
1/2 teaspoon salt
1 cup canned whole cranberry sauce
3/4 cup honey or wheat beer (Try different beers to vary the taste.)
2 tablespoons grated orange peel
3/4 cup chopped walnuts

Cream the butter, sugar, and egg in a large mixing bowl. Mix the dry ingredients together in a medium mixing bowl. Combine the cranberry sauce, the beer, and the orange peel. Add the flour mixture and the cranberry mixture alternately to the butter, sugar, and egg mixture. Add walnuts. Bake in an 8-inch loaf pan in a preheated 350°F oven for 60 minutes. Cool the bread before cutting. This recipe keeps well. You can also add half a cup of diced dried apricots if you are so inclined.

CRANBERRY CAKE

3 tablespoons butter
1 and 1/3 cups brown sugar
2 cups fresh or frozen cranberries
3/4 cup of white flour
3/4 cup whole wheat flour
1 and 1/2 teaspoon baking powder
1/4 cup soft butter
1 egg
1/2 cup milk
1 teaspoon vanilla

Melt 3 tablespoons of butter in an 8″ by 8″ pan. Sprinkle one cup of sugar over melted butter, add berries and set aside.

Cream remaining butter with 1/3 cup brown sugar, add egg, then dry ingredients alternating with milk. Spoon over berries and spread to cover. Bake in preheated

350°F oven for 35 to 45 minutes. When done invert onto a plate while hot so topping comes out. Serve with whipped cream or vanilla ice cream.

TRIPLE GINGER LOAF

This recipe comes to me by way of Hank Nielsen. I included it because it keeps well, everyone likes it, and it's healthy.

1 and 2/3 cups flour
1 teaspoon ground ginger
1 teaspoon cinnamon
1 teaspoon baking soda
1/2 teaspoon cardamom
1/2 teaspoon salt
6 tablespoons minced, crystallized ginger
2 tablespoon peeled, grated fresh ginger
1/2 cup applesauce or oil
1/2 cup brown sugar
1/2 cup white sugar
4 egg whites or 2 whole eggs
1/2 cup buttermilk or yogurt
1 cup chocolate chips (optional)

Sift dry ingredients. Combine wet ingredients separately. Mix both together, and add crystallized ginger and optional chocolate chips. Pour into lightly buttered 8-inch loaf pan and bake in preheated 350°F oven for 50 minutes. Let cool in pan before removing.

ABOUT THE AUTHOR

Isis Crawford was born in Egypt to parents who were in the diplomatic corps. When she was five, her family returned to the States, where her mother opened a restaurant in upper Westchester County and her father became a university professor. Since then Isis has combined her parents' love of food and travel by running a catering service as well as penning numerous travel-related articles about places ranging from Omsk to Paraguay. Married, with twin boys, she presently resides in Hastings-on-Hudson, New York, where she is working on the next Bernie and Libby culinary mystery.

We hope you have enjoyed this Large Print book. Other Thorndike, Wheeler, and Chivers Press Large Print books are available at your library or directly from the publishers.

For information about current and upcoming titles, please call or write, without obligation, to:

Publisher
Thorndike Press
295 Kennedy Memorial Drive
Waterville, ME 04901
Tel. (800) 223-1244

or visit our Web site at:

http://gale.cengage.com/thorndike

OR

Chivers Large Print
published by BBC Audiobooks Ltd
St James House, The Square
Lower Bristol Road
Bath BA2 3SB
England
Tel. +44(0) 800 136919
email: bbcaudiobooks@bbc.co.uk
www.bbcaudiobooks.co.uk

All our Large Print titles are designed for easy reading, and all our books are made to last.